DIFFERENT THIS TIME

Anne followed Kurt down the porch steps, hating to let him go. He turned and swept her into his arms for one last kiss, before he disappeared into the darkness. She heard the murmur of his truck's engine and saw the lights heading toward town. She sighed and glanced up at the stars—the same stars that shone above them in the gazebo.

It had been different this time. She felt no guilt, no confusion over their lovemaking.

She hadn't felt this way in years. In fact, she didn't think she had ever felt this way at all. It was all she could think about as she took a long, leisurely bubble bath. He was all she could see.

"God," she murmured, sitting up in the tub. "I'm not falling in love, am I?" Then she slid back down, smiling and letting the warm water from her sponge run down her shoulders and arms.

"What if I am?" she asked, staring into space and letting her mind consider all the possibilities. "Would that be so awful?"

Somehow, tonight, with the memory of Kurt's hands and body, with the taste of him still on her lips, she couldn't imagine anything awful about it.

She couldn't remember ever being so happy.

IT'S NEVER TOO LATE FOR LOVE AND ROMANCE

JUST IN TIME (4188, $4.50/$5.50)
by Peggy Roberts

Constantly taking care of everyone around her has earned Remy Dupre the affectionate nickname "Ma." Then, with Remy's husband gone and oil discovered on her Louisiana farm, her sons and their wives decide it's time to take care of her. But Remy knows how to take care of herself. She starts by checking into a beauty spa, buying some classy new clothes and shoes, discovering an antique vase, and moving on to a fine plantation. Next, not one, but two men attempt to sweep her off her well-shod feet. The right man offers her the opportunity to love again.

LOVE AT LAST (4158, $4.50/$5.50)
by Garda Parker

Fifty, slim, and attractive, Gail Bricker still hadn't found the love of her life. Friends convince her to take an Adventure Tour during the summer vacation she enjoys as an English teacher. At a Cheyenne Indian school in need of teachers, Gail finds her calling. In rancher Slater Kincaid, she finds her match. Gail discovers that it's never too late to fall in love . . . for the very first time.

LOVE LESSONS (3959, $4.50/$5.50)
by Marian Oaks

After almost forty years of marriage, Carolyn Ames certainly hadn't been looking for a divorce. But the ink is barely dry, and here she is already living an exhilarating life as a single woman. First, she lands an exciting and challenging job. Now Jason, the handsome architect, offers her a fairy-tale romance. Carolyn doesn't care that her ultra-conservative neighbors gossip about her and Jason, but she is afraid to give up her independent life-style. She struggles with the balance while she learns to love again.

A KISS TO REMEMBER (4129, $4.50/$5.50)
by Helen Playfair

For the past ten years Lucia Morgan hasn't had time for love or romance. Since her husband's death, she has been raising her two sons, working at a dead-end office job, and designing boutique clothes to make ends meet. Then one night, Mitch Colton comes looking for his daughter, out late with one of her sons. The look in Mitch's eye brings back a host of long-forgotten feelings. When the kids come home and spoil the enchantment, Lucia wonders if she will get the chance to love again.

COME HOME TO LOVE (3930, $4.50/$5.50)
by Jane Bierce

Julia Delaine says good-bye to her skirt-chasing husband Phillip and hello to a whole new life. Julia capably rises to the challenges of her reawakened sexuality, the young man who comes courting, and her new position as the head of her local television station. Her new independence teaches Julia that maybe her time-tested values were right all along and maybe Phillip does belong in her life, with her new terms.

CLARA WIMBERLY
ANGEL UNAWARE

ZEBRA BOOKS
KENSINGTON PUBLISHING CORP.

ZEBRA BOOKS are published by

Kensington Publishing Corp.
850 Third Avenue
New York, NY 10022

Zebra, the Z logo, and To Love Again Reg. U.S. Pat. & TM Off.

First Printing: October, 1994

Printed in the United States of America

One

Anne Benefield stepped out of the cool interior of Broussard's, an elegant downtown dress shop that had been one of her favorites for years. Her arms were filled with boxes tied with elegant satin ribbons. She jaywalked across the middle of the block, waving nonchalantly at the honking cars and trying to find her keys as she juggled the packages in her arms.

"Oh, hell," she said as she approached the dark green Jaguar parked at the curb.

There on the spotlessly clean windshield was a buff-colored piece of paper, stuck beneath the windshield. Anne knew what it was. She had a drawerful of them at home.

She pushed the button of her car alarm and heard a quiet chirping noise and the click of opening locks. Impatiently, she threw the packages into the backseat and stepped toward the front of the car to pluck the parking ticket from beneath the wipers. She took a look around, tugging at the jacket of her linen summer suit, before sliding into the car and closing the door.

She lifted her chin, frowning as she saw Sylvia Jordan walk down the sidewalk and smile toward the car. She knew she'd seen her take the ticket off the windshield.

Anne forced a smile to her lips, but it was gone as soon as Sylvia was out of sight.

"Bitch," she muttered.

She wondered how long it would take for Sylvia Jordan to run to her husband, who just happened to be a judge. "Wild Will," they called him—Will Jordan was the hanging judge in town, even though his cases were mostly civil. He had a reputation for being fair and honest, but exceedingly tough.

Anne had always found him a bit pompous, just like Sylvia, who'd often behaved as if she were a little princess when they were in high school together more than thirty years ago. Anne couldn't stand her then and she couldn't stand her now.

She tossed the parking ticket into the glove compartment, turned on the ignition, and pulled out into traffic. Two blocks away she caught up with Sylvia and couldn't resist blowing the horn at her as she hustled across the street, holding her frosted pageboy hair against the wind, her pencil-thin legs bent at the knees as she tried to run.

Sylvia jumped and turned with a glare toward the green Jaguar, and Anne smiled broadly and wiggled her fingers at her. Sylvia was angry, just as Anne had intended her to be, but the judge's wife only smiled weakly before lifting her chin and hurrying across the street.

"Snoot-face," Anne murmured, still smiling.

She turned the car west and headed out of town. Clayburn, Georgia, was still a small town, for all its progress over the past thirty years. She could remember standing on the same street corner where she'd just gone shopping when she was a girl. Instead of a fashionable boutique there had been a corner grocery and a furniture store, owned by one of the old families and operated with old money. Everyone knew everyone else in Clayburn.

Here on this street the country people stood around on Saturdays, waiting for a ride back home. Most of them didn't own a car; neither had Anne's mother.

"Not that she'd have bothered picking me up anyway," Anne muttered.

Anne remembered those times of waiting . . . the many hours in the blazing summer sun or the bitter winter cold, hoping for a ride, wishing everyone wouldn't stay in town all day. It was a tiring thing, waiting. Frightening to a young girl who was alone and too shy to ask for a ride. Humiliating.

Anne lifted her chin. Her teeth were clenched so tightly, her jaw ached.

"Anne Benefield, what's wrong with you?" she asked, gazing into the rearview mirror.

Sometimes she just had to remind herself who she was now. The memories that flooded over her so quickly were disturbing, and for a moment she felt inadequate. She felt like a poor, shy little country girl . . . a nobody. It was a feeling she'd just as soon forget, and there were times she'd just as soon forget, too.

She glanced briefly at her perfectly styled blond hair, the blue eyes that had grown paler with the years. And she thought that even the most expensive makeup couldn't disguise the lines at the corners of a woman's eyes forever.

Turning fifty in a few months wasn't something she looked forward to.

"You're more beautiful now than you were as a girl," her late husband Baxter used to say. "Prettier even than when I married you and took you out of that dismal job you had."

What Baxter hadn't added was that he felt responsible for making her that way.

Anne grimaced at the thought. He *was* responsible, in many ways. Baxter Benefield had come into her life more than fifteen years ago—during her independent period, as she liked to call it. He'd somehow seen through her coldness and sarcasm—Anne always thought it was because he was twenty-five years older than she, and more experienced. She could remember him telling her that age took away the luxury of indecision. He was a busy man, and he simply didn't have time for any of that garbage. But whatever his reason, when Baxter Benefield saw her working at his lawyer's office he knew what he wanted.

And even later, when Anne agreed to marry him, against the protests of her friends, she had made it clear to him that she didn't love him . . . maybe never would.

Her mother, as she recalled, was the only one who approved. Anne's marriage and her ultimate change in status was the one thing that had ever won her mother's approval. And by then Anne didn't give a damn.

But Baxter had accepted Anne's attitude, and he'd accepted her. Even over the years, when he had wanted to hear her say she loved him, Anne stubbornly had refused to lie to him. Nor did she try to hide the truth when she spent his money indiscriminately and laughed at his desire to have a child with her. She realized now, after he was gone, that Baxter was the only person in her life ever to love her unconditionally.

She hadn't appreciated it then. It had

taken his sudden death three years ago to make her feel ashamed and remorseful. And only to herself could she admit that it had also made her even more withdrawn. She was a fraud—plain and simple. The cool, elegant lady the residents of Clayburn saw wasn't the real Anne. She'd become a pretty damned good actress over the years. Sometimes, when she looked in the mirror, she even believed the charade herself.

Anne turned up the stereo and gunned the engine, racing through the town's last traffic light and zooming out the country road that led to the Benefield estate. She didn't want to think about any of that today. She wanted to enjoy the drive and she wanted to enjoy her new car.

That was all she had now and it was enough. Things. Expensive, beautiful things that made her feel secure and safe. Accepted, at least in a small town that had always regarded its wealthy citizens as symbols of perfection. And that made her believe she was just as good as anybody in Clay County.

"I'll have a party," she said, her eyes

brightening immediately. "That's exactly what I'll do."

She hummed to herself as she drove, her mind envisioning a summer party beneath the old trees, her white antebellum house the perfect setting in the background. An old-fashioned Southern lawn party, with men in tailored white slacks and tasseled loafers, and women in gauzy pastel-colored dresses and wide-brimmed, flower-bedecked hats.

But no children. Definitely no children at Benefield to spoil the aesthetics or to trip over the tables and topple her very expensive Steuben punch bowl.

Everyone in town would be trying to wrangle an invitation. It would be the most elegant, the most talked-about party of the year.

By the time Anne turned into her drive and smiled at the reflection of her house in the still, unrippled lake out front, her memories of the past were forgotten. As forgotten as the parking ticket that lay unnoticed in the Jaguar's glove compartment.

For the next few weeks Anne threw herself completely into preparations for the party. She made arrangements with her favorite caterer from Atlanta; she hired cooks and maids and waiters for the big day. The striped tents were ordered and would be shipped from Savannah to arrive the day before the party so that they could be erected and decorated with just the right blend of flowers. The string orchestra that she liked so well was available.

The tiny Austrian crystal baskets to be used as favors would cost a fortune. But what did it matter? It would take her ten lifetimes to spend all the money Baxter Benefield had left her. He had wanted her to enjoy it—had been the one to smile and urge her to indulge herself at every turn.

Anne thought now that perhaps it was the only joy she ever really gave him.

A few days before the party Anne received a letter in the mail about the overdue parking fines. Standing in the huge kitchen with a basket of roses in front of her, she opened it impatiently and stared at it for a moment before tossing it into a nearby wastebasket. She'd have to remember to tell her lawyer to pay it. That was probably the only way they were ever going to leave her alone. What was the big deal anyway? It wasn't as if she was destitute and *couldn't* pay the fines, for heaven's sake. She was busy, that's all.

On the Thursday before her scheduled lawn party the phone rang. When the maid came to tell Anne it was for her she picked it up, but she didn't have a chance to speak before she heard her lawyer's voice on the other end of the line.

"Anne, have you lost your mind?"

"Well, that's been a debatable point in this town for a long time now, Roger. Is there anything specific you had in mind?" She couldn't help her teasing sarcasm with Roger Finnell. He was always so serious— too serious, she often told him.

"I just got a call from the chief of police," he said, his voice exasperated and disbelieving. "Why didn't you tell me you had another parking fine? Better yet, why didn't you just pay the damned thing?"

"Oh," she said, frowning. She looked at one of the maids, who was cleaning some silver. "No, Jessica, for heaven's sake, not that one. The silver tray with the gold handles . . . yes, that's the one. Now, Roger, what were you saying?"

"Dammit, Anne, will you listen to me?"

"Why, I am listening, Roger dear. You were asking about the parking fines and wondering why I hadn't paid them yet. I just forgot, that's all. Tell Chief Barrows we'll put a check in the mail right away. You can—"

"I'm afraid it's not going to be that simple this time."

"What do you mean . . . this time?" The solemnity in his voice caused Anne to stand very still for a moment, holding the phone tightly against her ear.

"That's just what I'm trying to explain to you."

"Well, explain it then, Roger, and get on with it. I have a million things to do before the party Saturday. You are coming, aren't you? I sent yours and Janet's invitation . . . you should have gotten it by now."

"Anne, if you don't take care of this, there might not be a party, unless you plan on performing your hostessing duties from a jail cell."

His words finally quieted her and she waited, even though she was tapping her foot restlessly.

"You're being summoned to court to-morrow morning at nine o'clock sharp—"

"What? Summoned to court? Oh, Roger . . . really, this is ridiculous. Just call Judge Jordan and explain to him. Tell him—"

"I'm afraid that won't be possible. Will Jordan is the one who signed the papers. If you had told me about the fines in the first place . . ."

"You're serious," she said. She sat down at a small tiled table that looked out over the gardens and the pool. "I can't believe this. If I find out that Sylvia Jordan had anything to do with this—"

"Listen to me now. Chief Barrows called me as a courtesy. He's not going to serve a warrant, on my promise that I'll have you in court Friday at nine. I want you to be there early and I want you to dress conservatively; no jewelry, no furs—"

"It's summertime, dear," Anne said sarcastically.

"You just be there. Jordan's up for re-election this year and people say he's gunnin' for bear. We don't want you to be the first one he bags."

"How quaint you've become in your speech, Roger."

"And if you make one snooty, sarcastic remark in court, Anne, I swear, I'll—"

"You'll what? Dismiss me as your client? Let some other lawyer collect all Baxter's residuals? Oh, I hardly think so, Roger. But don't worry. . . . I'll be there."

Anne was more irritated than worried when she hung up the phone. She'd been in trouble before over her parking fines. The worse she'd have to do was pay court costs and promise it wouldn't happen again.

Friday morning she was at the court-house at eight forty-five. She was even there when her attorney walked in, carrying a fine leather briefcase and looking as frazzled and harried as usual.

"You get thinner every time I see you, Roger," she said, reaching out to straighten his tie. "Doesn't Janet feed you any more? And you know, contacts would be much more flattering than those silly wire-rimmed glasses you wear."

Roger Finnell's smile was weak and a bit forced, she thought. As he placed his briefcase on a table, he glanced up at the clock, then let his brown eyes linger on Anne's face before wandering down her elegant but understated sand-colored suit and back up to her plain gold hoop earrings.

"Very nice," he muttered.

"Thank you," she said, not bothering to hide her sarcasm. She glanced at her watch. "How long will this take? I swear, I still have a million things to do before—"

"Shh," Roger said, nudging her as the bailiff walked into the courtroom. "Smile . . . not too big, that's right."

Anne rolled her eyes toward the ceiling, thinking there was no species on earth quite so silly as lawyers, or quite so concerned with winning every game they played, at any cost. But she smiled anyway, just as the judge strolled into court, his black robes billowing out behind him.

Her case was the first one. She sat rather impatiently as Roger began what she expected would be a cut-and-dried matter.

"How do you plead?" Judge Jordan asked dryly, peering over his reading glasses at Anne.

Anne stood up. "Hello, Will," she said, smiling.

Roger nudged her as the judge sat unsmiling, staring at her.

"How do you plead?" Will asked again.

"Guilty," Anne said with a shrug of her shoulders and what she hoped was her most winning smile.

"Huh, we'd like permission to pay the fines, your honor and—"

"How many does this make, Mrs. Benefield?" the judge asked. "Four . . . five this year?"

"I really don't know, your honor," she said humbly.

"Six, your honor," Roger said, clearing his throat.

"Six?" The judge glanced down at his desk, shuffling through papers before looking up again and glaring at Anne.

"What seems to be your problem, Mrs. Benefield? Do you think these fees are for everyone else in town except you?"

"No, of course not, but—"

"Perhaps you don't have the money to pay the fines." His voice was sarcastic, as were his dark accusing eyes.

Anne knew Will Jordan very well. He

had been one of Baxter's best friends, and they'd often gone to the club together on Saturday night. She thought he must really be enjoying this.

"No, sir," she said, her voice purposefully meek and quiet. "I think I can afford to pay the fines."

There was a quiet titter of laughter in the gallery behind her.

"Yes, I'm sure you can," he said with a quirk of one bushy eyebrow. "But next year I expect we'll see the same paperwork with your name on it come shuffling through the police department and through several other departments before it finally winds up on my desk. Do you think we don't have more important things to do than try to collect parking fines from you, Mrs. Benefield? Or from anyone who seems to have such a total disregard for the law?"

Anne frowned. He was serious. His voice was stern and he was dead serious.

"I'm sure you do, Will," she said, forgetting herself until Roger nudged her again. "I mean, your honor."

"I don't want to see any more late notices with your name on them. Do I make myself clear? You might have money to burn, ma'am, but I can assure you the city and county do not."

"Yes, sir," she said. Anne breathed a sigh of relief and grinned at the judge, thinking it was over.

"And to make sure you remember it next time the court is going to impose another penalty above the fines; one that can't be paid with money."

Anne's blue eyes widened. She turned to Roger and saw his worried look before he shrugged and nodded for her to pay attention to the judge.

"You are hereby sentenced to three months of community service at the halfway house in the third district of this city. You will report for duty Monday morning to Kurt Bonner, the director for the house. He will assign you to your duties at his discretion. I'll forward the papers to him this afternoon," he said with a concluding nod to Anne's lawyer. "Service shall be forty hours a week, weekends free, until sentence is fulfilled. Any questions, counselor?"

"No, your honor," Roger said.

Anne gasped and stared at the judge's

bench. What on earth was he talking about? A halfway house? With—yuk— kids?

"But Will . . . your honor . . ." she said, taking a step from around the table.

She jumped as his gavel banged loudly against the wooden desk.

"Next case." Then, to Roger, Judge Jordan said sternly, "You may escort your client from the courtroom, counselor."

"Yes, sir. Let's go, Anne," Roger said, taking her arm and pulling her with him.

She couldn't help seeing the grins on the faces of the few people in the court- room. Everyone thought it was funny. She wondered just how funny they'd think it was if they were the ones being sentenced to community service with a group of dirty, wild little kids. Well, she wouldn't stand for it.

Outside she stopped, dragging her arm away from Roger.

"Do something, Roger," she de- manded. Her face was flushed, her blue eyes wild with alarm.

"At this point I'm afraid there's not a damned thing I can do."

She thought there was a glimmer of

pleased satisfaction in his eyes, and that made her more angry.

"There has to be! I can't work at a place like that. You know how I am with children. What on earth will I do there? You have to find a way to get this dismissed. Bribe somebody if you have to," she said beneath her breath.

Roger Finnell tilted back his head and laughed aloud, the sound of it echoing against the marble walls and floors. When he finally stopped laughing he took off his glasses and wiped his eyes.

Anne stared at his uncharacteristic laughter. Had he lost his mind? Didn't he realize how serious this was?

"Oh, Anne . . ." he said, still chuckling. "Baxter Benefield would be proud of you. Bribe a judge over a puny parking fine . . . that's a good one. And, on the other hand, your lawyer is shocked and dismayed by your suggestion."

"Roger, this isn't funny. What am I going to do?" she said, frowning up at him.

He wasn't going to help her. She could see it in his eyes. He was going to let her suffer through this as some kind of silly lawyer's lesson.

He was still laughing and shaking his head as he turned to walk away from her. He swung his briefcase like a kid in a schoolyard and glanced back at her over his shoulder.

"I'd suggest you show up at the half-way house bright and early Monday morning. And I'd also suggest you behave very humbly with Kurt Bonner." He turned around completely, grinning at her as he walked backwards. "I hear he's a man who takes his job quite seriously. And don't whine, Annie. They say he tolerates very little complaining from his employees." He laughed again and turned to go.

Anne was speechless, simply livid with disbelief as she watched her lawyer, her last hope of deliverance, walk away laughing, as if she didn't pay him a fortune in fees every year.

Two

Anne refused to let the prospect of working at the halfway house keep her from enjoying her party. By midmorning on Saturday the tents were all in place and the portable air-conditioning units were installed at both ends of all the open-structured canopies. Her friend Cecile had been horrified that she was spending so much money on such a thing as air conditioning for a lawn party.

"For heaven's sake, we're going to be outdoors, Anne," she muttered on the phone. "Do you expect to cool the entire world? How does it work, anyway? Why couldn't you just use fans?"

"Because I didn't want to use fans. I want it to be cool inside the tents—you know how hot and humid it gets at this time of year. Besides, nothing but the best will do for a Benefield party. If you like the fresh open air so much, you can stroll in the garden and sweat to your heart's content. But as for me, I'll take air conditioning, no matter what the expense."

"Well, it's your money," Cecile muttered. "But Barney would skin me alive if I ever suggested such a thing."

Anne ignored Cecile. Everyone in town knew that for all Barney Loudermilk's money he was as tightfisted as Scrooge himself.

Her guests wouldn't be arriving until late afternoon. She hoped there would be a spectacular sunset across the west meadows after supper—a sky filled with rose and gold that would reflect in the lake and cast rosy shadows against the beautiful old two-story house.

Sitting at her dressing table, she sighed with pleasure, letting her imagination wander and plan. She wanted everything to be perfect and she wanted everyone to realize what a perfect house she had . . . what a perfect life.

She had coveted this house since she was a small girl. It was in the area where she had grown up, and every morning on her way to school she would stare at the house, imagining who lived there . . . how it must look inside, what its occupants would wear. She wanted a house like that. She wanted a life like the lives of the people who lived there.

But she'd married right out of high school, to a man who turned out to be as much a bully at home as he was at school. After ten years of abuse her divorce had been ugly and frightening, and she had just about given up her dream of ever having anything decent. She'd forgotten about this house and she'd even forgotten her childhood dreams of owning a home of her own, much less one like the house at Benefield Farms.

She was proud of the way she had pulled herself out of that bad time, the way she went back to school, became a paralegal. But it was still a struggle, and she hadn't trusted anyone to help her through it.

Until Baxter Benefield came along, like a guardian angel, and rescued her.

"Oh, Bax," she whispered, remembering his generosity. She stared at herself in the mirror, seeing the sparkle of tears in her eyes.

No one ever saw her cry. Even Baxter had rarely seen her cry. Most people in Clayburn County would agree that Anne Benefield was as hard and cynical about life, as self-centered, as anyone they'd ever met.

She wiped her eyes angrily, determined that nothing and no one would spoil this day for her. And nothing would spoil her perfectly lovely life, not even the threat of working at a halfway house with a group of yelling, screaming, obnoxious children.

By the time Anne walked out onto the wide front porch and glanced appreciatively at the wicker furniture and green ferns she had quite forgotten her apprehension and her memories.

A light breeze rustled the leaves of the huge old trees around the house and carried the scent of magnolia blossoms toward her. Small flags atop the tents on the lawn flapped quietly in the breeze, and for a moment Anne stood listening, hearing the sounds of summer, smelling the grass and the flowers and the hint of moisture from the lake.

By the time the first car pulled into the long circular drive she was ready. She quickly smoothed her flowered, peach-colored silk chiffon skirt and stood waiting as more and more cars turned off the main road and onto Benefield property.

The lawn party was a success; Anne knew that as soon as the elegant cold supper was served and there was an immediate murmur of approval arising among the linen-covered tables. Waiters moved through the tents, lighting hurricane lamps at the tables, quietly serving wine. And later, after dessert and champagne, everyone moved outside to the wooden dance floor that had been erected beneath colorful Chinese lanterns. There was a hush as the sunset captured everyone's attention, and the orchestra began to play softly in the background.

Anne felt Cecile touch her shoulder.

"It's perfect," she whispered. "Just as you hoped."

"Just as I planned," Anne corrected.

Cecile laughed, her plump cheeks quivering.

"Oh, Anne," she said. "Still holding on so tightly to everything. Barney says you're only fooling yourself if you think you can control life."

"Oh, Barney," Anne said. "What does he know?" She refused to let stuffy old Barney Loudermilk interfere with her pleasure tonight.

"He just doesn't want to see you hurt, honey, that's all."

Anne shrugged her shoulders and looked down at her best friend. For all her money Cecile always seemed to choose plain, frumpy clothes for every occasion. On her petite figure the high ruffled neck of the dress she wore only emphasized all the wrong things.

Anne put her arm around Cecile's plump shoulders, hugging her against her. Despite all her money, Cecile Loudermilk had welcomed Anne into their circle of friends from the beginning, unlike most of Baxter's country-club friends. Cecile was the kindest, sweetest person Anne knew, and she would do anything for her.

"I know," Anne said, smiling at Cecile.

"What does he think about my having to do community service?"

"Well, Barney doesn't know you the way I do," Cecile said, glancing away from Anne's blue eyes.

"What does he *think?*" she asked again.

"He thinks you will wilt like an unwatered petunia beneath the hot Georgia sun." Cecile's drawling voice was purposefully wry and teasing, but Anne knew she was telling the truth. Barney didn't think she would be able to take it.

Anne grunted softly, humorously. She'd show him. She'd show them all that she wasn't about to wilt. After all, she'd done it before, hadn't she? Pulled herself up—got an education and a job—married the richest man in town? Besides, what did she care what anyone in this stuffy, stilted little town thought?

Just then Anne saw Judge Will Jordan talking to a group of people nearby.

"Excuse me, dear," she whispered to Cecile. "There's a man I want to see."

"Now, Anne . . ." she heard Cecile say as she walked away.

Anne waved her hand over her shoulder, brushing away Cecile's warning as if she were a small mosquito, buzzing harmlessly around one's ears. She was smiling when she reached the "hanging judge."

Just then a waiter passed by carrying a large silver tray. Anne reached out and plucked a frosty stemmed glass of champagne from the tray and handed it toward Will.

"Judge," she murmured, still smiling.

He turned to her and saw the glass in her outstretched hand. With a quirk of his lips he took the champagne, sipping it as he peered over the edge at Anne Benefield.

"Anne," he acknowledged, nodding coolly at her.

The people gathered around him grew silent; waiting for a confrontation, Anne supposed

"I wasn't sure you'd be here, Will," she said.

"Why not? Surely you don't think I'd let business interfere with my pleasure . . . or our long friendship."

There were a few speculative glances among the small group of people—and a few smiles. Anne knew they loved nothing better than a bit of juicy gossip. And Will

Jordan's sentence of three months of community service for one of the town's wealthiest women was bound to have everyone talking.

"Of course I didn't," she said, her voice calm and easy. "In fact, I'm sure I'll enjoy the . . . huh, work you've assigned me. After all, we should all do our civic duty, and I'm more than willing to do mine."

The judge's look was amused, even a bit challenging, as he lifted his brow, but he said nothing else. As Roger had already warned her, he *was* up for reelection this year, and Anne knew he had to tread carefully with all potential voters.

"Where's your lovely wife this evening?" she asked, more than willing to change the subject now that this confrontation was out in the open.

Will tilted his head to the side, but he didn't turn his gaze from Anne.

"She's around here somewhere," he said. "Enjoying your delightful party, like the rest of us."

"Why thank you, Will," Anne murmured wryly. "I hope so. I truly hope so."

She turned then and walked away, smiling to herself when the buzz of conversation began again behind her. These people hardly knew what to make of her, she thought, even after all their years of association. She knew that some of them had never accepted her. And some had accepted her only because she was Baxter's wife. Now that he was gone their old skepticism about her had returned, it seemed. Some of them obviously couldn't forget that she was not "born to wealth," or that she could sometimes be brash and bold, not quite as refined as they thought they were.

Anne merely gritted her teeth and forced a smile as she mingled and nodded and made small, polite conversation. When the dancing began she had just as many offers as any of the others. And what did it matter if they were dancing with her as an obligation . . . from curiosity even. She didn't care. She hadn't really cared about such trivialities for years now.

She hadn't allowed herself to care.

The next day was quiet after the initial bustle of workmen removing the tents and carting them away on big trucks.

Anne didn't go to church, but opted instead to walk through her lush gardens
and sit quietly at the lake, watching the
ducks swim past.

She walked along a well-worn path beside one of the pasture fences, coaxing
the mares and their foals to her and feed-
ing them pieces of apples and carrots
that she always carried in her pockets.
She leaned against the fence, watching
the sleek, well-kept animals, feeling that
sense of peace that she always felt when
she was at the farm alone.

"Hiding out," Cecile often teased. Ac-
cording to her, Anne had been hiding
out for the past three years, ever since
Baxter's death.

Maybe even longer than that, Anne
thought.

But the farm was what she loved . . .
and the surrounding landscape was what
she enjoyed best. It could be stormy and
fierce or calm and soothing, like today. But
it never disappointed her, and it never
made her feel inadequate about herself.

She guessed she was still a country girl
at heart, despite her designer clothes and
expensive cars. And that was something

not many people in Clay County knew about Anne Benefield. She didn't want them to know her secret—they'd probably only use it against her when and if it suited them.

The next morning, Anne dressed very carefully for her first day of community service, choosing white slacks and a striped pink-and-white silk blouse. She took off her red nail polish and re-painted her nails a glistening pearl pink that matched the blouse and her new ear-rings. Then she gave herself one last look in the mirror before going out through the kitchen to the garage.

"I'll be gone all day, Jessica," she called over her shoulder as she went out. "Tell Mrs. Hargis to leave a salad in the refrig-erator for dinner. I'll probably eat party leftovers with it."

"Yes'm," the girl said, glancing for only a moment at her employer.

Anne knew Jessica was aware of where she was going, as was everyone else on the estate. But no one had said a thing, especially not Jessica, who was so shy, she rarely spoke at all.

Anne wasn't close to any of her employees; she chose to keep her distance. If the truth were known, she still felt a bit awkward giving them orders, having them fetch and carry for her. If it weren't for the big house and large acreage, she probably wouldn't have help at all, but she supposed to others it seemed her aloofness was for different, more snobbish reasons.

She found the halfway house easily and parked the car, making sure she was in a free parking zone. She didn't plan on giving Will Jordan any other reasons to reprimand her.

She stood for a moment, staring at the large, rambling house at the end of a quiet residential street. It was a nice neighborhood, very peaceful at this time of morning. Anne was surprised that the people living here had allowed such an establishment in their midst, and she wondered if the children who lived here ever caused them problems.

The house itself was old but surprisingly well tended for a place meant to offer only temporary shelter to children with family problems. The front yard was small and green beneath old trees. And the sidewalk leading to the front door was lined with colorful impatiens that formed dewy mounds and made the place look as homelike as any of the other houses in the neighborhood.

She could see that the back area contained a larger yard that was surrounded by a white picket fence. Only the sign above the front door would keep anyone from thinking this was a normal house for a normal family.

That notion was dispelled as soon as Anne walked in the front door.

There was very little furniture in the house, and what there was looked old and well used. The oak floors, probably lovely when the house had been new, seventy-five years or more ago, were faded, scratched and marred, no doubt, by heavy traffic.

And it was noisy.

The children were seated at a table in a long, narrow room to the left of the entry hall. They appeared to be all ages, from toddlers to teenagers. For a moment Anne felt panic wash over her.

What on earth was she doing here? And how, dear Lord, would she ever be able to cope with such a rowdy group of youngsters?

She glanced quickly to the right into what looked like an office. There were papers and folders on the wide, masculine-looking desk, and a carved wooden nameplate that read KURT BONNER.

Quietly, she stepped to the door and peered around the corner. She saw a man standing with his back toward her. Without thinking, she let her eyes move from his broad shoulders down to his faded but neatly pressed jeans. He was talking on the phone, holding the receiver between his head and shoulder while his hands shuffled through a sheaf of papers. His motions were quick and impatient, and for a moment Roger's warning came back to haunt her. He did, indeed, look like a man who took his job seriously. He looked as if he took *everything* seriously.

Anne stood for a moment in the doorway, wishing she could turn and run; wishing she could get out of this somehow. When the man on the phone hung up and turned around his gaze raked over her as he moved back to his desk, and she was aware of a certain impatience in his gray-green eyes.

"Yes?" he asked. He began to look through some other papers on his desk, and when he glanced up there was a wrinkle between his brows.

"I . . . I'm Anne Benefield," she said. Why on earth was she stuttering like a schoolgirl? She supposed he was handsome in a rugged kind of way, with those broad shoulders that hinted at an athletic background. But he was hardly her type; his sun-streaked hair was thinning. But it was his eyes that made her feel so inadequate; there was something extraordinary in the way he looked at her. His attitude was cool and dismissive, but his eyes, an unusual pale green color, were quick and alert, intelligent—and for some reason they made her feel slow and uncertain.

"Come in," he said, waving her toward a chair that was covered with books.

She placed the books on the floor and sat down, waiting for him to acknowledge her and the reason she was there.

He scribbled something on a piece of paper, then got up and walked back to the phone, dialing a number as if she weren't even in the room.

Anne could feel her impatience growing, could even feel her cheeks growing warm with irritation. Didn't he know who she was . . . why she was here? She watched him out of the corner of her eye, noting the trim fit of the jeans he wore, and the shining but obviously worn loafers, and she wondered why a man like him would choose a job like this. It was obviously not a well-paying one, she thought, as her eyes wandered over the shabby office. And she thought the noisy children across the hall would be daunting to any man.

Kurt Bonner slammed the phone down and Anne jumped. He was cursing beneath his breath when he turned back toward her and came to sit on the corner of the desk, swinging one leg restlessly as he leaned toward her.

He was close enough now that she could see those eyes more clearly, see the flecks of brown in their green depths.

"Mrs. Benefield, huh?" he asked, his eyes trailing over her with a certain measure.

"Anne," she said. "You . . . you do know why I'm here?"

"Oh, yes," he said, leaning back slightly. He smiled then, showing white, even teeth that made him look altogether more appealing and boyish, although Anne thought he must be near her own age. "You're my new dishwasher, I believe," he said with a quick grin.

"Dish . . . dishwasher?"

"Right through the dining room and through the swinging door," he said, pointing toward the hallway. "Gabby will tell you what to do."

Anne glanced down at her white, very expensive slacks and even more expensive silk blouse.

"But . . . I—"

"Better ask him to find you an apron," he said wryly, seeing her look as his glance moved quickly over her clothes. Then, just as quickly, he turned away, going to his desk and picking up some papers, seeming to dismiss her completely.

Three

Anne stood up and grabbed her purse. She didn't look back at the man at the desk but walked resolutely into the hall, hesitating only a moment before stepping into the dining room filled with the chatter of children.

Some of them fell silent, and one of the boys tossed a piece of toast across the table, causing a loud outbreak of giggles.

"Good morning," Anne said, nodding to the group.

There were at least twelve children seated at the long table. The food looked plentiful and healthy enough, ranging from scrambled eggs to cereal and a large stack of pancakes that had become tilted from the children's eager hands.

Anne's gaze fell immediately on a small child, probably the youngest at the table. She looked no more than four, and her hair hung in straight, stringy wisps about her syrup-smeared face. Anne thought she had the biggest blue eyes she'd ever seen, and now they stared at her with a mixture of fear and curiosity.

Those blue eyes followed Anne all the way down the room and until she started to push the door open into the kitchen. Suddenly the door swung open and a short, heavy woman appeared, carrying a tray with glasses and a pitcher of orange juice. She seemed friendly enough as she smiled at Anne, who stepped aside to let her through.

"Can I help you?" the woman asked, going to set the tray at the end of the table. She began to pass the glasses around, not looking back at Anne, but at the children.

"Mr. Bonner said I could find someone named Gabby in the kitchen?"

"Oh, sure," the woman said. "You must be the new lady, come to help in the kitchen."

Anne smiled. "I'm not sure how much help I'll be. I'm not very good in the kitchen."

Having finished passing the juice

around, the woman straightened and brushed her hair out of her eyes with the back of her arm.

"Whew, gonna be a scorcher today. If Kurt don't get the air conditioner fixed, I swear, we're all likely to melt. I don't envy you having to work in the kitchen." Her eyes wandered over Anne's clothes, just as Kurt Bonner's had. "Guess they didn't tell you what you'd be doin'," she said softly.

"No, they didn't," Anne said. "I guess I just assumed I'd be working in an office or . . ." She shrugged, her voice trailing away.

"It doesn't matter. You'll do fine," the woman said. She wiped her hand on her apron before extending it to Anne for a handshake. "I'm Vivian . . . everyone here just calls me Viv."

Anne was aware of the children listening, their eyes glancing her way. She thought the little girl with blue eyes hadn't looked away from her since she stepped into the room. Some of the older boys seemed determined to catch her attention by roughhousing or teasing the other children.

"I'm Anne. What do you do here, Viv?"

"Oh, a little bit of everything, I reckon. I help Gabby, when I can stand bein' around him. He's the cook. I serve the children. We've got a big crowd right now. Sometimes we have two or three, sometimes ten. We've had as many as twenty kids here on a hot weekend."

"Hot weekend?"

"Guess I mean that two different ways. Hot meanin' busy, and hot weather, too— seems to bring out the nastiness in some people." She lowered her voice then, as if she didn't want the children to hear her discussing their personal problems.

"Viv!" A scratchy, growling voice came from the kitchen, just before the door burst open and a man appeared, hands on his hips, glowering at them. "How long does it take to carry a load of juice in here? Oh, didn't know we had company."

"Gabby, this is Anne, the lady the court sent over to help us."

The old man's graying, bushy eyebrows lifted and his mouth quirked to one side. Anne could see that he had no teeth, and his tired old eyes looked weary and solemn.

"Oh, yeah. The rich 'un that thinks she don't have to pay parkin' tickets," he muttered.

Anne's mouth flew open. She couldn't believe the animosity in his tone of voice or the way his gaze seemed to dismiss her as useless.

"Don't pay any attention to him," Viv said. She reached out to swat the old man on his sleeve. "Behave yourself, Gabby. Haven't you ever heard the one about lookin' a gift horse in the mouth?"

"Wouldn't know a gift horse if I was to see one, let alone look it in the mouth. Now that right there, Vivian, don't make a lick of sense."

"Oh, never mind," the heavy woman said, rolling her eyes toward the ceiling. "Come along," she said to Anne. "I'll show you where to put your stuff."

Anne decided that the inside of the house was the most depressing place she'd ever been. Besides the obvious lack of anything personal to give the interior a homey touch, it was too dark to suit her taste . . . too gloomy. The kitchen was no exception; although it was large and spacious, it was cluttered with boxes of canned food and other supplies. A large table in the middle of the room was covered with an oilcloth and piled high with vegetables. There was a knife and a big aluminum bowl nearby. The equipment was old and outdated, the cookware that hung from a rack above the stove dented and discolored.

She didn't know how she was to endure three months of this.

The old man followed them into the kitchen, grumbling beneath his breath as he went to the table to work. He picked up a knife, waving it in the air toward Anne.

"Well, don't just stand there gawkin', sis. Reckon you can see for yourself we got a sink full of dirty dishes. Get yourself an apron and have at it."

Anne's gaze turned to the sink and she felt her heart drop to the pit of her stomach. There were mounds of dirty dishes. It looked as if the old man had used every pot and pan in the kitchen; some of the dishes looked to be from yesterday's supper.

Her eyes must have given away her apprehension for when she turned to Viv she saw sympathy in the woman's dark eyes.

"Every day won't be this bad," she said quietly. "We're just a little shorthanded right now, that's all. Here, let me take your purse—I'll put it right over here in this closet, on the top shelf."

"For Pete's sake, the woman ain't an invalid, is she?" Gabby growled, still waving the knife.

Anne thought she was beginning to dislike the old man very much.

"Let her hang up her own purse. Probably what's wrong with her anyway . . . always had somebody waitin' on her, doin' for her. Let her do it herself."

Anne met his eyes, staring at him with open hostility. She had to bite her lip to keep from shouting out her frustration and anger. She didn't want to be here any more than he wanted her here. But she wasn't a dimwit, for heaven's sake.

"Yes," Anne said, walking toward the closet. "I can do it myself, Viv. But I appreciate your help . . . and your kindness," she added, glancing pointedly at the old man.

She heard his grunt, but she was determined not to let him get to her, any more than he already had.

"Are the aprons in here, too?" she asked.

"On the bottom shelf, there," Viv said. "Would you like a cup of coffee . . . juice or something? Anything you'd like to eat or drink, just feel free to help yourself." The woman glared at Gabby, almost daring him to dispute her offer. "Well, I'd better get back out to the kids before they wreck the entire dining room. I'll talk to you after awhile, Anne," she said. "You, too, crabby . . . I mean Gabby," she said, giggling as she went toward the dining room.

"Durned smart-mouthed woman," Gabby muttered. "Never could stand no smart-mouthed woman." His bleary old eyes glanced up resentfully at Anne, but she said nothing.

How did this strange little man find his way into such a job? For the life of her she couldn't understand why Kurt Bonner, a seemingly intelligent man, would allow the cantankerous old coot to work here.

As she turned on the hot water and

began to pour dishwashing detergent into the sink, she thought she might actually hate Will Jordan for what he'd done to her. And she'd decided that paying the parking fine definitely would have been easier than this.

By the time Anne finished the first batch Viv had brought in two other trays of breakfast dishes. It was hot in the kitchen, and Anne could feel rivulets of sweat between her breasts and beaded on her forehead. Her feet hurt and she wished she hadn't worn panty hose under her slacks. She blew a puff of air between her lips and wiped her arm across her head. She thought she'd never been so hot or so miserable in all her life.

"They's some rubber gloves under the sink," Gabby advised from the table. He had a mound of potatoes and carrots scraped and peeled in front of him. He seemed relatively cool and unbothered by the heat.

"I can't work wearing rubber gloves," Anne growled.

"Suit yourself. It's your hands."

Just then the door to the kitchen swung open. From the corner of her eye

Anne saw Kurt Bonner stroll in and pick up a carrot from the table. He brought it to the double sink and swung the water faucet over toward him, rinsing off the vegetable.

He smelled cool and clean, like sun-drenched linens and spicy cologne. She wondered if he knew how hot and grimy she felt . . . or how his cool presence enhanced that feeling.

"How's it going?" he asked.

Anne twisted around and watched him from the corner of her eye as he walked back to the table. She didn't take her hands out of the sink as she glowered at his back. She saw Gabby's toothless grin and had a feeling that the old man was just waiting for her to complain and get her comeuppance.

"Fine," she muttered. "Just fine."

The door swung open a second time. All of them were surprised to see the small, blue-eyed girl rush through, arms outstretched. Her face was crumpled and forlorn and she was crying.

"Oh, honey," Viv said. "What's wrong?" She put down the dishes that she had in her hand and turned to the little girl.

But the child ran past her, straight to Anne. She wrapped her small arms around Anne's legs, causing Anne to stagger slightly. She held her dripping hands out of the water, feeling totally helpless and inadequate, and totally surprised by the little girl's actions.

When Anne felt the child rub her nose against her white linen slacks she shuddered. Vivian handed Anne a towel, and she dried her hands, then bent to try and remove the girl's arms from around her legs.

The little girl was trembling and her sobs were quiet, choked little sounds of misery. Nothing Anne said or did could unfasten the girl's grip on her.

Anne looked helplessly toward Vivian, not knowing what to do.

"Talk to her," Viv suggested, nodding her head toward Anne. "Her name is Tracy."

Anne bent toward the girl, patting her back awkwardly and trying not to wince when she felt the sticky swipe of syrup on her slacks.

"Here, now," she muttered. "What's wrong? What's wrong, Tracy?"

"They . . . they said my mama's dead,"

she sobbed. "They said she's never comin' back to get me. They said they was puttin' me up for 'doption."

Anne looked up, frowning toward Kurt Bonner, who had obviously been enjoying her initiation with one of the children. But at the girl's anguished words she saw the smile leave his face, saw him straighten and toss the carrot from his hand onto the table as he came forward and bent to one knee beside the child.

"Hey," he murmured softly. His hands on the girl's shoulders seemed large, but Anne couldn't deny the gentleness with which he touched her. "You know the boys are just teasing you. Your mama is fine, sweetheart. She's just gone away for a little while . . . don't you remember us telling you that when you came?" He glanced up at Anne as if he needed help.

But Anne was frozen. How could she explain to him how totally inadequate she felt around children . . . around anyone who was suffering and in pain? She had no idea how to comfort the girl, or how to help her.

"Why don't you let me take you upstairs, sweetie pie," Viv said, bending over the girl, too. "You can take a nice cool bath if you like and put on something light, and I'll read to you 'til you go to sleep."

The tiny girl shook her head and put her fingers into her mouth.

Kurt reached forward and lifted her chin with his fingers. "What is it you want, angel?" he asked.

She looked at Anne then, and as Anne gazed into the big blue eyes of this sad, dirty-faced little creature, she felt her heart melting against her will.

"You want Mrs. Benefield to take you upstairs?" he asked, seeing Tracy's wistful look.

She nodded her head then, reaching one sticky little fist to latch onto Anne's slacks once again.

"Would you mind?" he asked, glancing up at Anne, his green eyes shadowed in the dimly lit kitchen.

"I . . . I'm not sure I know what to do," she whispered.

"It'll come to ya," Viv said. "Just take her up and talk to her . . . be nice to her. Workin' with these poor little ones makes you appreciate your own, doesn't it?"

Anne didn't answer, but she took Tracy's hand. The child started toward the door as if she couldn't wait to go upstairs.

"Don't take too long," Gabby said, nodding toward the new trays of dishes that Vivian had brought in. "They's lots of work to be done in here afore we can feed these younguns their supper."

Anne sighed and shook her head, aware of Tracy's light tug on her hand, aware of Kurt Bonner's cool, clear eyes watching her.

If she had expected a little appreciation for helping the child, she certainly wasn't going to get it from Gabby, or Kurt Bonner either, for that matter.

Four

Anne let the little girl lead the way upstairs and into a bedroom that contained three narrow cots. There were toys at one end of the room, and ruffled curtains on the windows. The room had the look of one used only by smaller children, and Anne guessed they were separated by age here.

"Is this your room?" Anne asked.

Tracy gazed up at her and nodded, her blue eyes shining now and clear of tears.

There was a doorway open at one end of the room, and Anne could see that it was a bathroom. She freed her hand from the little girl's sticky palm and walked to the bathroom.

"Why don't you sit on your bed?" Anne asked when she saw the girl begin to follow her. "I'll find a washcloth and we'll get you all cleaned up. Won't that feel better?"

Tracy didn't say a word and she didn't go to her bed, but followed right behind Anne.

With a wet washcloth in one hand Anne took Tracy back into the bedroom and sat her on the end of one of the beds. The little girl's look was adoring as Anne began to wash her face and then her sticky hands.

"How old are you, Tracy?" she asked.

She couldn't help smiling into the blue eyes. The child had such a sweet, innocent look about her. Anne couldn't imagine anyone ever being cruel or abusive to her. But she knew that something had to be very wrong with the little girl's life for her to have been brought here.

"Free and a half," Tracy said, holding up five fingers proudly.

"Three and a half?"

Tracy nodded her head wildly and Anne laughed. Then she put down the wet cloth and took the girl's fingers, tucking her thumb and little finger in toward her palm.

"There," Anne said. "That's three."

"Free!"

"That's right." Anne laughed again;

she couldn't help it. There was something so sweetly silly about Tracy that she couldn't help responding to it.

"That's a nice sound."

She turned toward the door and saw Kurt leaning against the doorframe. His hands were in his pockets and his gaze was steady and cool as he looked at Anne and Tracy.

"What?" Anne asked, feeling a bit foolish and wondering why her heart had suddenly accelerated.

"Laughter. Sometimes it seems we're more familiar in this house with the sound of crying, or angry screaming. We don't hear much genuinely happy laughter. Most of these kids haven't had what we'd call the all-American life, you know."

"Yes," she said. "I can imagine."

She turned to look down at Tracy. The child had her fingers in her mouth again and she was leaning against Anne.

"I think she's sleepy," Kurt said. "It's hard on some of the little ones, getting up so early."

"Shall I put her to bed? Is it all right to . . . to leave her here by herself?" She practically whispered the last words, not wanting to upset the child again.

"It's all right. Viv will come and check on her in a little while. Here . . . I'll help you."

He walked into the room and bent toward both of them.

"Here, angel," he murmured. "Let's scoot you up here where you'll be more comfortable."

Tracy made a quiet little noise of protest, reaching for Anne with her free hand. But it wasn't more than a minute or two before she closed her eyes and slept.

Anne stood up then, uncertain about what she should do. She felt out of place here, uncomfortable in Kurt Bonner's quiet, watchful presence. And she had to admit that part of that discomfort had to do with his very blatant masculine appeal. That was something she definitely hadn't counted on.

"Well," she said. "I . . . I suppose Gabby is wondering where I've gotten to." She couldn't help the note of irritability that crept into her voice.

Kurt laughed softly and touched her arm, moving with her toward the door.

Once outside he closed the door and stood looking down at Anne as if he had something to say.

"Gabby isn't as bad as he seems."

"Oh, really?" she asked dryly. "Wasn't that what they used to say about Mussolini?"

He laughed again. "You're a very funny woman, Anne Benefield. I can't quite figure you out."

She wasn't sure why his comment made her want to escape, or why she found it so difficult to meet his eye. But she was sure of one thing—she wasn't ready to have this man know all about her. She certainly wasn't in the habit of baring her soul to just anyone, and that wasn't about to change with a man she'd just met.

"Where are Tracy's parents?" she asked instead, hoping to change the subject and that look of speculation in his green eyes.

"She's never known her father. I'm not even sure Tracy's mother knows who he is."

Anne winced, hating to think of the sordid mess the little blue-eyed girl must have endured.

"The mother's a junkie. She's only

twenty-one and already she's been in and out of jail more times than I can count. This time it's a little more serious, I'm afraid. She was arrested for selling."

"Oh, my," Anne said, shaking her head. "But what if she goes to prison? What will happen to Tracy?"

"Well, if no relatives come forward who want her, I'm afraid foster care is the only alternative. We rarely keep children here longer than four weeks, unless it's on a specific order of the court."

Anne bit her lip, fighting back the flood of sadness that washed over her. She didn't want to get involved in any of the problems here, not even with a child as adorable as Tracy. She simply couldn't allow herself to.

"That's too bad," she murmured.

Kurt's eyes narrowed. He heard the coolness creep into Anne's voice and he could see her struggle to compose herself. This was one very unusual lady. He thought he was pretty good at figuring people out, being in his line of work. But she was different. For some reason she reminded him of some of the children who came here—hurt and angry and withdrawn. It took a long time to get through to some of them. And some would never allow him to get close enough to help. He wondered which side of the fence Mrs. Benefield would fall on.

"Well," he said, standing straighter and putting his hands in his pockets, "don't let it bother you. Before you leave us I'm afraid you'll see a great many kids come and go." He paused for a minute, looking at her as if he wanted to say something else. But he didn't. "If you'll excuse me, I have work to do, and I'm sure Gabby is anxious to have you back."

She clamped her lips together. Why did she feel so disappointed? What had she expected? Surely she didn't think one conversation with Kurt Bonner would send her from the kitchen to some other, more pleasant task in the household.

She watched him walk down the stairs. After he was gone she opened the bedroom door and stepped back inside. Her eyes softened when she walked to the bed and pushed a strand of hair away from Tracy's forehead.

What a beautiful child. Sweet and innocent and completely adorable.

And doomed, a voice whispered. She doesn't have a chance, living the life she's had, the voice continued.

Anne took a deep breath and turned to leave the room. Why couldn't something more be done for these children? Why couldn't Kurt Bonner manage to have a better place for them to stay until their lives were settled once again?

"It's none of my business," she muttered as she hurried down the stairs. "I don't care what he does with the place. I'm just here to do a job. Three months from now it will be all over. I can go home and forget this place ever existed."

Anne spent the rest of the afternoon washing dishes and trying to make a bit of order in the kitchen. She was quiet and thoughtful, her mind going again and again to Tracy and the work that was being done here. Necessary work. Probably unrewarding work. And she wondered again why a man like Kurt Bonner did it.

Viv took her outside at lunch and they ate a sandwich at a picnic table beneath towering oak and maple trees. The children played on a swing set and a wooden climbing platform in the fenced-in area of the yard. To watch them, you'd never know where they came from or why they were here in such a place.

"There's so much work to be done here," Viv observed.

"Yes, I've noticed," Anne said, glancing back at the house. "What do the children do at night? I haven't seen any house parents."

"Oh," Viv said, frowning. "House parents. You wouldn't believe what a time Kurt has with that problem. We can't keep them. The last couple who were here quit suddenly last week . . . just up and left in the middle of the night. Seems one of the bigger boys pulled a knife on them."

"Pulled a knife?" Anne gasped.

"These are angry, disturbed kids we get here," Viv said, frowning. "But that doesn't mean they can't be helped. Still," she continued, "I guess I can't blame the couple for being scared out of their wits. But it left us in quite a fix, I can tell you, what with a houseful of kids."

"But who's staying with them at night now?"

"My husband and I are doing it temporarily. Kurt has an interview this afternoon with a couple. I'm just keeping my fingers crossed that they take the job before my husband loses his patience and asks me for a divorce."

"Oh," Anne said, smiling at the woman. "I doubt that."

Anne thought that Viv had a pretty face, and even though she was heavy there was a feminine shape to her. Now that she knew the woman a little better, she thought she was rather attractive and sweet-looking.

"Do you and your husband have children?" Anne asked.

"Oh, yes. Four—two boys and two girls—but they're all grown and out of the house. Kevin—that's my husband—he says he's already raised his family and that it's time for me and him to spend some time alone. So you can imagine that he doesn't take too kindly to my bringing him here to baby-sit kids he doesn't even know."

"I can imagine," Anne said, nodding sympathetically.

"And I can tell you," Viv said, lowering her voice, "living here is pure hell on a ied couple's love life."

Anne laughed, enjoying Vivian's company and the conversation. She even enjoyed the plain cheese sandwich and the respite of being out in the breeze, away from the hot kitchen.

"You have kids?" Vivian asked.

"No," Anne said quickly. "No kids . . . from either marriage."

"Oh, you were married once before. I didn't know that."

"Yes . . . I married very young, actually, right out of high school." Anne glanced back at the children. "He made my life a living hell for ten long years."

"I'm sorry," Viv said.

"It's okay. That was a long time ago, another lifetime ago it seems."

"I guess you can relate to these kids, then, having lived through that."

"Why do you say that?"

"Well, you must know what it's like, being trapped in a miserable life, unable to do anything about it. I mean, it's bad enough for a grown woman—just imagine how it must be for kids. They don't have any say about what happens in their lives . . . not really."

Anne had never considered it before.

Perhaps she just hadn't wanted to consider it. But it was true—she should be able to relate to these kids and what had happened in their lives. But she knew she didn't want to; she didn't want to get involved. That was the same reason she'd never wanted children. She was too afraid she'd be like her own mother—cold and unemotional, incapable of loving anyone except herself. After all, she hadn't loved Baxter, and she certainly hadn't loved her first husband, although in the beginning the physical side of their relationship had been exciting and exhilarating.

But she had been young then. She doubted that even that kind of excitement was out there for her anymore—at her age, it probably never would be again.

Five

It was a long afternoon. Long and hot and miserable, even though Anne had to admit it was made somewhat more bearable by the delicious aroma of food cooking in the oven.

A little after four, Viv came into the kitchen and walked to the cupboard to get her things.

"I'm going home to take a break before Kevin and I have to be back to spend the night," she said.

Anne wasn't sure if Viv were addressing her or Gabby. She had finished with the dishes now, and she had to admit that even though she was hot and grimy, she felt a certain satisfaction at the clean, orderly countertops and empty sinks. She wouldn't let herself think of what would be waiting for her tomorrow morning at eight.

"I know you're probably tired and anxious to get out of here," Viv continued, coming to stand beside Anne. "But you're welcome to stay for supper."

Anne started to protest despite the growling in her stomach, which had grown worse as the delicious smells of the kitchen increased.

"Kurt wanted me to be sure and tell you that," Viv said, her voice coaxing.

"I don't want to impose," Anne said.

"Oh, but you wouldn't be. Actually, it would be more of a favor to us than anything. We always try to have supper with the kids, kind of like a family meal. It's something most of them have never had, and Kurt thinks it's important. The kids seem to really enjoy it. And since I can't be here, it would be nice if you could."

Anne wondered why she felt such a rush of disappointment. Had she really thought that Kurt Bonner might enjoy her company . . . that that could actually be his reason for asking her to stay?

"Don't beg her," Gabby growled. "The woman probably ain't used to the kind of rough grub we have."

Anne turned on the old man. She was

tired and suddenly fed up after a day of his hateful remarks. She had listened to him without a word, but now it was more than she could stand.

"And what would you know about the kind of food I'm used to?" she snapped.

He grunted and went to take a pan of fragrant yeast bread out of the oven. The hot, rich scent of it actually made Anne's mouth water.

"I know your kind," was all he said, not bothering to look at her.

"You don't know me," Anne said, practically shouting. "And in the future I'd appreciate your keeping your comments about me to yourself."

"Huh," he muttered, finally glancing at her from the corner of his bleary eyes. "Highfalutin and a mite touchy, too."

"Oh," Anne said, feeling her frustration growing.

"Look," Viv said, her voice low, "don't let the old man get to you. He doesn't mean anything by it."

"Meant every word," Gabby growled.

"Gabby, will you please be quiet a minute? Or shall I tell Kurt the way you're behaving?"

The old man grunted then and wiped his hands on his grungy apron. And even though he eyed Anne resentfully, he said nothing else.

"Please," Vivian continued, "it would mean so much to the kids, and it would be a great help to Kurt. I feel guilty leaving him alone this way."

"You shouldn't feel guilty . . . not the way you work around here. And you have your own husband, your own household to take care of," Anne began. "This is only a job."

"I know, but it's hard to remember that sometimes when I look at these kids," Viv said, nodding. There was a pleading look in her dark eyes and a wistful little smile on her lips.

"Oh, all right," Anne said. "But I hardly feel like sitting down to dinner. I'm dirty and hot and I look terrible."

"Kids don't care how you look," Gabby said sarcastically. "This ain't exactly the Ritz."

"I can see that," Anne snapped, her gaze moving pointedly over his dirty apron.

She thought the old man actually

laughed then, but if he did he covered it with a cough and turned back to his stove.

After Vivian left Anne went upstairs and washed her face, letting the cool cloth linger on her neck for a moment. She was tired, and for a moment she wished she hadn't agreed to stay. All she wanted was to be at Benefield Farms, to take a long cool bath in rose-scented water, and stretch out on the chaise in her upstairs bedroom.

Later, when she walked into the dining room, the children were just taking their seats. Kurt stood at the head of the table. He nodded to her and smiled.

"Why don't you sit there?" he asked, motioning to the other end of the long table.

She wasn't surprised to find little Tracy following her to that end of the table. She wasn't sure why the child had formed such a strong attachment to her so quickly.

Anne helped Tracy into her chair, and when the little girl got up and pulled the heavy chair even closer to her, Anne bit her lip to keep from smiling. For such a little girl, she was so sweetly solemn and so sincere. When Anne looked up Kurt was watching her.

The food was already on the table, and two of the older boys—the ones who had been rowdy at breakfast—began to reach for the platters of roast beef and potatoes before everyone was seated.

"Wait," Kurt said quietly, his gaze turning to the teenager.

The boy hesitated, staring at Kurt as if he might defy him.

"Sit down, Jeremy, and wait for the others." Kurt's voice was firm but not unkind.

The boy plopped down into his chair, sulking and throwing resentful looks at first Kurt and then Anne.

Anne was surprised when Kurt gave a quiet blessing after everyone was seated. Then, with a smile at the boy he had reprimanded, he picked up a platter of food and handed it to him.

"Why don't you begin passing the food around, Jeremy?"

All during dinner Tracy's adoring eyes looked to Anne every time she needed anything. By the time Gabby, minus his grubby apron, brought in dessert, Anne had decided there was no escaping the little girl's attention and had given in to it.

She spooned a small portion of nutmeg-scented peach cobbler onto Tracy's plate.

"Do you like peaches, sweetheart?" she asked. When Tracy took a bite her eyes lit up, and she quickly took another.

"It's good, huh?" Anne asked, turning slightly toward Gabby, who was just walking past. "Pretty good cooking, even if it isn't the Ritz," she murmured, intending Gabby to hear.

He just grunted and walked back into the kitchen.

Anne was amazed at how much she enjoyed supper. Maybe it was because she'd worked all day; maybe it was because she was so exhausted, but she thought it was the best meal she'd had in ages. The roast beef was so tender it melted in your mouth, and the vegetables were fresh and flavorful. The light, yeasty bread brought a sigh to her lips when she bit into it, and she thought she'd never had better peach cobbler in her life.

She'd have to give the old man credit

for one thing—he certainly knew how to cook.

After supper, Anne felt a bit of awkwardness as she rose from the table. She hardly knew how to leave or what she should say to Kurt. Should she thank him . . . ignore him?

As it turned out, he made the decision, in the same way he seemed to make all the decisions in the house. After sending the kids down the hallway to what he called the family room he walked with Anne out onto the small front stoop.

"That wasn't too bad, was it?" he asked. He was leaning back against one of the porch supports, his arms crossed as he gazed up at the trees that surrounded the house.

"I'm not sure what you mean," she said. "The work or the supper?"

"Both." His eyes were cool and unreadable as he turned his head to gaze down at her.

She took a deep breath and shrugged her shoulders. Then she lifted her hands in front of her.

"I'm not sure my hands will ever be the same." The withered look was gone now, but her hands were still red and slightly swollen.

Kurt reached forward and took one of her hands, and Anne gasped with surprise. His hand was big and masculine as it closed over her fingers with surprising tenderness. "We have some lotion inside," he said quietly.

"No." She pulled her hand away much too quickly and saw his slight smile. "I . . . I can do that at home."

She stood looking at him, not knowing what to think or what to make of this man.

"But you did enjoy Gabby's supper?" he asked.

She smiled then and shook her head. "It was amazing. Who'd ever think from looking at him that he has such a gift. I've known chefs who couldn't match that meal."

"Looks can be deceiving, as they say," he said.

"Yes . . . yes, they can. Well, I should go." Why did she feel so awkward, so out of her element with this man? Feeling confident was something she had worked on for years . . . something she thought she had perfected by now.

"Sleep well, Anne," he said, pushing himself away from the porch support. "We'll see you in the morning."

He went back into the house, and Anne stood for a moment, staring at the closed door. She was going to have to work on this, she told herself. This man disturbed her . . . tempted her as a man more than she'd been tempted in years.

By the time Anne got home the big house was empty. Her cook, Mrs. Hargis, did not live at Benefield Farms, but drove out each day from town. Jessica and her husband, Elmer, lived in a cottage behind the house. Elmer did all the odd jobs on the estate and helped with the horses when he was needed.

There were other day employees and other quarters on the grounds, empty now since Baxter's death. Anne preferred having only Jessica and Elmer living here full-time. They didn't have children and were very quiet and settled.

When she unlocked the back door her telephone was ringing.

"Hello," she said breathlessly.

"Where have you been?" Cecile asked.

"I've been calling and calling. I'm dying to know how it went."

Anne sighed and gave a little grunt of laughter.

"Oh, Cecile," she said. Where should she begin?

"What?" Cecile asked, her voice breathy and expectant. "What happened? Did something go wrong to make you so late?"

"I ate supper at the halfway house. And no, nothing happened. Just a long, miserable day of backbreaking work."

"You're kidding. I figured you would be doing a little filing or at the very worst reading books to the children."

"Ha. Most of them couldn't sit still long enough to be read to." She thought of Tracy and smiled. "But I did take care of one little girl . . . sort of."

"I want to hear all about it."

"Listen," Anne said, feeling her feet beginning to ache. "If I don't take a shower soon and get out of these dirty clothes, I think I'll die. Let me call you back."

Later, in silk pajamas and with her bare feet stretched out against the cool material of the chaise, Anne called Cecile. She explained how she had washed at least a million dishes, not to mention the caked pots and pans. She was surprised to hear the laughter in her voice when she spoke about Gabby, since she hadn't found him or his comments the least bit funny at the time. And she told her about Vivian and how she was doing double duty at the house.

"And what about him?" Cecile asked slyly.

"Him?" Anne knew who she meant. Every woman in town had heard about Kurt Bonner. Anne had thought before she met him that it was only his divorced status that caused so much attention. But after having seen him . . . after having been close enough to catch the seriousness in those odd green eyes, she knew it was more than that.

"You know very well who him," Cecil muttered. "Kurt Bonner. Is he as gorgeous as everyone says? Is he nice?"

"He seems nice," Anne said, frowning. She was having difficulty describing him. She certainly didn't want to go overboard and give Cecile the wrong idea.

"Oh." Cecile's voice lowered with disappointment. "Then he's not handsome?"

"Well, yes . . . actually, he's very attractive," Anne said. She didn't want to be having this conversation. Kurt Bonner was the last thing she wanted to think about tonight.

"Anne, what's wrong with you? You sound as if you're in la-la land somewhere. Are you that tired?"

"I'm exhausted," Anne replied, relieved that she had an excuse not to discuss Kurt. "I'm sorry . . . perhaps you can come out this weekend. I'll have Mrs. Hargis fix us a nice lunch and we'll sit under the trees and gossip. Right now, believe me, that sounds like heaven."

"I'll hold you to that. Now . . . you get some rest. Gee, I hope tomorrow isn't so bad for you, especially since Barney and I have a little bet going."

"A bet? You and Barney have a bet about me?"

"About how long you'll last," she said, giggling, "Barney thinks you'll go begging on your knees to Judge Jordan and ask him to commute your sentence."

"Well, you can tell Barney Loudermilk not to hold his breath."

"Atta girl," Cecile said, still giggling. "You hang in there, sweetie. If I don't talk to you before, I'll see you Saturday."

"Yes, Saturday," Anne said, her thoughts already somewhere else.

Anne lay on the chaise, unable to move. She'd never been so tired in all her life. She slathered lotion on her hands, gallons of it, it seemed, and chided herself for being too stubborn to wear the gloves that Gabby had offered. Lord, how she dreaded tomorrow. If it weren't for seeing Kurt . . .

Anne's eyes opened wide and her heart skipped a beat before returning to its slow, steady rhythm.

Where had that thought come from and how on earth had that little tingle of anticipation appeared in her chest . . . that long-forgotten pounding of her heart?

Slowly she let out her breath and leaned back on the chaise, which was positioned in front of the bay window facing the lake. She could see the tops of the trees and the intermittent twinkle of stars through the leaves when the wind blew. She was so intent on distracting herself that she didn't even realize it when she closed her eyes and slept.

Six

Anne woke next morning to the sound of the telephone ringing. For a moment she didn't know where she was . . . couldn't remember falling asleep in the chaise. She practically fell to the floor as she groped for the phone, glancing at the crystal clock on her nightstand.

Eight o'clock! Dear Lord, she'd overslept. It was probably someone calling from the halfway house now to ask where she was.

"Hello?" Her voice sounded husky with sleep. She cleared her throat and spoke again. "Hello."

"Anne, where are you?" It was Vivian. Her voice was a mere whisper, as if she held the phone right against her lips.

"Oh, no," Anne groaned. "I'll be right there. Tell him I've had car problems. Tell him I'm stuck in traffic."

"Actually, he doesn't know you're late yet," Viv said.

"He . . . he doesn't?"

"I was going to tell him that I asked you to stop by the store on your way here to pick up some dishwashing detergent and several rolls of paper towels. But I thought it might be a good idea to get our stories straight in case he asks. He probably won't."

"Do you really want me to?"

"No," Viv said with a laugh. "We have plenty. But when you get here come in the back door. It was a rough night and I don't think Kurt is in any mood to deal with a late employee . . . temporary or not." She was laughing when she hung up the phone.

"Oh, dear," Anne said. She turned around twice, not sure what to do first. Her head was practically reeling from being awakened so suddenly.

Anne was dressed and going out the door within twenty minutes. She only had time to grab a banana from a bowl on the kitchen countertop. Lord, but she had forgotten how it was to have to be at work at a certain time. What a hassle, and how humiliating at her age to have to make excuses for being late.

She vowed then and there that it was something she wouldn't have to do again, even if she had to set her alarm for five o'clock in the morning.

She'd dressed more practically this morning, pulling on loose-fitting cotton pants and a pale green knit top. She'd had to look for a few moments before finding a pair of sneakers stuck in the back of her closet. They looked as if they'd hardly been worn, but they felt soft and comfortable.

Anne parked her car on the street and slipped around the side of the house to the back. She didn't like sneaking; it wasn't in her nature. But then, that in-your-face attitude of hers was probably what had gotten her into so much trouble in the first place. Besides, she thought Viv was right. Maybe she shouldn't take a chance on making Kurt angry first thing this morning.

Gabby was the only one in the kitchen. Anne quickly put her purse in the cupboard and went without a word to the sinkful of dirty dishes and turned on the water.

She sensed Gabby looking her way and once when she turned around she caught him watching her with a wary expression in his sad old eyes.

"Where did you say those gloves were?" she asked.

"Under the sink."

She worked without speaking and when Viv came in later they exchanged a quiet look between them.

"Why don't you take a break?" Viv asked. "Gabby has some biscuits left over from breakfast. Would you like some orange juice?"

"That sounds good," Anne said, wiping her forehead. It was already sweltering in the kitchen, and she was glad she'd worn looser, more comfortable clothes.

She was hungry and the biscuit, still warm and dripping with butter, was wonderful.

"Ummm," she murmured with her mouth full. "Gabby, you're a master baker. These biscuits absolutely melt in your mouth and the yeast rolls we had last night were about the best things I've ever eaten."

Gabby turned a doubtful gaze her way, grunting disdainfully as he moved about the kitchen.

"Buttermilk," he muttered. "Never use nothin' except buttermilk in biscuits."

Behind his back, Anne rolled her eyes, wondering why she even bothered to try and compliment him. It was obvious the old man didn't like her, hadn't liked her since the first moment he saw her.

"So," she said, turning her attention to Viv. "You said it was rough last night. What happened?"

"Well, in the first place, Kurt didn't hire the couple he interviewed yesterday. Said there was something about them he didn't trust. But we need someone so desperately that he agreed to check them out really good before he says no for sure. Lord, I hope it's soon. Last night the two Miller boys—"

"Which ones are they?"

"Oh . . . that's right, I guess you don't know all the kids' names yet. Jeremy and Keith. Jeremy is the oldest."

"The one who always causes trouble at the table."

"And in the playground . . . and in the

family room and just about anywhere else he is. He's an angry, troubled young man, and his little brother does everything he says, although I think he's as terrified of him as the other children are."

Anne bit her lip. Somehow she hadn't thought of the dangers for the other children, living in a place like this, among strangers, actually. For the small, unprotected ones like Tracy, it was bound to be a frightening experience.

"Don't worry," Viv said. "Kurt knows what he's doing. He wouldn't let any of the kids harm one of the little ones."

"But he can't be here all the time."

"More than you'd think, although it's true he doesn't live on the premises. He manages to be here several nights a week, though, and luckily last night was one of those nights. He jokes that he doesn't have a life of his own anyway since his divorce."

"He's divorced," Anne said thoughtfully. "Recently?"

"No, it's been a couple of years. I gather it was a mutual agreement; a friendly divorce, if there is such a thing. Anyway, as I was saying, the two Miller boys crept into the hallway last night. They were sneaking a smoke and the cigarettes set off one of the smoke detectors. The other children bolted out of their rooms, terrified and crying. Kurt was about ready to skin those two boys alive."

"I can imagine," Anne said, thinking of how dangerous a real fire could be in a place like this. "What will be done about the boys?"

"There's usually a reprimand—no TV, confinement to their room . . . things like that. But Kurt tells me the boys will be leaving at the end of the week anyway. They've been placed in foster care."

"Oh, how sad."

"Actually, I think this is just what those boys need. They've been dragged from pillar to post all their lives. Both of them have been beaten and abused so many times. Their mother has left them off and on with relatives all over the country—whoever would take them in. And this is a nice family who's taking them—a good, patient man and woman with several children and a big old house just filled with sunshine and laughter. I only hope the boys don't drive them crazy first."

Anne made it through that second day much better. She hardly saw Kurt Bonner since he was in and out all day long. And she was a little disappointed that she wasn't asked to stay for supper again. She actually laughed at herself about that as she drove home.

"Why would I want to have supper with a room full of wild kids again anyway?" she muttered. "And why would I want to spend an extra minute in that dark, depressing house when I have a place like Benefield Farms?" Still not convinced, it seemed, she went on. "I have all that wonderful gourmet food in the freezer, and no doubt a big pitcher of freshly made iced tea. No one to bother me. No one to wipe their grimy little hands on me . . ."

She took a deep breath then, thinking of Tracy. Feeling, against her will, a warm tug at her heart and a smile on her lips. Oh, how she prayed that the little girl would find a good home, too, just like the Miller boys. She supposed that with all the problems these children suffered, it was the best thing one could hope for.

As it turned out, Anne learned only a few days later that Tracy had found a good home. But that didn't make Anne feel any better when Viv told her about it. She was surprised at her feelings of anxiety and loss when Viv told her the little girl would be leaving sometime the next week.

"Oh . . . but she's so tiny . . . so helpless. Who are the people who're taking her? Have they been checked out? Does Kurt think they're okay?"

"Does Kurt think who's okay?"

Anne turned around and saw Kurt standing in the kitchen doorway. For a second she wondered if he knew how attractive he was in his faded jeans and a shirt that made his eyes look more blue than hazel. She blinked and tried to sound sane when she answered.

"The couple who are taking Tracy. Have you talked to them? Has Tracy met them?"

He looked at her for a moment with a soft, amused look in his eyes. Then he pushed himself away from the door and came to stand in front of her.

"Why, Mrs. Benefield, don't tell me you're beginning to develop a heart?"

She'd made it clear during the past week that she didn't want to get involved with any of the children. And she'd made remarks to Viv and Gabby about how she couldn't wait until her three months were up and she could get away from this place for good. But all along she'd had the feeling that Kurt didn't believe her, and now he was teasing her about it.

"Only where Tracy is concerned. So don't get your hopes up," Anne said saucily.

"Oh," he said, still smiling. "Well, as a matter of fact, I have met Tracy's foster parents, although I don't always do that. I know from past experience how hard it is to let some of these kids go, even though they don't usually stay here that long. Tracy's foster parents are very nice, a young couple who can't have children. She'll get plenty of attention, and I think that's just what she needs. Tracy liked them right away, especially the young woman."

Anne frowned and turned away. What on earth was wrong with her? Had she expected the child to stay here forever? To continue tagging around after her and grabbing hold of her pant legs whenever she was near?

"Good," she said. "I'm very happy to hear that." She went back to the dishes as if she actually enjoyed them.

Kurt and Viv exchanged glances, and Viv got up from the table and left the kitchen. Gabby made a big pretense of not noticing Kurt and Anne, and in the process managed to make plenty of noise with his pots and pans.

Kurt stood leaning against the kitchen cabinet for a moment. He bent his head to look down into her face.

"Don't take it so hard," he said, his voice still amused. "Everyone discovers they have a heart sooner or later."

"That's not funny," she said, her voice a mere whisper.

"Hey," he said, his face growing serious. "It's all right to have feelings for these kids, you know. It just shows you're human."

Anne turned to glare at him. She made sure there were no tears in her eyes, and if anything her look expressed anger rather than the hurt she was actually feeling.

"Maybe I don't want to be human," she said stubbornly.

"Why? Because it hurts too much?"

She didn't answer, turning her attention back to the dishes.

"I wonder about you sometimes," he said.

"Why? What do you wonder?" She frowned up at him, trying to decide what he meant.

"Oh, little things—like why you're so defensive, so closed off from your emotions. Like who or what hurt you so deeply that you feel safer being cold and unfeeling."

"Oh, please," she snapped. "If there's one thing I can't stand, it's a shade-tree psychiatrist. I'm only here because the judge forced me to be. In less than three months I'll be gone and you'll never have to see me again. So don't try to psycho-analyze me, Mr. Bonner. I have no intention of getting involved with any of these children. My life is perfect just the way it is, with no involvements and no complications."

"Is that right?"

"Yes, it is." The knowing look in his

eyes angered her. "I am happy," she said. "I don't need anything or anyone else to make me that way."

"You're a real tough lady, aren't you?" His voice was soft and filled with a certain curiosity.

"Yes," she said, meeting his eyes stubbornly. "As a matter of fact, I am. I hope that doesn't offend your male ego."

His gaze held hers for a long, quiet moment before he turned and walked out of the kitchen.

Seven

Anne managed to avoid Kurt Bonner for the rest of the week, and when Viv asked her to stay and be the chaperone again for Friday night's supper, Anne refused.

"I'm sorry," she said, "but I've already made other plans."

"Oh, it's all right. I understand . . . you have a life of your own."

That's right, I do, Anne wanted to shout. She didn't owe anything to this place; not even to Viv, who had been so kind to her.

But the truth was she didn't have any other plans, and telling a lie nagged at her after she left and almost made her change her mind and turn the car back around.

Anne had seen the disappointment in Viv's dark eyes, heard it in her voice. She knew how hard the woman worked at the house and how much she must long for a free night to have supper with her husband and a little time alone with him.

But it wasn't her responsibility, Anne told herself as she drove home. In a few weeks she'd be out of the place for good.

By the time she got home she had a splitting headache. She took some aspirin and a long, cool bath, then went straight to bed.

On Saturday she thought she had never appreciated her home so much. It was glorious having nothing more to do than sleep late and have a leisurely breakfast.

"Mrs. Hargis," Anne asked as she sat in the breakfast nook, gazing out toward the gardens and sipping a cup of coffee, "can you make biscuits?"

"Huh?" the woman said distractedly. She turned around from the sink and picked up a dishtowel. "Biscuits?" She laughed then, and Anne thought it was one of the few times she'd heard the quiet older lady laugh. "Why, 'course I can make biscuits. You just never asked for 'em, that's all. Any self-respectin' Southern cook knows how to make biscuits so light and fluffy they practically float off your plate."

Even though she wasn't hungry, Anne felt her mouth actually begin to water, thinking of Gabby's biscuits. About how light and flaky they were, how white the insides were, and how they practically melted in her mouth.

"Do you use buttermilk?" Anne asked.

"Sure do." Mrs. Hargis laughed again. "What's this all about? I know you've had biscuits before."

"Oh, sure," Anne said, smiling at her cook. "When I was a kid, we ate biscuits a lot. And you used to make them for Baxter, as I recall."

"I did . . . yes, I did. Mr. Benefield loved his biscuits. As a matter of fact, I'd never heard of those things you like for breakfast 'til I started workin' here."

"Croissants," Anne said with a smile.

"Yeah. They're good, though. Don't know but what I might like them better. But sometimes a person just has a natural hankerin' for a soft, fluffy, hot biscuit. Guess it's our Southern roots."

Anne's smile was wistful as Mrs. Hargis turned back to her work. Southern roots. That was something Anne hadn't thought about in a long time. It was certainly nothing her mother had ever instilled in her. In fact, it was something Anne had tried to ignore over the years.

The afternoon with Cecile was all Anne had hoped it would be. They sat in a small gazebo beneath the willow trees while Anne told her friend all about her week at the halfway house.

"My," Cecile said with wide-eyed curiosity. "It sounds very interesting. I can see how you might get involved with the place and with those poor children."

"I'm not involved," Anne said, clamping her lips together. "And I don't intend to be."

Cecile's look was skeptical, but knowing Anne as she did, she said nothing.

"You haven't said much about your boss . . . Kurt Bonner."

Anne shrugged. "There's not much to say. He's a very busy man who seems to be quite efficient at what he does."

"Efficient," Cecile said with an amused lift of her brows. "Anne Benefield, you can't fool me. I've known you too long, and we've spent too many hours talking about our needs and our frustrations."

Anne's gaze darted Cecile's way.

"Needs? Please, don't use that word in the same breath with the name Kurt Bonner."

"Oh," Cecile said knowingly. "He *does* get to you. I thought so," she said gleefully. "I've thought so since that first day you were there."

"He doesn't *get* to me, Cecile. Unless, of course, you consider making me angry as 'getting' to me. He thinks I'm heartless and cold and unfeeling. And he thinks he's going to analyze me and figure me out; then I suppose he thinks he's going to help me *find* myself somehow."

"Ummm."

"Oh, for heaven's sake." Anne fairly leapt from her cushioned window seat and walked to one of the arches of the gazebo that faced the lake. "I didn't mean it that way. He's not like that. He's not a flirt. He's . . . serious and committed to his work. I doubt he even notices me that way . . . as a woman."

Cecile sat for a moment, watching Anne, seeing the faraway look in her eyes. She wondered if Anne realized what wistfulness lay in her voice or how restless and distracted she seemed when she talked about Kurt Bonner and the halfway house.

"Anne Benefield, I can't believe you."

"What?" Anne said, turning to frown at her friend.

"You know very well that you're an attractive woman. You have absolutely no reason to feel insecure in that area. Need I remind you that you've had several offers since Bax died?"

"Offers of what?" Anne said with a disdainful sound. "Offers to share the wealth my husband left me? Oh, yes, you're right about that—I certainly have had several offers in that regard."

"What about John Taylor? He's divorced. He owns three banks of his own in town. I hardly think he needs your money, or anyone else's, for that matter."

"You're right, he doesn't," Anne said with a wry look. She went back to the table and poured herself another glass of iced tea. "John wasn't interested in my money. And I wasn't interested in what he had in mind."

"Oh, you're kidding," Cecile gasped. "Sex?" she said in a conspiratorial whisper.

Anne laughed softly. "Isn't that a laugh? Can you imagine—a woman my age meeting the town banker on Thursday afternoons, hiding from his grown children and the rest of Clayburn for a quick roll in the hay?"

"Well, it might not be so bad." Cecile laughed. "Besides, what do you mean, 'a woman your age'? Good gracious, Anne, you're the same age as me. Forty-nine is hardly over the hill as far as enjoying sex goes—just ask Barney," she said with a girlish giggle. "I think our love life is better now than it ever has been in our lives. The kids are gone, we don't have any financial worries, we have the house to ourselves. It's wonderful."

Anne gritted her teeth. She hardly knew what to say to Cecile when she brought up the subject. And although her friend knew that she had married Baxter strictly for security and companionship, she thought that deep down Cecile still carried the fanciful, romantic notion that everyone shared the same kind of relationship she had with Barney.

But that easy kind of love was something Anne had never had, not with her first husband and certainly not with Baxter Benefield.

"It was never that way between Baxter and me," Anne said finally. "You know that. He was older, and later he had . . . problems with his health."

"I know," Cecile said.

Why did it bother her so much that there was sympathy in Cecile's dark eyes? Did she really think that not being intimate with a man for several years was such a great loss? After all, it had never been that good with Bax to begin with.

"But there's no reason you can't see other men, Anne. And no reason at all that you can't enjoy a healthy, active sex life."

"Oh, please," Anne said, forcing a smile. "Let's not talk about this any more."

"Lord, you are so stubborn sometimes. After all, this is the nineties, you know, and we're long past all those taboos about men and sex."

"Speak for yourself," Anne said, ignoring Cecile's look of exasperation.

Anne had to work very hard the rest of the weekend to get that conversation out of her head. It was the last thing she needed to think about when she went back to the halfway house.

It didn't help any that she had had an odd, puzzling dream that woke her and left her feeling breathless and hot. And even though she couldn't remember the dream, she knew that it involved Kurt, and that it had been sweet and intimate and disturbingly sensual.

She supposed that was why, on Monday morning, she was even cooler than usual with the man who had featured in all those disturbing and forbidden images in the night.

She could catch his eyes on her, studying her, trying to figure her out, she supposed. But she would look away with her most aloof expression, pretending that her heart didn't beat faster when he was near. Or that she hadn't wondered a hundred times how it would feel to have him touch her, kiss her, pull her against him in that intense way with which he did everything.

His seriousness excited her, and his quiet looks left her feeling oddly perplexed and needy, until it became a constant struggle to control her thoughts.

By the middle of the week the workmen had finally arrived to repair the cooling unit in the house. The construction foreman was a man Anne knew; he often did work at Benefield Farms. She almost laughed at the look on his face when he saw her standing at the sink, washing dishes. Kurt had just walked into the kitchen and she was very aware of him watching her and listening to her exchange with the man.

"Anne Benefield? Well, hello—I didn't expect to see you here."

"I didn't expect to be here, Mr. Chase," she said with an amused grin. "Will Jordan thought I might remember to pay my parking fines in a more timely fashion if I worked here at the halfway house for a few months."

"Is that right? Whew," he said, glancing ruefully at the stack of dishes. "Looks to me like it would have been easier just to pay the damned things."

Anne smiled up at him. Bill Chase was a talker, a big man who enjoyed his work and seemed to enjoy conversing with his customers even more. He leaned against the sink now with his arms crossed over his chest.

His eyes wandered down over the apron she wore, and lower to the legs of her jeans.

"Well, I must say, it suits you. You're looking mighty good."

"Why, thank you, Bill," she said with a pleased look of surprise.

She heard Gabby grunt and saw him glance disapprovingly toward her.

Bill leaned closer to her, but his murmured words weren't a whisper and they were clearly audible, even in the noisy kitchen.

"What say you and me run out to the lake one evenin'? Might even stop at Scooter's on the way back, have a beer . . . catch a slow dance or two."

Anne couldn't help being amused by his invitation, and flattered. It had been a long time since any man had come on to her so blatantly. And she had to admit that having Kurt hear it did wonders for her ego.

"Why, Bill, I'm not sure your wife would approve of that at all."

"Hell," he said, moving closer. "What she don't know won't hurt her."

"I'm really flattered. But no, I don't think so," she said. Even though she was still smiling her eyes were cool, and there was no doubt that she meant what she said.

"Well, never hurts to ask," he said, nudging her with his elbow before he sauntered out of the room.

It was so quiet, the sound of water dripping in the sink was loud and annoying.

Anne was aware that Kurt had walked across the kitchen and stood leaning against the cabinet, very close to her, gazing down at her. When she finally glanced up there was such a look in his eyes that she caught her breath for a moment.

"What?" she asked. "There's nothing in the court order that restricts me from talking to someone, is there?"

"No," he said quietly. "Nothing at all." He let his gaze move over her face and down to the low cut vee of her blouse. He turned his head, deliberately, it seemed, to look down at her snug-fitting jeans. "Bill was right about one thing, though," he murmured, a teasing light in his eyes.

"You do look good in jeans. But if you want my opinion—he's not your type."

Her heart was pounding and she could feel her cheeks growing hot beneath his steady gaze.

"I don't want your opinion. And what would you know about my type, anyway?"

"Oh, I think I know," he said, handing her a towel as she finished the last dish and let the water out of the sink. "Remind me sometime; I'll tell you all about it."

His eyes held hers until the very last minute, until he turned and, with his usual ease, picked a carrot out of one of Gabby's ice-filled bowls.

"Now there's a man for you," Gabby said after Kurt was gone. The toothless, knowing grin he gave her was the first one she'd actually seen that was directed her way.

"Not for me," Anne whispered, shaking her head.

"Oh, yeah." He nodded. "Straightforward. Don't play no games. Serious." As he spouted off all Kurt's virtues, he waved a paring knife in the air, keeping time with his words. "Proud; don't need no woman keepin' him up. Yes, sirree.

Looks to me like the kind of man a woman like you needs, all right."

"A . . . a woman like me?" she sputtered. "You're out of your mind. I don't *need* any man." She turned away, picking up a dishtowel to fan her burning face.

She heard Gabby's soft grunt of laughter and practically ran from the kitchen.

"It's hot in here," she said as she went out the back door. "I'm going outside for some air."

"Hotter'n you think," Gabby said, chuckling to himself. "Yes, ma'am. Hotter'n you think."

Eight

Tracy's foster parents were coming for her on Friday evening. Anne came in early that morning, bringing with her a small gift-wrapped box tied with bright blue ribbons. She intended to show it to Viv, but she wasn't there, so she started to take the box up the stairs to Tracy's room.

She met Kurt on the stairway.

"Good morning," he said. His gaze shifted from her face down to the box in her hands.

"I . . . it's a gift . . . for Tracy."

There was only the slightest hint of surprise in his eyes.

"That's nice," he said. "Oh . . . I'm sorry. Perhaps I shouldn't have used the word *nice.*" He leaned closer, his look teasing. "I wouldn't want to insult you . . . or ruin your reputation."

"Very funny." She brushed past him

and moved on upstairs, trying to pretend she hadn't heard his soft laughter behind her.

Tracy was dressed, and she and two other girls, who were a little older, were struggling to make up their beds. Anne put the gift on top of a dresser and went to help.

The little girl's blue eyes shone when she saw Anne, and she came to hug her.

"Hey, darlin'," Anne said, bending to put her arms around the child. "This is a big day for you, hum?"

Tracy shook her head, but Anne could see the fright in her eyes, and the confusion. No one would ever know how that look wounded Anne, and she didn't want Tracy to know, either. It would only make it harder for her to say goodbye.

She took Tracy on her lap and sat on the bed, wrapping her arms around the girl and rocking her back and forth.

"Oh, you're going to have such a good time at your new home. You'll have a nice big room, all your own, with lots and lots of toys to play with. You'll like that, won't you?"

Tracy nodded, and for the first time her eyes brightened.

"And you'll have a mommy and a daddy who will love you so much."

"They read to me," Tracy said, putting her fingers in her mouth.

"Yes, they will," Anne said. "And take you on picnics and to the movies." Suddenly the emotion was too much for Anne. The open trust on the child's face was heartbreakingly sweet. Anne prayed that she would never know another moment's fear or sorrow, and that after awhile the couple who were taking Tracy would be able to adopt her. She wrapped her arms tightly around the little girl, trying desperately not to cry. She didn't want Tracy to see her crying and be upset.

"Well," she said, blinking her eyes against the tears. "I've brought you a going-away present. Do you want to see it?"

"Yay," Tracy said, slipping down from Anne's lap.

Anne took the gaily wrapped box from the dresser and handed it to Tracy. The other two girls had gathered around to see, and when Anne sat back down on the bed they came to sit very close, snuggling on each side of her.

Anne frowned, feeling guilty that she hadn't thought to bring at least a small gift for them, too.

Tracy sat on the floor, trying to rip the ribbons off the box but having trouble because of her small hands. Anne bent to help and laughed when Tracy brushed her fingers away.

"I can do it."

"Of course you can," Anne whispered. She reached out to touch Tracy's hair, pushing it away from her eyes.

When the box was finally open, Tracy sat for a moment, staring at the blue dress inside. Her eyes looked huge when she turned to Anne.

"Is it mine?"

"Yes, darling, of course it's yours. Do you like it?"

Tracy didn't answer, but simply nodded her head wildly. Then she jumped up from the floor, pulling the new dress with her amid the rustle of tissue paper.

"I wear it now?"

"Well . . ." Anne hesitated. She didn't want to spoil Tracy's enthusiasm, but she could just imagine what the dress would look like by evening if Tracy wore it all day.

"I thought you might want to wait until after supper. Then you can come upstairs and take a nice bath and put on your new dress and wait for your new mommy and daddy. How does that sound?"

Tracy nodded, but still she held the dress tightly against her.

"Would you like me to hang up the dress now?"

Tracy didn't want to part with it, but finally Anne was able to persuade her to hang it on one of the dresser drawer pulls.

"There. You can see it whenever you like and you can reach it by yourself."

Tracy and the other girls looked with wonder at the blue dress with its lacy underskirt that hung just below the hem. They spoke about it in quiet whispers and stepped forward to touch the lace and the tiny pink rosettes at the waist. Anne decided right then and there that nothing would do but new dresses for the other girls as well, and as she watched them she made mental notes about their size and coloring.

"Are you ready to go down to breakfast now?" she asked at last.

Their excitement about the dress seemed to have set the tone for the day, and Anne was delighted that it was such a happy beginning. Even Tracy laughed as she ran down the stairs with the other girls, and for the first time she didn't seem distracted by Anne's presence.

Anne watched them go into the dining room and take their seats at the long table. She remained at the bottom of the steps, her elbow resting against the banister as she gazed wistfully at Tracy through the wide doorway.

Anne felt Kurt behind her, felt the touch of his hand at the back of her waist, and for a moment she felt like turning and throwing herself into his arms; letting someone hold her and comfort her, letting herself cry openly and fully for the first time in years. Instead she stiffened, and she felt him take his hand away.

"She's going to be all right, you know," he said softly.

"I know. I know she will. But oh, Lord . . ." She turned toward him then, and all the fear, all the pain she was feeling was there in her eyes for him to see.

"What if they're not good to her? What if they're rigid and unyielding, Kurt? You read about it every day in the papers, about how someone is so nice on the outside and at home . . ." Her voice trailed away when she saw the warmth and understanding in his eyes.

"Don't you think I've asked myself that question about every child who's ever left this house?"

"Have you?"

"God, yes," he said with a soft laugh. "But I've learned that as much as I'd like to, I can't control the world and I can't protect every child who needs it. All I can do is provide the safest, best place possible for them to stay until they either go back to their parents or to what will hopefully be a permanent home."

"I know you're right." She sighed. She turned to look at Tracy again. "But she's so little and sweet . . . helpless, really. I don't think I could stand it if anything happened to her."

"All we can do is pray and try to believe that she'll be all right."

"Is that what you do?" she asked. "Is that your secret?" She turned and looked up into his eyes. And she thought, when he wasn't teasing her, that he had the kindest, most expressive eyes she'd ever seen.

"A lot . . . yeah."

She took a deep breath and lifted her shoulders. She could do it, too. She could let Tracy go with her prayers and her hopes, and she would try to be happy for her and expect the best.

"All right," she said. "I guess it's back to the kitchen for me."

"Anne," he said, touching her arm. She stopped and turned back to face him. "Viv has a virus of some kind and won't be in this morning. Her husband called and said she was up all night. I hate to ask, it being Friday night, but do you think you might chaperone for supper again?"

"Sure," she said. She supposed it was the conversation they'd just had and her renewed hope that made her answer so quickly and so positively.

"Tracy's foster parents are driving over from Smithville, and it might be late when they arrive."

"Oh, but I don't . . . I hadn't planned—"

"You hadn't planned on being here when she left?" His voice was soft, and there was such understanding in his eyes.

"Oh, Kurt, don't ask me to . . . I can't . . . it's just too much."

"I need you to do this. And if you'd stop and think for a moment, it's what Tracy needs, too."

"But it will only be harder for her if I'm here," she said.

"No, it won't. I think your being here to say goodbye might make all the difference in starting her new life off in the right direction."

Anne closed her eyes for a moment and actually reached for the banister for support. Damn him; why was he doing this to her? Why was he forcing her to feel things she'd never wanted to feel?

"Just think about it," he said, forcing himself not to touch her. "That's all I'm asking. If you decide it's something you just can't do, I'll understand." He looked into her eyes for a moment before going into the dining room.

She could hear him talking to the kids, his voice energetic and happy as he spoke to each and every one of them. She watched him touch one's hair, pat another on the shoulder, and she saw the respect and adoration in their eyes when they looked at him. And she realized that Kurt Bonner was the first really decent father figure some of these kids had ever known. For the first time she had some idea why he stayed in what she had thought of as a thankless, dead-end job.

Anne glanced around the house, noting again the work that could be done to make it more attractive and more comfortable. She might not be able to make a difference emotionally to these children, but she had enough money to make a difference materially in the house where they stayed. And that was exactly what she intended to do.

She was very quiet the rest of the day, not even bothering to respond to Gabby's badgering as she usually did. Kurt came into the kitchen several times, and his gaze often caught hers, holding her for a moment with a questioning look.

"What's wrong with you today?" Gabby asked Anne finally. "You sick or somethin'?"

"No, I'm not sick."

"You're acting funny."

She turned to the old man with a wide-eyed stare, making a face at him.

"Do you mean odd funny or ha-ha funny?"

"Ayy, now she's bein' cute. Can't stand a durn cute woman," he muttered.

"From what I've seen you can't stand anyone."

"Huffy, too, ain't she?"

Anne thought there was a speculative glint in his droopy old eyes as he looked at her.

She sighed and went back to her dishes.

"I'm just trying to make a decision," she said. "And I guess I'm a little distracted."

"Well, if you want my opinion, and you probably don't, I think you oughta stay tonight and see the little girl off."

Anne frowned at him, a look of utter disbelief on her face.

"How did you know—"

"Well, it ain't hard to figure out, sis," he said, waving a large spoon in the air. "Everybody around here knows that little

Tracy has sort of latched onto you, and that she's leavin' tonight. It'd take a fool not to see that some of us is gonna miss her." He looked away then, and Anne heard him clear his throat.

"Why, Gabby," she said. She dried her hands and went to the table where he stood working. "You old fraud. You're going to miss her, too, aren't you?"

He cleared his throat again, and when he spoke Anne thought his words were the quietest she'd ever heard from him.

"You miss 'em all. Wouldn't be human if you didn't. But like Kurt says, you can't hide from what you're feelin'. Builds up inside you . . . makes different people act in different ways. In my case, when I got down and out, I'd drink . . . too much." His glance darted upward, meeting hers for a moment before looking away sheepishly.

Anne couldn't say a word. It was the most the old man had ever said to her, and this time it was real, with no bantering and no sarcasm.

"Well . . ." she said finally, letting the word out softly to hang in the air between them. "I guess you've helped make up my mind, Gabby. Thank you."

She smiled to herself when she turned back to the sink and heard his soft grunt. But he didn't fool her. This time his grouchy demeanor didn't fool her at all.

Nine

That day, Anne spent as much time as she could with Tracy. She usually ate lunch in the kitchen or outside with Viv, but today she went out to the dining room and sat with Tracy, laughing and teasing her. She noticed that the other children were grinning at her. Their faces were so expressive and so welcoming. There was almost an adoration in their eyes when they realized that an adult actually wanted to spend time with them, as if they weren't used to such positive attention.

Be careful, Anne said to herself more than once. Not too much or you'll be sorry.

She caught Kurt's gaze on her several times. He was smiling, eyes filled with a quiet warmth and approval. Finally Anne smiled back at him, then looked away, feeling as shy as a teenager with her first serious flirtation.

Supper was a cheerful affair, but Anne found her stomach churning as the time grew nearer to Tracy's departure. She found herself chattering away senselessly, not that the children noticed. But she was certain Kurt did, just as she was certain he understood.

Anne was amazed at the way nothing seemed to bother the kids. If they had grown attached to Tracy and would miss her there was no sign of it, and she decided that they'd had so much disappointment and pain in their young lives, they were probably immune to it. Perhaps that was the only way they could survive.

Like me, she thought.

That realization made her pause for a moment and sit quietly, staring around the table at each of the children. They were too young to feel the way she did, she told herself. Too innocent to feel as if nothing mattered, as if one's feelings didn't matter. And she found herself wanting to persuade every one of them that they did.

After supper they took the children out

to the backyard to play awhile before dark. Kurt wouldn't allow them to watch television too much, and Anne thought that was a good idea. Children needed to be outside, enjoying the silent blink of lightning bugs and the sound of the crickets.

She had helped Tracy to change earlier and had cautioned her about keeping her dress clean while she was outside. She needn't have worried, for the little girl sat on a swing, pushing her feet lightly against the ground and sitting very still. Anne would see her stop occasionally and run her hand down the blue material of her dress.

Anne and Kurt sat at the picnic table, watching the kids, and now she felt at ease with him. Perhaps it was the dim light of evening that made her feel less self-conscious.

"How did you become involved with the halfway house?" she asked.

"I have a friend who's on the Board of Directors for Angels, Incorporated, the group that runs the house."

"Angels, Incorporated?" Anne said, frowning. "Why, I believe my husband was a member of that board. I know I've heard him mention it."

"He was," Kurt said. "Just as you, as his widow, are a member now." His expression was cool and speculative.

"Me?" She frowned, trying to remember all the organizations Roger had told her about after Baxter's death. "But I . . . I . . ."

"Didn't want to get involved," he finished. "It's all right. Roger Finnell does a very nice job as a representative of Benefield's."

Why did she feel that his words, although very politely spoken, were an indictment of her and her way of life?

"Who's the friend you mentioned?" she asked, trying to change the course of the conversation.

It wasn't someone she knew, and Kurt explained that the man was from the next county.

"I didn't realize it was such a large organization."

"It's getting there," he said. He gazed off toward the children as he spoke. "Angels was formed by a group of tri-county residents who saw the need for such a place. In fact, your husband was one of the founders. This one in Clayburn was the first; there's another in Granger and a third is being opened next month in Smithville."

"Angels, Incorporated," she said. "Quite a name."

"The sponsors are quite a group of people. Most of them are wealthy, and I'm sure they could find other, less stressful ways to spend their time and money."

Anne stared at him, feeling guilty against her will about her lack of participation over the years. She was certain his words were a hint about how she spent her own time and money. But if he meant it that way, it didn't show on his face.

"Is this what you've always done . . . be the director of such places?"

"Hardly, or I'd have lost all my hair," he said with a laugh, running his hand through his thinning, sun-streaked hair. "I was a high school counselor . . . and a science teacher. But over the years I found that teaching began to take second place. So I took more classes and began to counsel full-time."

"Was your wife a teacher also?" she asked, not knowing if she should or not.

Kurt looked into her eyes for a moment before he answered.

"No, Darlene was an administrator for a government agency. I suppose, during her career, she saw a lot of fraud and waste, and as a result she thought every person who needed help was lazy and calculating." His eyes were narrowed as he gazed out at the children, and Anne could see a muscle in his jaw flexing and releasing.

"She resented your work," Anne asked very quietly, "the time you spent with the children?"

He sighed and shrugged his shoulders. "Not resented. I don't know. Maybe it was time for us to move on, or who knows . . . maybe all those years we spent together were a complete waste."

"But you have children, don't you? I thought Viv said—"

"Two boys." His face lit up when he mentioned his sons. "They're grown now. Greg is twenty-five and married; Tim is twenty-three."

"Then the years you talk about couldn't have been a waste."

She couldn't explain why she wanted to make him feel better, or why she was letting herself be drawn into such a personal conversation.

Slowly Kurt turned toward her, looking at her intently. There was a sparkle in his eyes and a faint smile on his lips.

"Be careful, Mrs. Benefield," he said teasingly. "Someone might accuse you of actually giving a damn."

She laughed weakly. "Not likely," she said. "I was just making a practical observation."

"I know in reality that those years weren't wasted," he said, turning serious again. "And I thank God every day for my sons. I have a very good relationship with both of them, although believe me, there were times when I wondered if we'd ever reach this point."

"You're a good man," she said without thinking. "And of course your sons have recognized that about you all along."

He looked into her eyes and for a moment, in the dim light of sunset, she saw a warmth and tenderness there that almost took her breath away.

She wasn't sure what might have hap-

pened if they hadn't heard the slam of a
car door out in front of the house. Kurt
stood up, pulling his gaze away from hers
as if to break a spell.

"That must be them." He let himself
through the gate and jogged around the
side of the house. Anne could hear his
deep voice, and then she saw him coming
back with a young man and woman following behind him.

Anne stood up, clasping her hands together to keep them from shaking. She
studied the couple before they reached
her, and saw that they were as anxious
as she was, probably more so, as their
eyes searched the children for Tracy. But
the little girl had already seen them, and
now she hopped down from the swing
and ran forward.

When she reached Anne she stopped,
becoming suddenly shy and wrapping her
arms around Anne's legs. Anne touched
her hair, making no effort to stop the
girl from clinging to her. Rather she
stood smiling as Tracy's new parents approached.

"Anne," Kurt said. "This is Phil and
Regina Thomas. This is Anne Bene-

field . . . one of our . . . assistants." He smiled as his eyes met Anne's.

Anne thought that the Thomases would probably not even remember meeting her later. Their eyes and their attention were focused completely on the little girl who clung to Anne.

"Sweetheart," Regina Thomas said. "Do you remember us?"

Tracy nodded her head, and Anne could see that she had put her fingers in her mouth, as she always did when she was feeling shy.

"Go say hello, honey," Anne urged, gently pushing against Tracy's shoulders. Regina Thomas bent down and her husband knelt on one knee as they looked at the little girl. They were an attractive, well-dressed young couple, and they seemed quiet and easygoing. Anne tried not to let any doubts about them creep into her thoughts.

Suddenly Tracy released her grip on Anne and ran into Regina Thomas's outstretched arms. When the woman looked up at Anne there were tears of joy in her eyes.

"Oh," she whispered, turning then to

her husband, who put his arms around his wife and the little girl.

Anne held herself rigid as the young couple said goodbye.

"Her things are in the hallway at the front of the house. We can go through the house from the back here," Kurt said.

He called the other children to come in for the evening; then he looked at Anne to see if she wanted to come inside the house, too. She shook her head. Somehow she couldn't bear to be confined in a small area, not when she watched Tracy go and tried so hard to pretend it didn't hurt.

As they were going toward the house Tracy turned once. She was holding Mrs. Thomas's hand and with the other she made one sweet little waving motion toward Anne.

"Oh," Anne said, feeling a catch in her throat. "Bye," she whispered, waving back at Tracy. "Goodbye, little darling. Have a wonderful life," she added to herself.

Anne walked to the childrens' swing set, trying to choke back the tears. Her throat ached and her eyes felt hot and swollen. She saw something lying on the ground and bent to pick it up; it was one of the tiny rosettes from Tracy's new dress.

Anne turned toward the house, and for a moment her heart urged her to go to Tracy. But she closed her eyes and clutched the pink rosebud in her fist. And finally the tears came.

"Oh . . . God," she gasped. She couldn't seem to control her sobs. They shook her and stole her breath away, and still she could not stop crying.

She had to get away. Suddenly she felt an overwhelming need to be away from the house, away from the sound of children laughing upstairs in their rooms.

She ran into the kitchen and retrieved her purse, then came out the back, hoping to avoid Kurt and the Thomases as she went around the house to her car. But she needn't have worried—the flash of their taillights could be seen going down the street. She supposed it was only natural that they were anxious to get Tracy away from the house and to their own home.

"Please, let her be happy." Anne sighed. She was still trying to stop the sobs that made her chest feel heavy and weighted.

She saw Kurt then, standing in the doorway at the front of the house. She was sure he had seen her, but she hurriedly opened the car door and slid into the seat.

"Anne," she heard him shout. "Anne!"

She slammed the door and started the engine, pulling away from the curb quickly. She didn't look back to see Kurt walk out toward the street and stand staring after her.

Ten

The house seemed quieter than usual, more empty. Her nose felt stuffy and her eyes were swollen. All she wanted was a cool bath. She hesitated in the kitchen and took a bottle of wine from the refrigerator, then rummaged through the cabinets for a glass. It would help her sleep. And she had a feeling that tonight she was going to need it. Then she dragged herself up the stairs.

She took a long bath, letting the tepid water and the scent of roses soothe her. But still she couldn't get the image of Tracy out of her mind or out of her heart. She could still see those wide blue eyes, the sweet way she had stopped what she was doing and proudly run her hand down her new dress.

Anne sobbed anew at the memories.

"Stop this," she said, sitting up in the

tub. "What's gotten into you? You're getting absolutely maudlin in your old age."

Later, after she'd put on a peach-colored silk gown and peignoir, she sat for a while, sipping her wine. She switched on the television in her bedroom and found her attention straying after only a few moments. Finally, feeling restless, she stepped to the windows that overlooked the lake. There was a moon tonight and the light of it brushed the water and the tops of the trees with silver.

Anne pushed her hair back behind her ears and impulsively took the bottle of wine and her glass downstairs. She let herself out onto the wide covered front porch and set the bottle she carried on a wicker table. She hadn't bothered with slippers, and the floor of the porch felt cool and smooth beneath her bare feet.

Sipping from her glass of wine, she walked to the huge fluted columns that supported the porch roof and leaned back against one of them, gazing out at the lake.

She felt better here and thought wistfully of her childhood and how she would sometimes spend the night outdoors on their front porch on hot nights. She wished she could do that now; she wished she had someone to share it with.

"For heaven's sake," she muttered in disgust.

Suddenly she straightened. She thought she saw car lights turn off the main road into her drive. Sometimes people made a turnaround here; that was probably all it was now.

But she saw the lights coming on, moving rather swiftly, she thought, toward her house.

For a moment she was afraid. Baxter was always cautious about anyone who came to the house at night, even if it was someone he knew. She thought she probably should go back inside.

But Anne hesitated for a moment, staring at the vehicle that came to a stop in the circle drive, no more than fifteen yards from where she stood. She recognized the red pickup truck. She'd seen it often enough at the halfway house, and she'd seen Kurt Bonner driving it.

For a moment she felt only anger that he had come here, that he was checking up on her. Then, with a catch in her chest, she realized he might be coming because something had happened.

That thought swept away any anger there was and made her rush down the steps to meet him.

"Is anything wrong?" she asked, breathless with worry and anxiety.

Kurt stopped. The dim light of the moon was behind Anne, and in it she could see his face clearly. She saw the frown between his eyes, saw his gaze move over her negligee and down to the wineglass she still held in her hand.

"That's what I came to ask you," he said, reaching for the glass.

"What about the kids?" she asked. "Surely you didn't leave them there—"

"They're not alone," he said. "I'd have been here sooner if that were the case."

She felt his hand, warm and reassuring, against hers and she let the glass go. He took it and set it on the wide walkway away from them.

"Do you think that will help?" he asked, nodding toward the glass.

Anne took a deep breath of air. She didn't need his disapproval, not tonight. Tonight she felt fragile and exposed. Having finally allowed herself the release of tears, she was afraid she might never be able to stop again.

"Yes, as a matter of fact, it does," she replied. "Is that why you came? To judge me?"

"No," he said. He took a step closer and his hand lifted toward her, then stopped. "Anne," he whispered. "I know how you feel . . . how you felt tonight with Tracy."

"No, you don't," she said. "You can't imagine how I feel." She had held herself so tightly in control for years, and tonight had been like opening the floodgates. How could he possibly know about that?

But he did know, his eyes seemed to say. And when he reached out to touch her face she felt all those emotions breaking free again.

It was only the slightest sound she made, the smallest hint of a sob that escaped her lips at his touch. But it was all it took.

He stepped toward her so quickly, she was in his arms before she fully realized what was happening. She couldn't stop the sigh that escaped from her lungs at the feel of his strong body against hers, at the security in his arms wrapped around her.

"It's all right," he murmured, his lips against her hair. "You don't have to pretend anything with me," he whispered against her ear.

All she could do was move her head back and forth against his shirt as she tried to shake her head. She didn't want to cry anymore. Didn't he understand that? Still, she clung to him, taking his strength and his comfort.

She felt his lips at the corner of her jaw, heard his soft murmur as he kissed her cheek. And when his mouth moved toward hers she turned to meet it with a hunger and a fiery need that surprised her.

It had been so long since she'd been kissed. Really kissed.

Still, she held back. She had her hands on his arms, ready to push him away, ready to end it if her old fears overtook her.

Kurt pulled his mouth away, only slightly out of reach, and looked down into her eyes. He could see the need, the want in her eyes, and yet he sensed a reluctance there as well.

"Why can't you let it go, Anne?" he whispered. "Can't you see you're safe with me? Don't you know I'd never hurt you?"

She did know that. She thought she'd known it from the first moment she met him. And she was so tired of holding everything back. So damned tired.

With a quiet sound of surrender she reached her arms upward, sliding them around his neck as his arms came around her waist, drawing her tight and close against him. His hands moved up her back to her neck and he cradled her head.

Anne let herself be lost in that kiss and in his touch. Lost and breathless and out of control, the way she hadn't been in years. It was what she wanted and needed. Kurt was what she wanted.

"You are a contradiction, woman," he said, pulling away and looking down at her.

"Why's that?" She didn't bother moving away from him, but stood close, loving the feel of his legs against hers through the silky gown, the way the muscles in his back moved beneath her fingers.

"I don't think you're nearly as tough as you pretend."

"Could we not talk about me tonight? I don't want to think about what I am or what's best for me. If I did I might run into the house and hide. I might never see you again."

"Would that bother you?" he asked. "Never seeing me again?"

"More than you could ever guess," she admitted.

"What is it you want, then?" He tightened his arms around her and kissed her lightly on the mouth. "Tell me, Anne."

She could feel the hardness of him against her. He wasn't shy about his needs and his wants. And, at her age, she shouldn't be either. Only for a moment did she hesitate, thinking about the few extra pounds she could never seem to lose, about the fact that her skin was not as smooth and supple as it once was or that it had been years since a man had made love to her.

But then he kissed her again and she could see, could *feel* that it didn't matter to him.

"You," she whispered beneath his mouth. "I want you."

Upstairs in her bedroom, she softened the lights and turned to Kurt, lifting her arms to him. He walked to her and gathered her close and there, in the quiet intimacy of her room, his kisses were even hotter and more urgent.

He pushed the peignoir off her shoulders, trailing kisses along her bare skin and slipping his fingers beneath the thin straps of her gown.

Anne felt hot. She felt an urgency that surprised and delighted her. It was thrilling and exciting, something she had not let herself feel in years. Somehow with Kurt she could not seem to stop it. It was as spontaneous as a spark of fire near fuel, and just as powerful.

She closed her eyes, feeling the heat of his kisses along her neck as she touched the buttons of his shirt. She was trembling as she unbuttoned them and pushed the material away from his chest. Hungrily, she let her mouth trail along his smooth skin, tasting him, reveling in the scent of him.

He groaned and took her head between his hands, his fingers tangling in her hair before he pulled her face up for a long, slow kiss.

The straps of her gown had fallen off her shoulders and now, urgently, he pushed the material away, letting it fall to the floor in a soft shimmering mass about her feet.

She held her breath as his head dipped and he touched his mouth to her breasts. With a quiet moan he pulled her closer, tighter, his hands running smoothly down her back to the curve of her hips as his mouth explored and teased and made her gasp with the pleasure of it.

"Kurt," she whispered, feeling her legs grow weak beneath her. She moved toward the bed, still holding him, still reluctant to have his mouth leave her.

He undressed quickly and moved with her to the bed, murmuring softly to her as his hands explored and as he pulled back to let his gaze wander over her.

"God, you're beautiful," he whispered. "So beautiful." He touched her full breasts almost reverently before giving in to his needs and crushing her against him.

There was no awkwardness between them now, no need for questions. He seemed to know that she was ready for him, just as she knew he could wait no longer. It was an exciting, exhilarating feeling for Anne, that of being wanted so blatantly and being accepted. More than accepted . . . desired.

He hesitated only a moment as he looked down at her. There was such heated pleasure in his eyes . . . a connection that frightened Anne as much as it fascinated her. She wasn't sure what was happening between them. But she knew that this tonight with Kurt was more than just sex. Oh, so much more.

Only for a moment did she feel that old fright returning, that fear of commitment, of allowing anyone to get close to her. But then it was too late. She felt the walls tumbling down, the very earth beneath them shattering out of her grasp and out of her control.

Kurt groaned and closed his eyes as he felt the heat of her body. Anne felt it too. She opened her eyes wide and stared into his, moaning softly as she clasped her arms around him and gave in to the urgency that his body made her feel.

Neither of them could stop it now. The wild, completely out-of-control power joined them together. Kurt's movements were strong and sure, certain of what she needed and what she wanted. She was trembling beneath him and as he kissed her, he urged her on, whispering wild, erotic words into her ear until she thought she might actually scream with the longing and pleasure that swept through her.

This was new to her. Completely and wonderfully new, and if there was a part of her that urged control, there was another that yearned to feel every response, every delightful bit of emotion there was to feel. And in the end it was that feeling of yearning that won out.

She felt the sensation of heat and power building in her body, felt it coming from somewhere deep in her soul, threatening to lift her to the heavens. The power of it was overwhelming as she felt the erotic, pulsating rhythm begin, as she heard Kurt's voice softly coaxing her.

She cried out, rising up to meet his

body and calling out his name, her hands reaching out to clutch the sheets as she felt his own trembling begin.

Afterward Anne felt dazed, stunned by what she had just experienced. She had never dreamed anything . . . any man could be this way. She turned her head to stare at him and found his gaze warm and tender on her face.

She moved her head against the pillow, staring into his eyes with something akin to awe.

"I can't believe this has happened," she whispered. "That it's happened to me."

"I gather this is not something you do often," he said, smiling at her in a sweet, teasing way.

"Hardly," she said softly, pulling her eyes away from his.

"I only came here to comfort you, you know," he said.

"You certainly accomplished that," she said, almost shyly.

Kurt's look was questioning. Getting her into bed *wasn't* what he had intended tonight, although it was certainly something he'd thought about. Touching Anne, holding her, making love to her—he knew it was something that had been in the back of his mind since the day she came to the halfway house. But she was a complicated woman, puzzling and complex. And he was afraid, now that it had happened, that she would pull away and retreat again into that hard, protective shell she'd erected around herself.

He didn't want that. He wanted this Anne. This responsive, passionate, sensual woman who made him feel good about being a man.

She snuggled against him, putting her arms around him and resting her head against his chest.

"I never wanted to feel what Tracy's leaving made me feel tonight," she said in response to his comment.

"I know that." He touched her hair, pushing the damp strands back from her face. "But now that you have?"

She sighed. She didn't know what she would do. Or how she could possibly cope with all the emotions that Tracy had opened up. It was rather like pouring salt into a wound. And now, after this night with Kurt, she wasn't sure she could ever feel safe again.

"I don't know," she whispered. "You have to understand how my life has been. I've been careful not to let anyone in, Kurt. No one." She lifted her gaze toward him, and there was almost a plea for understanding, as if she wasn't sure she could sustain this level of emotion for long.

"Why is that? Do you want to tell me?"

"It's just . . ." She shrugged, hardly knowing where to begin. It had been so long, she wasn't even sure anymore why she was the way she was. Maybe it was just her nature to be closed off and emotionally cold.

Like her mother.

She pulled away from Kurt, frowning at the thought.

"What?" he asked, reaching for her. "What is it?"

She slipped out of bed and picked up her robe from the floor, quickly slipping her arms into it before she turned to look at him again.

"Don't analyze me, Kurt," she said softly. "Not tonight. Can't we just enjoy what we have? What we've found?"

He was quiet for a moment, his eyes speculative and troubled. Then he pushed the sheet on her side of the bed out of the way. He was propped up on one elbow and with his other arm he reached out toward her, his eyes changing and growing warm.

"Come back to bed."

Eleven

Anne was asleep when she felt Kurt move in the bed and his lips brush against her cheek.

"I have to go," he said. "The people I asked to stay with the kids will be wondering where I am."

"What time is it?" Anne murmured, turning over and snuggling against him.

"Almost midnight."

"Hmm. I can't seem to wake up."

"Sleep then," he whispered against her ear. "I'll see you in the morning."

Anne smiled as she watched him get out of bed and walk to retrieve his scattered clothing. Moonlight spilled through the windows, casting a soft light across the room and over Kurt's naked form.

He was a beautiful man—inside as well as out. And she still couldn't believe he had actually wanted her. She continued to watch him, not wanting to let him out of her sight. After he was dressed he came back toward the bed and she lifted her face for his kiss.

"Are you asleep?" he asked.

"No. I was watching you."

He laughed and bent to kiss her and, as had happened before, the kiss turned serious and heated as soon as their lips met.

"I wish I could stay," he whispered.

"I wish you could, too. But I'm afraid my cook might be shocked to find herself preparing breakfast for two after all this time."

He kissed her again and rose from the bed.

"Good night. Sleep well."

She lay awake, hearing his footsteps in the hall and the quiet closing of the front door. Long after the sound of his truck's engine had died into the distance Anne lay staring at the ceiling.

She went over every word, every touch, every sweetly delicious minute of their lovemaking. It seemed as if the quiet of the house made thoughts race through her mind. She found that it took being alone only a few moments for her self-doubts to return. And she wasn't sure she'd ever be able to go back to sleep.

Anne was tired the next morning, but she showered and dressed quickly. She found herself envisioning Kurt's expressive hazel eyes, imagining the way they would light when he saw her, and that made her hurry. She had the most frightening feeling that this was simply too good to be true.

He was in his office when she arrived. There was a teenaged boy seated in front of Kurt's desk. Probably a new resident, Anne told herself.

Kurt seemed busy and didn't see her, so she went on back to the kitchen.

"Hi, Vivian," she said, seeing the woman at the kitchen table. "I'm so glad you're back. Are you feeling better?"

"Oh, yes," Viv said. "I think I was just worn out. I'm so glad the air conditioning is fixed, though, or I might not have come back so soon. I still feel weak and tired."

"We'll help you," Anne said, putting her things away. "Won't we, Gabby?"

"I reckon," Gabby said in his usual grouchy way.

Anne found that as the morning progressed she could hardly keep still. She looked toward the door several times, wondering where Kurt was and why he hadn't come into the kitchen as he usually did. But they were all exceptionally busy, and she told herself that he must be as well.

Just before noon Vivian stepped to the door.

"Anne . . . Kurt would like to see you in his office."

"Oh," Anne said. Quickly, she dried her hands and turned to a small mirror near the sink. In the reflection she could see Gabby's wry, watchful expression as she pushed her hair back and smoothed her brows.

When she got to Kurt's office she hesitated in the doorway. Then he looked up, and the light in his eyes was everything she had dreamed it would be. His smile, always attractive, was different . . . special this morning. Anne found herself feeling as nervous and silly as a schoolgirl as they stood looking at each other.

"Come in," he said, standing up behind his desk and waiting for her.

"Shall I close the door?"

"No," he said, smiling mischievously at her. "Don't tempt me."

"Viv said you wanted to see me."

"Viv has no idea how badly I wanted to see you."

His gaze never left her face. There was a look of tenderness and affection, a shared intimacy that practically took her breath away.

Anne put her hands up to her cheeks, moving to sit in the chair before his desk.

"I can't believe I'm blushing," she said. "I don't think I've blushed in years."

"Well," he said, grinning, "I guess I should be flattered." He sat back down and for a moment they just smiled at one another before Kurt finally spoke.

"Besides having an excuse to see you alone for a few minutes, I wanted to tell you that you've been promoted."

"Promoted?"

"I want you to be my assistant." He waved his hand about the room and toward his desk, stacked high with papers. "God knows I need an assistant. The position has just been approved and I want you to have it."

"Kurt . . ." She frowned at him, seeing the look in his eyes. "But what about the kitchen work . . . who will help Gabby?"

"I've found someone else who can do that, a young man who dropped out of school and is studying at night for his GED."

Anne didn't know why she'd always hated change. And she knew she should be elated about Kurt's offer. Being near him every day was what she wanted, and heaven knew she was sick to death of washing dishes and fending off Gabby's irritating remarks. But she didn't trust change—never had—and she began to wonder exactly why this one had come about. And why now.

"Why are you doing this?" She hadn't meant for her voice to sound defensive or disapproving, but as soon as the words were out, she knew that they were.

Kurt frowned and sat back in his chair, his eyes narrowed and cautious as they studied her.

"Why do I get the feeling you're not pleased? I thought you would be."

"I am," she said quickly, leaning toward him and wishing she could remove the doubt from his eyes. But how could she when she couldn't seem to keep it out of her own mind?

"It's not that," she said. "It's just . . . I wonder why you're doing this now. After last night . . ."

"After last night?"

"Well, yes. We were . . . we're . . ."

"Jesus, Anne, do you think I'm rewarding you for last night? Is that it?"

"Are you? Wouldn't it seem that way to anyone, knowing what happened between us last night?"

"No one knows what happened last night, Anne, except you and me." He got up and came around the desk, kicking the door shut impatiently. Then he sat on the edge of the desk, very close to her. "Do you want to tell me what this is all about? Have I made you angry? Insulted you somehow?"

Anne understood his frustration. After all, despite the fact that they'd been working together for weeks, he hardly knew her. They had taken a giant step last night, skipping over several usual preliminaries on their way to becoming lovers.

"The word you used before is a good

description, I think," she said, clamping her lips together stubbornly. "Rewarded. I *do* feel that way—as if you've just rewarded me for sexual favors."

"My God," he said, standing up and moving restlessly across the floor. He poured himself a cup of coffee and turned back to face her. "Do you really think that what happened last night could be paid for with a puny little job like this? Hell, I don't know who the bigger insult is to—you or me."

He placed his coffee on the desk and sat down in his chair, leaning back and staring at her. His look was one of disbelief and incredible curiosity. Finally he raked his hand down his face and leaned forward, propping his chin in his hand.

His voice was softer when he spoke.

"It just happened this way. All right? Last night when I got back there was a message on my answering machine about the position finally being approved. I already had the application for a dishwasher and I called him for an interview this morning. I thought you would be pleased."

Why wasn't she pleased? It was something Anne couldn't quite understand herself. All she knew was that she was afraid; more afraid than she'd been in years. She'd been afraid all along that this couldn't work, that an incredible man like Kurt could never really be interested in her for herself alone.

Opening up all those feelings, all those emotions with Tracy, had led to her vulnerability with Kurt. The emotions had always been there between them; that was why it had happened. Last night she had been feeling alone and sad, and he had been there. It had been a mistake from the beginning, and now she was paying for it with a terrible ache in her heart from which she thought she might never recover.

"I think I prefer the kitchen," she said in a low, quiet voice. "Besides, I won't be here long enough to do justice to the job you mentioned. You would just have to hire someone else after I go and—"

"I don't want anyone else. You were wonderful with Tracy, and I know you could be a tremendous asset to the center. I want you," he said, his voice lowering and becoming more personal. "We could work well together."

Anne fairly leapt from her chair, taking a step backwards toward the door.

"No," she said. "I can't."

The look of pain and disbelief in his eyes shook her, and for a moment she almost relented.

"Kurt . . . last night with you—" She closed her eyes, remembering. "Last night," she continued, "was astonishing. I want to see you again—I'm not saying that that part has to end. But our relationship here will. Working here is just a temporary thing—something I had to do to appease Will Jordan's misguided sense of justice."

"It doesn't have to be temporary. But I understand that a woman like you wouldn't want to be bothered with this job."

The look in his eyes was one of acceptance, as if he already knew he'd never be able to convince her. But she thought there was also the tiniest flicker of disapproval, the disapproval she'd seen in other people's eyes ever since she had married into the Benefield wealth.

"It does have to be temporary," she said firmly. "It does." She turned toward the door, then stopped and tossed her hair back in an artificial, haughty way.

"Good heavens, Kurt, do you really think I'd be interested in working here permanently?" She deliberately let her eyes wander over the shabbiness of his office and then she laughed. "You saw my house last night. Really, darling . . . buy yourself a clue."

She didn't want to see his reaction or the hurt in his eyes that she knew was inevitable. She walked out the door, closing it behind her and leaning against it for a moment to catch her breath.

Then she hurried to the kitchen. Where there were no commitments . . . no responsibilities. Where she would be safe.

Kurt sat for a long time staring at the closed door, stunned into silence.

He leaned back in his chair, propping his feet on the desk and raking his hand over his jaw. He shook his head and stared at the walls, wondering what had just hit him and what he could have done differently to avoid it.

He had miscalculated what happened

last night. And he had misjudged Anne Benefield. Not that he had believed her insinuations that she was too good to work here. That was her defense mechanism kicking in—he'd figured out that much about her already. That snooty, better-than-you attitude was a facade—it wasn't Anne. He'd suspected it all along. And whether she was ready to admit it or not, last night had convinced him it was true.

He had known from the first that she was complicated, that she withheld the deepest part of herself from other people, and that she was closed off emotionally. He had simply made the mistake of thinking all that could be whisked away with one night of passion.

Hell, he wasn't even sure now if last night had meant the same thing to Anne as it had to him. He didn't jump into bed with every woman he met. In fact, Anne was the first since his divorce. But they were adults, long past the need for games, and perhaps Anne expected a purely sexual relationship with no commitments, no real, deep affection between them.

"Dammit, Anne," he muttered, letting

his feet slide off the desk. "I can't do that. I simply can't do it. And I have a feeling you can't either."

He stood up and paced restlessly back and forth behind his desk. God, but she'd thrown him for a loop, and he hardly knew what to do about it.

"The first thing I have to do is cancel the paperwork for an assistant," he said, moving to his desk and picking up the phone. "And then, Mrs. Anne Benefield, you and I have some serious talking to do."

Twelve

Anne hardly saw Kurt the rest of the day, and that suited her just fine. She didn't know what to say to him, or how to react when he looked at her with those questions in his beautiful eyes. She didn't want him to be hurt, but dammit, she didn't want him treating her any different than anyone else or making her feel obligated. She couldn't just throw herself heart and soul into a relationship so soon. Didn't he realize that?

I should have thought of all that last night, a voice whispered inside her head. When he kissed me I practically dragged him into the house and into my bed.

Desperate. Needy. Dependent. All the things she hated and never wanted to be.

Giving in to her sexual needs had been easy; so very easy with Kurt. But it was the emotional commitment that she couldn't handle. And, if she could admit it to herself, she never had been able to handle. Wasn't that the reason she had married Baxter? So she would be secure and safe without the need for an emotional and physical commitment?

But Kurt is not Baxter, the nagging voice whispered. He's a strong, healthy, masculine man in the prime of his life. And she had known from the beginning that he had no need for games.

Why had she allowed this to happen? Why? It was a complication she didn't want in her life.

That afternoon she heard Viv say that Kurt had gone to the jail to pick up a child, a little girl.

"How sad," Anne said. She had been cleaning the cupboard and replacing the shelf paper and she stepped out into the kitchen, not sure Vivian had seen her when she came in. "Is it usual to pick up one of the children at the jail?"

"Oh, yes," Vivian said with a shake of her head. "It's sickening how common it is. This little girl was locked out of her house all night for some reason. The neighbors called the police and turned her mother in; they say it's not the first time she's done it. She's in jail now and the child has nowhere else to go. So Kurt's gone to get her."

Anne forgot about the conversation until that afternoon when she was going home. She passed Kurt's office on the way out the door. He was at his desk, his head bent as he wrote something, and in front of his desk sat a little girl.

Anne stopped, staring at the girl. The child, who looked to be about ten years old, was filthy, with straight, stringy blonde hair. She wore no shoes and her chubby ankles were crossed tightly and tucked back beneath the chair. She sat very stiffly, as if she were afraid to move, with her hands clasped rigidly in her lap. Her plump, round face held no expression at all as she stared straight ahead.

It was like looking at herself.

Except when she was that age Anne was never dirty. In fact, her mother could never tolerate a speck of dirt on Anne's shoes or clothes, and she was constantly lifting Anne's chin to inspect her neck and ears. She could remember the accusatory tone of her mother's voice when she came in from playing, as if getting dirty was somehow shameful, intolerable.

Anne had been plump, about the same size as this little girl. And it had caused her such agony that just looking at the child now brought it all back. She could almost hear her mother's biting criticisms. And she could remember feeling as miserable and as useless as any human could ever feel. She had felt ugly and not good enough. Never good enough.

Fighting her weight had always been a battle. She was still ten pounds or more too heavy, but she had learned to maintain it at least. It was a constant struggle to keep the pounds from creeping back on, and no one, not even Cecile, knew how panic-stricken or how sick inside Anne became if she gained an extra pound or two.

She frowned, remembering, and continued staring at the little girl. She wondered what her name was, what her story was.

Anne shook her head and moved to the front door and outside.

"Forget it," she muttered. "Just forget it. Look what happened with Tracy. Do you want that to happen again?"

But Anne found that she couldn't forget

the girl, or the sad, hopeless expression on her face, the way her eyes stared blankly. It made Anne's heart ache, and she cursed beneath her breath at the long-forgotten feeling. At all the forgotten emotions she'd been experiencing lately.

"Oh, Kurt," she whispered as she pulled into her drive. "I should have stayed away from you. I should have stayed away."

As soon as Anne walked into the house, she knew she wouldn't be able to stay home. Not after she stepped into her bedroom and the memories of last night came flooding back. She actually had to close her eyes for a few moments. Her mind played tricks on her and made her think that the scent of Kurt's cologne still lingered like a slow, sensual caress in the quiet room.

She opened her eyes, turning to walk to the bed and trace her fingers along the expensive comforter. The bed had been made and there was no physical trace of Kurt's presence anywhere in the elegantly furnished bedroom. But still she could feel him there. In her heart and soul, she could feel him, just as real as he'd been last night. She wanted nothing more than to fall on the bed and weep at her weakness where he was concerned.

Instead she took a long, steadying breath and went to the phone.

"A movie?" Cecile replied at Anne's question. "Sure, I'd love it. Wanna stop by the Riverside Grill for a salad before we go?"

"Sounds good," Anne said. "Let me shower and change. I'll pick you up in forty-five minutes."

It was a relief to have to hurry and get out of the house. But Anne had no idea what she would do after the movie. Or how she would be able to sleep in that bed.

Less than an hour later, she and Cecile walked into the small restaurant that overlooked the river and went to one of the tables near the windows.

"This feels good," Anne murmured as she slid into her chair.

"How's it going at the center?"

"Good," Anne said, picking up her menu. She knew Cecile was genuinely interested, but she didn't want to talk about the halfway house tonight.

She glanced up and caught Cecile's

questioning gaze. But neither of them said anything.

After they'd placed their order Anne gazed through the windows at the river tumbling over smooth rocks below them. There were ducks floating and dunking their heads beneath the water and song-birds perched in the tree limbs along the banks. It was serene here, and beautiful, and she could feel her tension beginning to melt away.

She listened quietly to Cecile's chatter and let her gaze drift aimlessly over the people in the restaurant.

She hadn't seen Kurt until then, sitting alone at a table at the farthest end of the restaurant. He was watching her with an odd, inquisitive look on his face.

She hadn't realized she'd made any sound until Cecile stopped talking and stared at her.

"Annie?" she asked. She turned then, following the direction of Anne's look.

"Don't—" Anne began.

But it was too late. Cecile had already turned around and seen Kurt. Just in time to see him lift his glass of beer their way in an amused little salute.

"What a good-looking man," Cecile whispered. She turned back around quickly and saw the look on Anne's face. "My goodness, is that him? Is that your boss?"

"You don't have to announce it to everyone in the restaurant," Anne said between clenched teeth.

"Why don't we invite him over. Ask—"

"No," Anne said.

She could still sense Kurt's gaze on her and she was afraid she might blush. What on earth would Cecile think if she saw how he affected her? If she saw her blushing, for heaven's sake.

"Why not?"

"I said no, Cecile," Anne muttered. "I see the man all day long. I really don't care to have to share dinner with him, too."

Cecile's lips quirked and she turned her head to one side as if she couldn't discern Anne's meaning.

"What's going on here, sweetie?" she asked quietly. "You can't fool me, you know. I know you better than anyone in this town. Besides, your hands are shaking."

Anne took her hands off the table and placed them in her lap. Then she frowned at Cecile, feeling annoyed and impatient.

"Nothing's going on."

"You mean nothing you want to tell me about."

"Just drop it, Cecile, okay?" Anne cleared her throat and turned to stare at the river. God, she actually felt as if she might cry. Why, she had no idea.

"Anne?" Cecile said, reaching across the table toward her. "Honey, I've never seen you like this. If you want to go, it's fine with me. Has he said something to upset you? I mean, he's not one of those—"

"No . . . no," Anne said, shaking her head. "Of course he's not. He's a decent, caring man and he—"

She couldn't seem to keep her eyes from turning toward him again. And this time his gaze met hers with the impact of a freight train.

"Oh, Cecile," she whispered, looking down at the table. "I think I'm in serious trouble here."

"Well, that much is obvious. I just never thought I'd hear you admit it."

"I never thought I could admit it. And

if you ever mention it to me again, I'll kill you. I don't know what I'm going to do about him. I think I'm completely out of my league with this man."

Anne couldn't believe it when Kurt stood up and began to walk toward their table. She actually had to grip the sides of her chair to keep from springing up and running away.

He stopped, just as she knew he would, and stood staring down at her. His manner was easy and cool, but one look into those hazel eyes and she knew that he was still hurt and still angry about what had happened between them.

"Evening," he said.

"Hi," Anne said, pulling her gaze up toward his. "Uh, Cecile, this is Kurt Bonner, the director of the halfway house. Kurt, this is my best friend, Cecile Loudermilk."

Kurt turned and smiled down at Cecile.

"Loudermilk . . . I've heard the name, I believe. Doesn't your husband own a couple of sporting goods stores?"

"Why, yes, he does."

"Ah. I'll have to take the two of you out to dinner one night . . . see if I can't twist his arm and get him to donate some equipment to the center."

Anne thought Cecile was practically twittering as she grinned up at Kurt.

"Why, that would be delightful," she drawled in her best Southern belle voice. "I'll tell Barney. I'm sure he'd be happy to do what he can to help out. We're very big on support for the community," she added. "Very big."

Kurt laughed then and nodded, letting his gaze linger on Anne just a moment longer.

"I'll let you ladies finish your dinner. Nice to meet you, Mrs. Loudermilk. I'll see you tomorrow, Anne."

They both watched as he paid his tab and walked toward the door.

"Oh, my Lord," Cecile sighed, her eyes still following him. "Those eyes . . . that voice. And he has the sexiest smile I think I've ever seen."

"Cecile," Anne said with just a hint of irritation, "try and control yourself. Have you stopped taking your hormones?"

She ignored Anne's sarcasm and when she spoke her voice was breathless and filled with curiosity.

"What gives?" she asked. "There are only two reasons a man looks at a woman the way Kurt Bonner just looked at you. Either he wants her and can't have her or he's had her and is coming back for more."

"Oh God," Anne groaned, turning away from Cecile's bright inquisitive eyes.

"My stars and garters, that's it, isn't it? He wants you and you're running away, just the way you always do. Anne, don't you think it's time you stop this foolishness? You're a mature, attractive woman. Don't you think you need something more in your life than that farm and cards at the club with the girls? Believe you me, if I had a man look at me the way he just looked at you . . ."

Cecile's voice trailed away as she stared at Anne, as she saw the misery and despair in her eyes.

"Honey, is there something else? You're worrying me. Now I want you to tell me what happened. Forget the movies. We're going to sit right here until they close or until you've told me what has you in such a state." She turned toward the waiter. "Would you please bring us two glasses of white wine?"

"Right away, ma'am."

"Oh, Cecile, I think I've made the worst mistake of my life."

"What?" Cecile asked, her voice low and urgent.

"It's a long story," Anne murmured, her voice a mere whisper. "But the gist of it is, Kurt is a caring, sensitive man who only meant to comfort me . . . about something that happened at work. I'm sure that's the only reason he came to the house last night. But there's been this tension between us, this . . ." Anne spread her fingers and shrugged, then looked away toward the river again.

"Sexual attraction . . ." Cecile finished, her eyes wide and filled with expectancy.

Anne only nodded.

"And . . . ?" Cecile urged. "And?"

"I don't know how it happened. I didn't mean for it to happen." Anne put her fingers over her lips and her eyes were tortured.

Cecile gasped and sat back in her chair. For a moment she could only stare at Anne, her eyes wide with surprise. Then she began to smile.

"Anne Benefield, you devil. You sly, surprising little devil. But I think maybe . . . just maybe, after years of fooling yourself, and being the loneliest woman in Clayburn County, you might just possibly have done something right."

"No," Anne said, shaking her head. "No, I don't think so."

"Listen to me," Cecile said, reaching across the table to take Anne's hand. "You deserve to be happy. And you deserve to have a man like Kurt Bonner paying attention to you. Can't you see what's happening?"

"I don't *want* anything to happen," Anne said. "I want everything to stay just the way it was."

"The way it was? You mean with you holed up in that big old house alone, night after night? Going to the club once a week to play cards with a bunch of widow women who have nothing better to do? Going to Saturday-night dances by yourself? Sleeping alone? Throwing expensive parties to keep yourself entertained? Spending too much money on clothes and on no one but yourself?"

"That's enough," Anne said, shaking her head against Cecile's onslaught of accusations.

"You have a chance to open up your heart, Anne. This could be the man—that one man you've never been able to have in your entire life. Are you going to let that chance slip through your fingers because you're afraid?"

"You're putting too much into this, Cecile."

"No, I'm not," Cecile declared, and for once her eyes were dead serious. "I can feel it, what's between you two. And you can feel it, too! You have to let go of the past, sweetie."

Anne had to close her eyes against the memories that Cecile's demand brought. They were almost the same words Kurt had said when he made love to her, an urgency for her to let go, to feel all the wonderful things that life had to offer.

"I can't," Anne whispered. "I'm afraid it's too late."

"You're not dead yet, are you? Or sitting senseless in a nursing home?"

"No," Anne said, laughing against her will.

"Then it's *not* too late. Not unless you make it that way."

Thirteen

Anne thought about Cecile's words all the way home. They seemed to haunt her dreams later that night, until finally she got out of bed and walked to the windows and stood staring out into the darkness.

By morning she had convinced herself that Cecile was dead wrong. She had always been fanciful and romantic. She'd probably only imagined what she wanted to see in Kurt's eyes.

At work his manner seemed to bear that out. He was coolly friendly, as if nothing had ever happened between them, as if he hadn't held her and kissed her until she thought she would shatter into a million pleasurable pieces.

He talked and he smiled at her. He kidded with Gabby when he came into the kitchen for his usual carrot snack.

"Good," Anne muttered to herself after he went back to his office without a word to her.

"What's that?" Gabby said.

"Nothing," she said. "Just talking to myself."

"You see the new girl in the house?" he asked.

Anne turned to the old man. She thought he was fond of the children, but it was unusual for him to talk about them very much. He had probably talked about Tracy more than most.

"I saw her yesterday, when she came in. Why?"

"Locked herself in her room this mornin'. Wouldn't come out."

"She did? How did Kurt finally persuade her?"

"Didn't."

"You mean—"

"Yep. Still in there."

Anne shook her head, thinking what a tremendous task Kurt had with these children. None of them were ever here long enough to allow him to make real progress. She wondered how he stood it, being only a temporary help to them. He was a compassionate man; she had seen that. She wondered how he could ever have a sense of completion, the way things were in the house.

"But . . . he didn't seem worried when he was in here a moment ago."

"Kurt? Not worried? Shoot, he's probably holed up in his office right now, pacin' the floor, or callin' the psychologist and askin' what he can do. But he ain't one to force something. He sure ain't the kind of man to drag the girl out by the hair of the head, if that's what you think."

"No," she said. "No, I didn't think that." What did she think? she asked herself. Normally she didn't bother getting to know someone intimately enough to have an idea what they thought or felt.

But with Kurt it was different. She found herself wanting to know everything there was to know about him. What he liked, what he didn't like. What bothered him or irritated him. The thought of him being worried and uncertain brought a tiny ache to her chest. And she found her gaze wandering more than once toward the kitchen door.

Should she offer to help? After all, Tracy had been fond of her. Perhaps she could relate to this girl, too. She did remind Anne an awful lot of herself at that age.

"No," she muttered, pushing a pan into the soapy water.

"Huh? What the heck's the matter with you today anyway, Sis? You been talkin' to yourself all mornin'. You hungry? Want a sausage and biscuit?"

When she turned to look at Gabby she thought she actually saw genuine concern in his weary old eyes, and she smiled.

She didn't need the calories or the fat that was in a sausage and biscuit. But she nodded at him and dried her hands before going to the refrigerator for the orange juice.

"When have I ever been able to turn down one of your biscuits, Mr. Harrison?"

"Mr. Harrison," he grunted. "You know don't nobody call me that."

"Where did you get the name Gabby, anyway?"

He stared at her for a moment, then went on kneading the bread on the smooth wooden bread table.

"Kurt give it to me, I reckon. Said I

looked like Gabby Hayes. You probably don't even know who he was."

"Of course I know who Gabby Hayes was. He was an old cowpoke . . . Roy Rogers's right-hand man. I used to watch them every Saturday at the movies."

Gabby actually looked impressed as he nodded toward her.

"That's right. Old Gabby didn't have no teeth and he was a mite grumpy, too, if you'll recall."

"But Roy Rogers loved him. They kind of looked out for one another . . . like you and Kurt," she said, dipping her head so she could see Gabby's expression better.

He grunted again and wiggled his mouth. Then, with his lips pressed together, he nodded toward her. There was a sweetly wistful look in his eyes and even the slightest hint of a smile on his face.

"I reckon you could say that."

"You care a lot about him, don't you?"

"Kurt? Why, sure I do. He's the salt of the earth. I reckon they ain't nothin' I wouldn't do for him, or him for me. He's the reason I'm here, you know."

"Oh, he knew about your cooking skills and—"

"Oh, hell no. Cookin' didn't have nothin' to do with it. Had to learn to cook. I'll tell you the truth; I was a drunk, missy. Just a sorry, worthless old sot, never had nothin', never wanted nothin' except a bottle. Couldn't hold down a job, lost my family because of it. Kurt Bonner found me on the street one winter. I was sick, mighty sick. He took me home with him, sobered me up and got me well, let me do odd jobs around his house. Even found me a place to live. And when he took this job, he asked me to do the cookin' for him."

Anne had set her glass of juice down and now she stared at Gabby.

"How long ago was it he took you in?" she asked softly.

"Goin' on five years now."

"Five years. So you . . . you knew Kurt's wife."

"Yep. A nice woman, real nice. Not friendly like Kurt, but nice."

"I'll bet she was very pretty."

Why had she asked that? It was none of her business what Kurt's ex-wife looked like. And what difference could it possibly make to her if the woman was pretty or not?

"Yep, she was. A right pretty woman."

Anne frowned and pushed the biscuit away, wishing she hadn't asked.

"It's hot in here," Anne said, pushing away from the table. "I think I'll go outside with Viv, watch the kids playing for a while."

She could feel Gabby's gaze on her as she walked to the back door.

"Hey, Sis," he said. "Didn't your ma ever tell you that it's what's on the inside that counts?"

"No," Anne snapped. "My mother is hardly the kind of person to ever say something like that."

"Well, it's true. The good in a person's soul shows through to their face, they say."

Anne turned and frowned at him.

"Well, you're a regular philosopher, aren't you?"

Gabby grinned at her; then his eyes turned uncharacteristically shy.

"Reckon you don't have to worry about it anyway," he said softly. "You look fine. I'd say beautiful if I was tryin' to be highfalutin'. Prettier when you ain't so crabby." He didn't look at her again, but busied himself with putting the kneaded bread into a large wooden bowl.

Anne didn't know what to say. She knew that in his funny, grouchy way, Gabby meant it as a compliment. And she considered it a high compliment, indeed, coming from him. For the life of her she couldn't explain why she had the urge to hug the old man, or the sudden, overwhelming need to be alone and cry.

She hurried out the door and into the backyard. She walked to where Vivian sat beneath the tree, watching the children. It was hot outside, but there was a light breeze that stirred the leaves of the tree.

"Hey," Viv said, turning to smile at her. "Have a seat. It's nice out here."

Anne sat for a while, watching the children play.

"Gabby said the little girl who came in yesterday locked herself in her room."

Viv's eyes glanced toward the upstairs level of the house.

"Yes," she said with a sigh. "She's certainly a rude, sullen little thing. I swear, I can almost understand why her mother locked her outside."

"You don't mean that," Anne said, frowning at her.

"Of course I don't," Viv said with a

quiet laugh. "But for whatever reason, some of these kids *are* unlikable, you know. They aren't all as sweet and lovable as Tracy."

"No, I know they aren't."

Why did she feel so defensive about Vivian's words? It was certainly nothing to her if the new girl was hateful and unlikable.

"What's her name?"

"Crystal Raburn. Her mother's a druggie. Father abandoned them years ago. Crystal has an older sister who some say is a prostitute in Atlanta. No doubt that's where this kid is going to end up, too."

Anne didn't say anything, but Vivian's words irritated her. So many adults did that to children, filled them with such doubt and disgust about themselves that they had no choice but to end up the way they did.

Anne had a lot of hang-ups herself; she'd be the first to admit that. Recognizing them sometimes was just as hard as trying to correct them. But she supposed she was lucky to have come away as sane as she was from her relationship with her own controlling mother.

For the first time in a long while, Anne felt guilty about her mother. She was an old woman now, in a retirement home with no relatives to visit her except Anne. And it had been months since Anne had been there. Every time she did go, there were the inevitable criticisms, and the just as inevitable arguments. Her mother was as critical and independent in her thinking as ever. The difference was, Anne didn't have to put up with it anymore.

"Which room is Crystal in?" Anne asked, standing up suddenly.

"First one on the right, top of the stairs." Viv flashed a doubtful look at Anne. "You won't be able to get her out. Besides, it might do her some good to stay in there awhile. Maybe she likes being alone."

"Maybe," Anne said. "But I think I'll give it a try."

"Good luck," Viv said with a wry smile.

Anne hurried back into the kitchen. Some little voice inside her head nagged at her, reminding her that she hadn't intended to get involved. Reminding her with a jolt of longing about Tracy and how she'd sworn she wouldn't let it happen again.

But there was something about this girl that cried out to her, something of the same lost child that Anne had been when she was young.

"Gabby," she said in the kitchen, "did you like chocolate when you were a kid?"

"Lord, woman, you're talkin' about more'n a century ago. How the heck do you expect me to remember that far back?"

Anne laughed. "I loved chocolate when I was a girl. Still do. The experts even say now that it's a comfort food."

"Well, hell," Gabby said, waving his hand toward the refrigerator. "I got them brownies I baked yesterday . . . there in the Frigidaire. Help yerself . . . get all the comfort you want."

Anne laughed again, going to the refrigerator. She didn't bother telling him that the chocolate wasn't for her. While she was there, she poured a tall glass of milk, too, and took it with her through the dining room.

She thought there was no one in that part of the house, but as she approached the stairs near Kurt's office, she could hear him talking. She peeked in and saw that he was on the phone.

His eyes brightened when he saw her, and when he saw the glass of milk and the plate containing two brownies, he smiled crookedly at her.

"Hungry?" he whispered, putting his hand over the mouthpiece of the phone.

"For Crystal," she said quietly, pointing up the stairs.

"I'll call you back," she heard Kurt say.

He came into the entry hall and stood at the foot of the stairs, his hands hooked into his belt as he watched her go up.

"It won't work," he said, his voice firm but not unkind. "I've already tried bribing her with food."

"Ah," Anne said with a teasing lift of her brows, "but have you tried chocolate? Don't you know how women absolutely crave chocolate?"

She stood at the top of the stairs, looking down at him. His smile was slow and sweet, and he shook his head at her as if he were completely enchanted with her new teasing manner.

"Lady, I can't figure you out," he said, keeping his voice as light as hers.

"Don't try," she said. "A true Southern lady is always mannered and polite, and as sweet as a ripe juicy peach on a hot summer day," she said, exaggerating her own Southern accent. "But," she said with a wicked little grin, "she is never predictable."

Kurt laughed then and came to stand leaning against the banister, looking up at her with a warm, intense look but making no attempt to follow.

Fourteen

Anne knocked on the door and stood listening. From inside she could hear a radio playing country music, blaring out the twangy sound of a steel guitar. She tapped the bottom of the glass of milk against the door again.

"Crystal? Would you open the door, please?"

There was no sound of movement and the music continued to blast unrestrained.

"Crystal, please turn down the music. I've brought you something to eat."

She turned and looked down the stairs. Kurt lounged against the banister, watching her, his look decidedly one of "I told you so."

"Crystal . . ."

Suddenly the music stopped and there was silence. Anne felt her heart begin to beat a little faster. Still, she heard no sound of movement from within.

"It's a beautiful day. Why don't you come outside?"

"I don't want to go outside," the girl's voice said. She sounded very close to the door. "It's too hot." There was a whining quality to her voice, and for a moment Anne understood Vivian's irritation with the girl.

"You can sit in the shade if you like. There's a big old oak tree out back and—"

"Who are you anyway?" the petulant voice asked. "I already said I'm not coming out, and I ain't."

Anne sighed and rolled her eyes. She turned to see Kurt shrug his broad shoulders as he grinned up at her.

"My name is Anne. Why don't you open the door and let me say hello? I'd really like to meet you."

"Well, I don't want to meet you. I don't want to meet anybody in this stinkin' place!"

There was such anger and defiance in the girl's voice that Anne wondered if it was too late, if anyone would be able to get through to Crystal Raburn.

Anne remembered her own anger as a youngster, how she had lashed out at anyone trying to get close to her. And she also remembered that most of it came from an intense pride, a desperate need to keep from making a fool of herself by begging for the attention she really wanted. Not many people even bothered trying after a while. Yet that was what she'd wanted. She'd wanted someone to try, to *force* her even into letting them into her painful little world. That was exactly what Baxter had done to win her.

Anne smiled. She'd been right about Crystal. She was more like her than she'd thought.

"But I want to meet you," Anne said quietly, leaning closer to the door. "I've brought some brownies and a glass of milk. I wish you'd let me come in long enough to give it to you at least. Then I'll go away and let you eat in peace."

The silence seemed to last forever. Anne frowned. She couldn't help being concerned about the girl. Locking oneself in for hours was a desperate act and she couldn't help worrying about Crystal's state of mind.

She started to leave when she heard the sound of the lock. The door moved open only a few inches, and Anne found herself face to face with the defiant little girl.

"Hello, Crystal," Anne said. Her gaze wandered over the girl's round face, noting the flushed cheeks and the stubborn glint in her blue eyes. "I suppose I should have brought something a little more nourishing than brownies and milk. Perhaps later you'd like to come down to the kitchen for a sandwich. That's where I work."

Crystal said nothing, but reached forward for the brownies and glass of milk. Anne could see her attempt at coolness, but her eyes gave her away as they focused hungrily on the food.

The girl had to open the door wider to get the food inside, and she glanced at Anne fearfully, as if she was afraid she might attempt to force her way into the bedroom. Anne stood very still, letting her know she had no such intentions. She noted the girl's appearance—her stringy, unwashed hair and her bare feet caked with what looked like days of dirt. Anne smiled at her.

Crystal clamped her teeth together and stepped back into the bedroom. Then she slammed the door hard, leaving Anne stunned.

"Well, you're welcome," Anne murmured to herself.

Kurt had come about halfway up the steps. She heard him behind her now.

"It's a beginning," he said.

She turned around to face him, and they stood for a moment in the dimly lit area. She walked over to the top of the stairs and looked down at him.

"I promised myself I wouldn't do this . . . get involved again after Tracy," she confessed quietly.

"I know." His gaze was steady as he looked into her eyes. There were so many questions there, so much doubt. "This is a big step for you. But I have to insist on one thing."

His words surprised her and she frowned at him. She wasn't used to hearing him sound like a boss.

"What?"

"Don't do this if you don't intend to stick it out. Don't reach out for Crystal and then, when the going gets tough . . . when it hurts, pull away."

Anne felt his words shoot straight to her heart.

"You mean the way I did with you?" She was stung by his quietly spoken words and she supposed it was evident in her eyes. She felt so vulnerable, standing there, staring him straight in the face and discussing what she had done to him. It would have been easier for her to ignore it and let time heal whatever damage she had inflicted. But he wasn't going to let her do that.

"I'm a grown man," Kurt said slowly. "Crystal is only a child."

"Oh," Anne said, her cheeks burning with humiliation. "I see. You can handle it, then." Why did she want to hear him deny that? Why did she suddenly need him to tell her he needed her and wanted her and would do anything to get her back?

"Yeah," he said with a confident lift of his brows. "I can handle it."

She hurried past him, practically running down the stairs.

"Good," she said breathlessly. "I'm glad you're such a big, tough guy."

She felt Kurt's hand on her arm as he stepped down one step and brought her to a halt.

"I mean it, Anne," he said, leaning closer to her. "You make up your mind about Crystal. And if you can't hack it, then I'll have to ask you to stay away from her. She's messed up enough without anyone here adding to her confusion."

Anne felt the adrenaline, the anger rushing through her. The blood pounded in her ears and made her eyes water as she stared into his determined eyes. Her jaws were clenched so tightly that she felt an ache beneath her ear, and it was all she could do to keep from lashing out at him.

Instead she took a long, steadying breath of air and spoke quietly.

"*Yes, sir.*"

His eyes were cool as he released her arm and stepped away. And he said nothing else as Anne jerked around and hurried down the stairs and toward the kitchen.

"Damn you," she muttered to herself.

"I don't intend to quit, Mr. Bonner. Not this time."

She was still angry when she slammed through the doorway into the kitchen.

Gabby made a face at her and leaned back, his gaze going up and down as he stared at her.

"What the heck's wrong with you? You look madder'n a wet hen."

"I'm just frustrated," she said, going to stand at the sink. "I have no idea what your boss wants. He doesn't like people who don't get involved and now that I *want* to get involved, he doesn't seem to want that either."

Gabby grunted. "I don't know who you're talkin' about, but it ain't Kurt Bonner. He's a man knows *exactly* what he wants."

"What are you saying?" she fumed. "Are you saying that I'm the one who doesn't know what she wants?"

" Sis . . ." he sighed, gazing at her wearily. "You ever heard that old song—'First you say you will and then you won't, then you say you do and then you don't'? "

She shook her head at his attempt to sing the song.

"Are you being funny?" She turned away and began to straighten the items sitting on the cabinet.

"I was scared, too, when Kurt took me in. Afraid I couldn't quit drinkin', afraid I couldn't stay long enough to have a home. Hell, I was afraid of everything, I reckon. Still am, sometimes."

"I'm not afraid," Anne said, whirling around to face him.

"The devil you say." As usual Gabby didn't bother looking at her, but continued with his work. "You're scared to death, girl. Scared of feelin', scared of bein' hurt, scared you're gonna fail." He did look at her then, staring her straight in the eye. "You might come in a nicer, prettier package than this old booze hound, but take my word for it, Sis. You're just as scared as I ever thought about bein'."

Anne stared at him, letting his words sink in and trying to decide if he was right or not.

"And I'll tell you another thing . . ."

"Please," she said wryly, "be my guest."

"Kurt is a special man. He expects a lot outta people, and most of the times he gets it. And when you really like somebody like him, when you begin to care about him, then you're scared of bein' the one to disappoint him."

Anne walked to the table and pulled out the chair opposite Gabby. She practically slumped into the seat.

"Gabby," she sighed. "How did you get to be so damned smart?"

"Genes," he said with a toothless grin. He pecked a gnarled finger against the side of his head. "Inherited. They say I'm a direct descendent of William Henry Harrison, the ninth President of these here United States."

She couldn't help grinning at him. "If I remember my history correctly, President Harrison took ill after his inauguration and died about a month later. He hardly had time to serve as President."

"Well, hell, he was still President. Ain't nobody perfect."

She stared at him for a minute, then picked up a green bean from the table and flung it at him, hitting him in the chest. She burst out laughing and soon Gabby was cackling right along with her.

"Oh," she said finally, still breathless from laughing so hard, "I needed that."

"Don't take yourself so serious," Gabby said. "For what it's worth, I don't think you're gonna disappoint anybody if you do what you know is right."

"Open up my heart, huh?" she said, remembering Cecile's advice.

"That's it," he said, nodding wisely. "That little gal upstairs, now she's got problems. It's gonna take somebody unselfish to help her."

"I haven't thought of anyone or anything much except myself for the last fifteen years," Anne said quietly.

"Heck, that don't mean you can't start thinking about somebody else now."

Anne took a deep breath, feeling her determination coming back. She could do this. She had to.

"Thanks, Gabby," she said. She stared at him, as if seeing him for the first time. "You know, I didn't like you much when I first came here. But I'm glad you let me get to know you. I'm glad you're not as snooty as I was."

Her look was tender and sincere and when Gabby looked up at her he quickly swung his gaze away and waved his hand toward the sink.

"Well, hell, you gonna let them dishes set there all day? We got work to do, girl. Can't set here yammerin' all day."

Fifteen

Crystal didn't come out of her room that day, not even for a sandwich, as Anne had suggested. When Kurt came into the kitchen to talk to all of them before Anne left for the day she could see the frustration and tension on his face.

He sat at the kitchen table, his hand covering his mouth and chin, his eyes thoughtful and filled with worry.

"The psychologist said to talk to Crystal periodically, be friendly, offer her our help, but in the end if she doesn't want to come out, we should leave her alone. He says she will come out sooner or later. The problem is what to do with the other two girls who were sleeping in that room."

"They can move across the hall," Viv said. "We can put cots in there temporarily. Surely Crystal will come out to-morrow."

"I hope so," Kurt said, raking his hand down his jaw.

Anne thought he looked weary, and there was such a disquieting look of defeat in his hazel eyes.

"And there's another problem," he said. Then he shrugged and laughed softly. "Actually, this should be a solution, but I'm not sure it will be. I've hired a man and his wife as house parents. She will be the one we'll deal with mostly—he has a day job and will continue that, although he understands he has to be here at night."

"The ones you interviewed last week?" Viv asked.

"Yeah. I had them checked out; all the references were good, but for some reason I'm just not really impressed. I don't know . . ." he said, shrugging again.

"Well, you don't have much choice," Viv said. "We have to have somebody and soon."

"I know. They'll move in tomorrow and then we'll see."

For a moment, Kurt traced his finger

along a crack in the wooden table. Then his gaze lifted toward Anne.

"Since you got more out of Crystal than any of us, would you like to try getting her to eat supper?"

"Sure," Anne said. "You mean take it up to her or—"

"I'll leave that up to you," he said. "Whatever you think is best."

"Well . . . I'll take something up there. Gabby, can you fix a plate for her?"

The old man grunted as he pushed himself up from the table and hobbled to the stove.

This time when Anne went upstairs she found Crystal's door slightly open. She hesitated, surprised that the child had finally relented. Then she pushed the door open and stepped inside.

The room was almost dark and it took a while for Anne's eyes to adjust. Finally she saw Crystal sitting in a chair in front of the window that looked out into the backyard.

"Crystal? Honey? I've brought you some supper."

"I don't want any," came the muffled reply.

"You have to eat."

The girl said nothing, just sat very still, staring out the window.

"I'll put it here on the table for you and—"

Suddenly Crystal turned, moving so violently that the chair almost came out from under her.

"I said I don't want it! Are you deaf or something? I don't want your stupid food and I don't want you being nice to me."

Anne put the food on a table and walked over to the girl, bending down and looking straight into her angry blue eyes.

"You know, you're behaving like a real brat. Everyone in this house is concerned about you. They want to help you. And all you can do is sit up here and pout. Really, I don't know why I bothered. I'll take the food back downstairs."

Anne turned to go and was almost to the door when she heard the girl's whispered words.

"Hey, lady," she said.

"My name is Anne."

"Anne," Crystal said very quietly. "I ain't a brat and I'm not pouting. It's just that. . . ." Her eyes were dark and troubled.

"What?" Anne asked. "You can tell me."

"My mama says if I keep eating I'll be as fat as a pig." The girl's voice was very soft, hardly above a whisper. "She said nobody loves a fat girl. I had to be punished when I ate too much."

"Is that why she locked you out?" Anne asked, her voice horrified. "To punish you?"

Crystal nodded. "She said fat people are the ugliest people on earth."

Anne felt her heart ache. There was such pain, such despair in those softly spoken words.

"Honey," Anne said, going back to Crystal, "you can't stop eating completely. Besides, this is good, nutritious food. It's not going to make you fat."

Crystal glanced at the plate, her eyes growing soft as she stared at the baked chicken and green beans.

"It will me. I always eat too much."

"Tell you what," Anne said. "How about I go downstairs and get myself a plate just like yours and I'll sit up here and have supper with you. I have to watch my weight, too, you know. It's always easier to do that when you have a friend to share with you."

Crystal's eyes wandered over Anne. There was still a stubborn reluctance in her eyes, and yet Anne knew she had to be terribly hungry by now.

"Okay?" Anne said.

Crystal nodded, and when she turned back to stare out the window Anne hurried out of the room. She wanted to get back before the girl changed her mind and locked the door again.

Later, as they ate, Anne tried not to stare as Crystal wolfed down her food. It was heartbreaking to see her lift her eyes toward Anne in an apologetic manner, then try to eat more slowly. Anne would smile and continue eating her own supper, and even though she tried to start a conversation, Crystal had nothing to say.

Finally Anne gathered up the dirty dishes. Crystal had gone back to the window.

"You know, Crystal, there were two other girls in this room before you came.

They had to sleep somewhere else tonight because you had the door locked."

Crystal turned sad, distrustful eyes toward Anne.

"No one is angry with you about that. But I'm sure they'd like their room back tomorrow." Anne couldn't read what was in the girl's eyes. They were blank, uncaring. "Breakfast is at eight o'clock, downstairs in the dining room. I hope I'll see you there. Vivian has left some clothes outside your door if you'd like to take a bath and change before bed."

Crystal said nothing. She wouldn't even look at Anne.

"Well, good night, Crystal. Sleep well. I'll see you tomorrow."

The house was relatively quiet when Anne went back downstairs. She could hear the sound of a television in the family room. But the dining-room table had been cleared and the chairs put back in order. The kitchen was clean and quiet.

Anne was tired so she just piled the dishes in the sink, got her purse, and turned out the lights.

Kurt's office was dark, too. She thought he'd probably already gone home.

But when she stepped out on the front porch she saw him, sitting on the bottom step, his forearms propped on his knees as he gazed up toward the night sky. Seeing him there brought a strange ache to her heart. He was always so brisk and efficient at work and yet, sitting here, his shoulders slumped forward, he looked alone and tired and vulnerable.

"Hi," she said. "I thought you'd gone home."

"Hey," he said, coming to his feet when he saw her. "I was waiting for you. . . . I wanted to see how it went with Crystal."

"I don't know," Anne said, shaking her head. "I thought at first she didn't want to eat because she wanted attention. But tonight she told me that she didn't want to get fat . . . that her mother told her fat people are ugly."

"God," Kurt said, closing his eyes and shaking his head. "After all this time, working with these kids, I'm still amazed at some of the things their parents do to them."

"It's not just their parents," Anne said thoughtfully. "This is a nationwide problem . . . mostly feminine, I'm afraid. Girls are blasted with this sort of 'thin is in' mentality from the time they're old enough to walk."

"What did you do?"

"I told her I had to watch my weight, too, and then I took my supper upstairs and ate with her. I tried to explain a little about eating nutritious food, but I don't think she was in the mood to listen. Poor thing was starving after not eating all day."

Kurt's eyes wandered from Anne's face down over her voluptuous figure.

"I can't believe weight was ever a problem for you."

"It was," she said. "It still is."

He made a soft noise in his throat, as if he didn't believe her.

"I don't think so," he said, smiling that odd, disquieting smile of his.

"You don't know anything about me, Kurt Bonner," she said, staring up at him with a glint of defiance in her eyes.

She said the words to get back at him, but she blushed as she saw the look in his eyes. He should know much more about her than he did, considering they had shared the most intimate act a man and woman could share. But still she was angry; she hadn't forgotten his earlier warning about her getting involved with Crystal. His criticism hurt more than she wanted to admit.

"I'm willing to learn."

"Oh, Kurt," she said, sighing. It wasn't fair to him, pretending that nothing had happened, pretending that the other night meant nothing, when both of them knew it had. "Do you have any idea how difficult this is for me?"

"I'm beginning to see that." He stepped closer, brushing her hair back and letting his hand linger just below her ear. "I can help."

She closed her eyes, feeling her legs trembling just from his nearness, his touch.

"This . . . this is not helping," she said, backing away.

"Why isn't it?" he asked. "Tell me why you're trying so hard to run away from me. You can't deny what you felt the other night . . . what both of us felt. And this deal with the assistant job—that was just your way of continuing to run."

"You think you're pretty clever, don't you?"

He smiled and brushed his fingers against her cheek.

"Sometimes it takes awhile, but yeah . . . pretty clever." He laughed, then, at himself, and she couldn't keep from smiling, too.

Cecile was right; he did have the sexiest smile she'd ever seen.

"I don't mean to be coy, or teasing, or any of those other things you must be thinking I am."

"I don't think that and I never have. I know there's a reason for all this. I just wish you'd tell me what it is and give me a chance to understand."

She ignored his words and his tenderness.

"I want to," she whispered. Oh, but he had no idea how badly she wanted to.

"Then do it," he said, taking her arms and pulling her toward him. "Talk to me, Anne. I'm a damned good listener, and believe it or not I have a lot of patience."

"Do you?" she asked, staring into his eyes, wanting to believe that he would wait, that he would be patient. And wishing even more that this time, with this man, she would be able to open her heart as Cecile had suggested.

Anne was afraid that, unlike Baxter, who had pursued her forever, despite her rejections, this dynamic man would soon lose patience with the waiting game.

"Try me," he whispered. He pulled her close, but he didn't make an effort to kiss her.

And Anne found that was what she wanted; more than anything she wanted to be held and kissed and caressed.

"Here? Now? I hardly know where to begin."

"Why don't we try a quiet dinner somewhere? Whenever you say. Wherever you want."

He was trying; she knew that. She could sense the tight control he held over his emotions, and the patience he had spoken of was evident.

"Let me think about it," she whispered, gazing up into his compelling eyes.

"Think about this, too," he said. He pulled her against him, cradling her tenderly with no forcefulness, and when he bent to kiss her she met his lips eagerly, hungrily.

"Oh, my," she murmured, finally pulling away. "I think that was what happened the last time."

"It was too soon." There was a question in his statement. "I should have seen that and backed off, but—"

"Yes . . . no . . . God, Kurt, I don't know. All I know is that for some unknown reason I'm changing. Part of that reason is you, I think. Where you're concerned I can't seem to think straight. But I've made too many mistakes with my life. I don't want to make any more."

"That's good," he said. "Promising."

"It's just that this is all so new for me. You can't imagine how new. I need to take it slow."

"Slow as you want. I'll let you lead . . . for a while, anyway," he said, laughing softly in the darkness. "Just say the word and I'll be there."

She was ready *now,* she wanted to shout. Ready for his kisses, for his lovemaking. And the only thing keeping her from telling him so was her own conscience. She couldn't keep moving toward him, then pushing him away. It was immature and foolish behavior for a woman her age. It wasn't fair to Kurt, and she couldn't expect him to accept it from any woman. As much as she wanted him, she couldn't do that to him again. The next time it happened—*if* it happened—it would have to be right for both of them.

Sixteen

Anne dreamed about Kurt that night. She could see him so clearly, see the glint of desire in his beautiful eyes. The dream was so real that when she woke she expected to turn and find him lying beside her. And she was disappointed when he wasn't.

She felt hot and restless. The dream had ended just before Kurt made love to her, and she found her mind experiencing all the emotions of it, her body still wracked with desire. She kicked the sheet off her legs and slid out of bed, walking to the windows and back again.

She had never felt like this about any man in her life. She'd always remembered sex with her first husband as being hot and exciting, but she realized now, since Kurt, that she had been naive. She'd known nothing about how good it could be between a man and woman. Her love life with Baxter had been practically nonexistent, and that was exactly the way she'd wanted it. She had fooled herself all these years into thinking all men were the same and that none of them could ever move her.

"Wrong, wrong, wrong," she whispered into the darkness. But now, after Kurt, she knew what she had been missing, and it came back to haunt her hour after restless hour as she lay alone in her bed.

She was amazed at the power of it. It had taken only one night of love for her mind and body to become addicted to him, to begin to crave his touch and his kisses. She thought now she would go crazy from the need.

It was very early in the morning before she finally managed to go back to sleep, and even then she tossed and turned until the alarm went off.

When Anne arrived at the center that morning there was a truck outside, and two men were carrying furniture into the house.

She met the new house parents just inside the front door.

"Oh, hello," the woman said. She was a tall, raw-boned woman, almost masculine in appearance. And she stared at Anne as if she were an intruder.

"Hi," Anne said, extending her hand. "I'm Anne Benefield. I work here . . . temporarily." Why did she get the idea that this woman would disapprove of her reason for being here?

"Oh, how nice. I'm Nancy Howard, and this is my husband Ed."

Ed was almost exactly the same height as his wife, perhaps an inch taller, and he was as meek-looking in his appearance as Nancy Howard was bold. He could hardly meet Anne's eyes.

"Benefield . . ." Mrs. Howard said, her eyes studying Anne. "You're not related to the late Baxter Benefield, are you?"

"Baxter was my husband."

"Oh . . . well. And you say you . . . *work* here?"

"Community service," Anne said, feeling irritable.

"Ah," the woman said.

But Anne didn't miss the look she threw toward her husband. She probably assumed that Anne had been arrested for drunk driving, and Anne didn't feel inclined to tell her any different.

"Well, everyone's glad you're here," Anne said. "It's been hectic, to say the least. I'm sure things will go much smoother once you've moved in."

"Oh, you can count on that," Nancy said smugly. "I run a tight ship, don't I, Eddie? Ed won't be here during the day— he has a regular job. That's why I say *I*." She glanced around the sparsely furnished house. "I can see I have my work cut out for me."

"I'm afraid so," Anne said. "If you'll excuse me, I'd better get to work."

The children were eating, as they usually were when Anne arrived, and she was surprised that the new house parents paid so little attention to them. Perhaps they'd already met the kids, she told herself. Perhaps Anne was being too critical.

When she saw Crystal sitting at the table a quiet feeling of relief washed over her.

Until she heard one of the boys teasing her.

"Fatty, fatty, two by eight," he whispered, leaning toward Crystal.

"Roy Lee," Anne said, marching to him and pulling him up straight in his chair, "you stop that right this minute. If I hear you making such ugly remarks to anyone else, I'll spank you myself."

"No, you won't," the boy said, glaring at her with youthful defiance. "You're not the boss. You just help old Gabby, that's all. You ain't gonna do nothin' to me."

"Come with me," she said, taking his arm and pulling him up from his chair. The boy was no more than seven, but even so he was hard to handle as he wiggled and squirmed to get away from her.

"Stop it," she said, pulling him into the kitchen. "Now, you sit right here until you think you can behave properly at the breakfast table."

The boy flopped down into one of the wooden kitchen chairs, crossing his arms and pursing his lips in an ill-tempered pout.

Gabby turned from the stove, frowning first at Anne, then at the boy.

"Roy Lee," he said, shaking a wooden spoon at the boy, "what you up to this time?"

"Nothin'!"

"Don't sound like nothin' to me. You been pesterin' Miz Benefield here?"

"No, I wasn't."

"Then who? I know you was pesterin' somebody, you little scoundrel."

The boy just glared at Gabby.

"He was making remarks to Crystal."

"Oh," Gabby said, nodding wisely. "Makes you feel like a big man, does it? Bein' mean to little girls?"

"She ain't little," the boy snapped. "She's fat."

"You hush," Anne said, taking the boy's arm and shaking him. "If I hear you say anything else like that to her, I'm going to—"

"Not to mention what Mr. Bonner is going to do if he hears you sayin' ugly things to her," Gabby interjected. "You won't be able to sit down for a week."

"Mr. Bonner don't whip nobody," the boy said. "He's nice."

Anne and Gabby exchanged glances, and then she sat at the table with Roy Lee.

"You like Mr. Bonner, don't you? He's been nice to you."

"Yeah, I guess."

"You'd hate to make him feel bad, wouldn't you? After he brought you here, gave you new clothes and a nice place to live?"

Roy Lee uncrossed his arms and shrugged, but the pouty look was gone from his face.

He was a cute little boy, and now that he was quiet and seemingly remorseful, Anne smiled at him. Without thinking, she reached over and hugged him.

"Now, you be nice to Crystal, Roy Lee. You hear? She's not very happy right now. Remember how you felt when you first came?"

He nodded, gazing into Anne's eyes and, surprisingly, leaning closer to her.

"When you talk to her try to remember how you felt, how sad and alone you were. And say things to her that you would have liked hearing. Can you do that?"

"I guess."

"Good," she said. She pulled him toward her and hugged him. Then she pushed his shoulder, and he slid down from the chair. "Go on; finish your breakfast now."

After the boy had left the kitchen Anne laughed and turned to Gabby.

"I see what you mean about Kurt being special. I think I've just found a secret weapon to use with these kids."

"He is that," Gabby said. He was looking at her steadily, taking note of the color on her cheeks and the sparkle in her eyes. "Looks like it might even be workin' on some grown-ups around here."

"Oh," Anne said, waving her hand at him. "Don't you start on me, old man. Just don't start."

She heard Gabby chuckling as she went to work.

Mr. and Mrs. Howard took charge immediately, and Anne had to admit, despite her doubts about the woman, that it was a relief having them there. It gave her and Vivian more time to clean and take inventory. It was then that Anne decided she was going to donate some furniture to the house, and she asked Vivian's advice.

"What do you think? Beanbag chairs in the family room or something nice?"

"Something comfortable," Vivian said. "And durable. You've never had kids, but

I can tell you, two or three together could destroy a Mack truck. What about the bedrooms? We could use new mattresses in some of the rooms, and I was thinking about asking Kurt if we had enough funds to turn the storage room upstairs into a nursery. We've had several babies, and we never have a proper bed or playpen for them."

"Funds are no problem," Anne said. "We can buy new mattresses for all the beds, and the nursery furniture as well."

She was standing in the middle of the family room, turning around slowly to make note of what was needed. She realized that Viv had grown silent and was looking at her oddly.

"What?"

"Do you know how lucky you are?"

"Lucky? Me? Oh . . . are you speaking of money, Viv?"

"Not just money, but that is a big part of it. My husband and I have always had to struggle. Even now, with the kids gone, there never seems to be much left over after bills."

"I know that feeling."

"Oh yeah, sure," Vivian muttered.

"I didn't always have money, you know."

"You didn't?"

"Before I married Baxter Benefield I was a working girl, just like you. I struggled to put myself through school and then I got a job and went to work. I was surprised at how little of my paycheck was left over at the end of the month."

"I hope you won't be offended at what I'm about to say, but you're nothing like I heard you were."

"Oh? And what did you hear?" Anne asked, smiling good-naturedly at Viv.

"Well . . . I'd rather not say."

"You can tell me," Anne urged.

"All right, then. I heard you were a rich bitch who married Old Man Benefield for his money." Viv's words came out in a rush.

Anne took a deep breath and walked away from her.

"Does that offend you?" Anne asked, not turning around. She pretended to be adjusting a cushion on the worn sofa. "That I married for money and not love?"

"Offend isn't exactly the word I'd use."

"What then?" Anne asked, turning to face Vivian.

"Uncomfortable, maybe. Puzzled."

"You're a romantic, Viv," Anne said, not smiling.

"I guess I am. I just can't imagine living with a man you don't love. Goodness, it's hard enough living with one you do love."

"Oh, I married for love once, too," Anne said softly. "Just out of high school. And to tell you the truth . . ." She stopped, thinking that she was saying too much, revealing too much of herself to a woman she had known less than a month.

"What?" Viv asked.

"To tell you the truth, I'm not sure which marriage was the more miserable."

"You just didn't find the right man, that's all."

"Oh, yes, I've heard that one time and again. But at my age I don't think I'm likely to find him now, do you?"

"Why, yes, I do. If you want to, at least. Heavens, you're not exactly old and decrepit, you know. That's what I meant about your being lucky. The money's part of it, but you just seem to be one of those women who has it all."

A woman who has it all. That phrase repeated itself in Anne's mind as she stared at Viv.

If she only knew, Anne thought. If she only knew how very little I do have, and how empty I've felt for years, she wouldn't be quite so envious, or so judgmental.

"I don't have it all, Viv," Anne said quietly. "I thought I did once. But for some reason I've been thinking lately that I really have nothing much . . . except money," she added.

"Huh," Vivian grunted. "I'd settle for that."

"No, you wouldn't," she replied.

They stood quietly for a while, and Anne turned to make a few notes about colors and dimensions.

"What do you think about the Howards?" she asked finally.

"Oh, I don't know. They seem nice enough to me, although I think he's a little bit henpecked."

Anne laughed and nodded.

"I'm so relieved someone is finally here that I guess I have no complaints," Viv said. "I just hope Kurt likes them."

"Do you think he doesn't?"

"I don't know. He's been kind of quiet the last few days. Can't seem to get anything out of him. You noticed that?"

"Well, I . . . I don't talk to him that much." Anne turned away in case Viv saw the flush on her cheeks.

"Maybe you should."

There was an odd note in Vivian's voice, and when Anne turned she found her smiling at her, rather slyly, she thought.

"He is single, you know. Not to mention handsome as the devil."

"Yes," Anne agreed quietly. "He is that."

"And he's a good man. Decent and compassionate and deeply committed." Viv was watching Anne closely. "But maybe women nowadays don't want decency and compassion. Too boring."

Boring? Kurt Bonner? Never, Anne wanted to shout. Not in a million years.

Instead she smiled at Vivian.

"Sounds pretty good to me," she said, thinking about Kurt and all the things about him that appealed to her.

"It's almost noon," Viv said, looking at her watch. "Why don't you go talk to

Kurt—tell him what we want to do and see what he thinks. I'll go help Gabby finish up lunch."

Seventeen

Anne stopped at Kurt's office doorway and looked in. He was alone, and for once he wasn't on the phone. He sat back in his chair with his feet propped on the desk, holding a pencil between his fingers and his teeth, staring off into space.

Anne took a deep breath and went in. "Hi. Could I talk to you?"

"Sure," he said, swinging his legs off the desk. His eyes, when he turned to her, were riveting. Anne felt sometimes that he could actually read her thoughts.

She felt her insides tremble as she stepped into the room and sat down.

His silence was disconcerting, and even though she realized he was only waiting for her to speak, she wished he would say something. Anything.

"I've been thinking for a while now that I'd like to do something for the center. And after talking with Viv and hearing about all the needs, I'd like to donate some furniture." She glanced up at him and saw him lean back in his chair, his eyes cool and expectant as he watched her.

"Vivian and I went through the house together this morning. I've made some notes." She started to pass the paper to him and realized that her hand was shaking. Quickly she put the paper back down in her lap. "She . . . she thought it would be a good idea if we cleared out the storage room upstairs and put in a nursery. For . . . for when there are babies . . ." What a stupid statement. Why else would they need a nursery?

She shook her head and took another gulp of air. Why was she finding it so difficult to talk to him today? Certainly his quiet assessment of her didn't help. And the way his gaze moved over her face and down to her throat. She could actually feel his caress from across the desk.

For a moment the room was so quiet, she could hear the faint, rhythmic ticking of Kurt's wristwatch.

"Well," she said. "What do you think?"

"I think it's a wonderful idea. Thank you," he said.

Thank you? Was that it?

"Well . . . where . . . where shall we start?"

"Wherever you wish. It's your dime."

"All right. I'll make a more detailed list. Would you like to see what I'm ordering? Does it have to be approved by the board?"

"You're a board member—I think that's sufficient approval."

"Still, I'd like your advice. You know more about what's needed here than I do."

"Is that an invitation?" he asked. His look was guarded and serious. "To go shopping, I mean," he added.

Anne couldn't think of a thing to say. She had never let a man disconcert her this way. The things he said were certainly not suggestive or flirtatious—why did she feel so exposed and vulnerable when she was with him? She felt hot and absolutely breathless and her knees had suddenly turned to jelly.

"If you'd like to go . . ."

"What would *you* like?" he asked, his

voice steady. "Do you want to go to Atlanta for the furniture this weekend?"

"No," she said quickly. A weekend in Atlanta with Kurt Bonner was exactly what she didn't want.

He smiled then, a slow, knowing smile that made Anne's breath catch in her throat. He could see right through her and he knew it.

"Where, then?"

"We can go here," she said, swallowing hard. "Whenever you can get away."

"How about this afternoon around three?" he said, flipping through his desk calendar.

"Fine," she said. She stood up, feeling awkward and unsure of herself. "Perhaps I could run home first and shower . . ." She stopped at the look in his eyes, then continued quickly. "I get so hot working in the kitchen and . . ."

"You have my permission," he said, seeming to take pity on her inability to say anything remotely sensible. "I'll pick you up at your house then . . . around three."

"Three," she said, backing out of the room.

She felt like running, like shouting. Going shopping for furniture was a very uneventful thing for most people. But Anne thought this invitation, such as it was, was the hardest thing she'd ever done. And she was excited at the prospect of spending the afternoon with Kurt.

It would be safe, she told herself. A nice, quiet, safe afternoon, free of any commitment other than buying furniture for the center.

When she got home she raced into the house, throwing her purse on the kitchen counter and glancing toward her cook.

"Oh, Mrs. Hargis, you're cooking," she said, standing and staring at the woman.

"Why, yes," the cook said, turning around slowly and looking at Anne as if she were demented. "That's what I do here, you know."

"I know. It's just that things have been so hectic for me lately. Mr. Bonner and I are going to look at furniture for the center this afternoon, so I doubt I'll be home for dinner. I'm sorry—it looks so good." She felt her stomach rumble as she gazed at the small pork roast that

Mrs. Hargis was stuffing with her special dressing.

"Well, goodness gracious, it'll keep. After it's done I'll just wrap it in foil and put it in the refrigerator for tomorrow. Maybe you won't even need me to come back for a day or two." Mrs. Hargis's gaze shifted uncertainly to Anne, then back to her work.

"Do you need to be off for a couple of days? It's no problem, you know. Heaven knows I've not had time for dinner lately, or parties either, for that matter."

"I would kind of like a day off," she said. "I've just had my first great-grandchild."

Anne stared at the woman for a long moment. Mrs. Hargis turned and smiled rather sheepishly at her.

"Why, that's . . . that's wonderful," Anne said. "A great-grandchild. You hardly seem old enough to be a grandmother, much less a great-grandmother." She realized that she really knew very little about Mrs. Hargis or her family.

Mrs. Hargis beamed. "My daughter

says the baby is a little angel. I can't wait to see her."

"You mean you haven't seen her yet? When was she born?"

"She's almost two weeks old now. And they live in Smithville, so—"

"But you should have told me," Anne said. "I'd gladly have let you off to be with your family."

"Well, I didn't want to bother you."

She went to the woman and put an arm around her shoulders. It was the first time she'd ever done such a thing, and she saw the surprise in Mrs. Hargis's eyes.

"Taking a day off to see your first great-grandchild wouldn't bother me. Family comes first."

She saw Mrs. Hargis's eyes widen before she managed to hide her stunned expression.

Anne laughed then, not only at Mrs. Hargis's reaction but at her own.

"I can't believe I said that either," she said, acknowledging Mrs. Hargis's surprise.

"It's not something I've ever heard you say before." The cook's gaze was kind and a little skeptical.

"Well, I'm changing," Anne said with a nod. "Yes, I am. I'm really changing." She turned to leave the kitchen, calling to Mrs. Hargis over her shoulder, "You go ahead . . . take your day, take two, if you wish . . . have a wonderful visit. Leave the roast in the refrigerator like you said. It will be fine." She met Jessica coming down the hallway toward her.

"Good afternoon, Jessica," Anne said brightly. "How was your day? How's Elmer?"

Jessica stepped to the kitchen door and turned toward her employer, then back again to Mrs. Hargis, who was standing with an odd, puzzled look on her face.

"Fine," Jessica said. "Just fine."

In a silent gesture toward Mrs. Hargis, she hooked her thumb toward Anne's retreating back and lifted her brows in a quizzical expression.

"Don't ask me," Mrs. Hargis said, shrugging her shoulders. "Maybe it's the heat."

After her bath Anne dressed carefully. She wanted to look especially nice, but none of her elegant designer clothes would quite do. She wanted something bright and casual, something that expressed the happiness and hope she was feeling.

Finally she found a pale yellow pantsuit that she had bought and never worn. It was still in the Broussard's plastic bag, and the price tags still dangled from the sleeve.

She quickly took the garment out of the bag and held it up, letting her gaze wander over the white piping that ran along the edges of the collar and lapels and short sleeves. The material looked cool, like iced lemonade on a hot summer day, and she loved the way the long jacket fit smoothly over the full pants.

"Very nice," she murmured as she threw her robe over a chair and began to dress.

She was almost ready when she heard Kurt's truck pull into the circular drive at the front of the house.

She glanced out the window quickly to make sure it was him, then she ran to the hallway and leaned over the banister.

"Jessica? Jessica, will you let Mr. Bonner in? Tell him I'll be right down."

Jessica came right away, walking toward

the front door as she glanced up at Anne. There was a puzzled little look on her face when Anne ran back into her room and shut the door.

Anne came downstairs less than ten minutes later. She was surprised that Kurt wasn't in the living room. She glanced out to the front porch, knowing his penchant for being outdoors on beautiful afternoons, even hot ones. But he wasn't there either.

Finally, turning around with a frown, she heard laughter from the kitchen. And one of the voices was definitely male.

Anne walked to the kitchen doorway. Mrs. Hargis and Jessica turned toward her, their smiles fading into awkward looks. Kurt rose from the table, where he had been drinking iced tea and having some of Mrs. Hargis's pound cake.

"Sorry to keep you waiting," she said, wishing she didn't sound so breathless.

"That's all right," Kurt said, smiling. "Jessica and Kathleen have been entertaining me quite royally." He turned to Mrs. Hargis. "You definitely have to teach Gabby how to make this cake."

The grandmotherly woman smiled.

"Kathleen?" Anne said with a shake of her head.

"It's my given name," Mrs. Hargis said, ducking her head as if she had offended Anne somehow.

"Oh . . . yes, of course. I knew that." Anne felt so foolish. If she had ever known Mrs. Hargis's first name, she had quite forgotten it. And it had taken less than ten minutes for Kurt, not only to be invited for tea and cake, but also to be on a first-name basis with the woman.

"Are you ready?" Kurt asked.

"Yes . . . ready." She smiled at him, aware of Mrs. Hargis's and Jessica's speculative looks. Aware of Kurt's eyes and the way they had moved slowly down the yellow silky pantsuit, then back up to her face. For a moment she wanted to laugh. She felt like a girl going to her first prom, with Kurt as her date and Jessica and Mrs. Hargis as her watchful surrogate parents.

Anne turned as she and Kurt left, waving to the two women who stood watching. " 'Bye . . . thanks."

When they stepped out onto the front porch and closed the door behind them

Kurt stopped, touching Anne's arm and looking into her eyes.

"Why do I get the feeling I should have promised to have you home early?"

Anne did laugh then.

"Oh," she said, shaking her head and trying to control her urge to giggle. "I don't know. I've never had this happen before. Actually, I've never been very close to either Kathleen or Jessica. Their curiosity and concern is so odd." She gazed up at him, still smiling. "But I think I like it."

"You're a very funny lady," he said, his eyes warm and mysterious.

"I am?"

"Unusual," he said. "I'm not sure I've ever met anyone quite like you. I find myself wanting to know more . . . to see more." His eyes couldn't hide his meaning.

"Oh," she breathed softly. "I thought we were going to proceed slowly."

"With great caution," he said.

"Then why do I feel as if I'm on a rocket, spiraling helplessly out of control?" She had meant her words to be teasing, but she wasn't at all sure they were.

"Does that bother you? Being out of control?"

"Scares me to death."

"I won't let you fall," he whispered. "I'll be right here."

"We'd better go," she said, unable to disguise her shaky voice. "I have a feeling my fairy godmothers are behind the curtains watching."

"Let them," he said. "Tell them I'm your boss and I'm entitled to a little attention."

"I . . . I'm not so sure how many women go shopping with their bosses . . . or how many get this kind of attention."

He took her hand and pulled her toward him, and as she stared up into his eyes, he tucked her arm into his.

"You know I'm harmless," he said.

"Oh, but I don't know anything of the kind," she whispered, her eyes sparkling as she slowly shook her head. "I think you might just be totally devastating to a woman's fragile heart."

"Are we speaking of all women's fragile hearts. . . ?"

"One in particular," she said quietly, looking up at him.

He gazed down at her for a long moment, his eyes serious, as if he were making a solemn pledge.

"I promise to take it slow . . . and to be very careful of your heart."

Eighteen

It took a while, riding in Kurt's truck, for Anne to be able to say anything. She was almost giddy with the pleasure of his words and the remembrance of his gaze on her, so serious and sexy, that even now, thinking of it, she felt a tingle down her spine.

Suddenly the world was brighter and she found herself commenting on everything. Houses, flowers, things along the same roadway that she drove every day and never seemed to notice until now.

There was a quiet smile on Kurt's face, and sometimes he would turn to glance at her with the oddest look of affection.

"I'm carrying on like a crazy woman, aren't I?" she asked finally.

"I like it," he said. "I've never seen you like this. But then, we didn't start out on the best of terms at the halfway house."

"I think I'm beginning to change. I thought about that just today," she said, feeling fear tugging at her chest even as she said the words. "I know it's hard to judge one's own behavior, but I don't think I've ever been this way, or felt this way."

He glanced at her from the corner of his eye.

"Being around children tends to change everyone, I think. Especially children who are so hurt and vulnerable and need our help so badly."

They were quiet for a few minutes while Anne thought about his words. It wasn't just being around the children that had changed her; she knew that.

"Why didn't you have children, Anne? If that's not too personal."

"Oh." She sighed. "It's a long story. I'm not sure it was something I made an actual decision about; it just sort of happened that way. But for the last few years I've thought that there were probably subconscious reasons."

"Do you like kids?"

"No," she said. Then she laughed at the look on his face. "Does that shock you?"

"A little, considering how good you were with Tracy and now with Crystal."

"That's different," she said, turning her gaze away from his and looking out the window. "They're sweet and lovable. I just seem to have a problem with obnoxious, ill-behaved children."

"I wouldn't exactly call Crystal a loving child," he said.

She turned to face him and saw the challenge in his hazel eyes.

"Oh, that's all a facade, a defense mechanism that Crystal has had to erect for her own survival."

"You sound as if you understand that."

"I do," she said softly. She hadn't meant to get into this, not today and not with him.

She turned and smiled at him. He was clever; he managed to get things out of people against their will. She'd seen him do it with the children, and she supposed it was why he was so good at what he did.

"But you don't want to talk about it," he said, his eyes questioning.

He pulled into a large parking lot and she saw the furniture sign on the side of the warehouselike building. She felt a rush of relief that they were here, and that she wouldn't have to answer any more of his questions.

"We're here," she said brightly.

Kurt smiled at the note of relief in her voice. He reached across the seat and took her chin in his hand, turning her face so that she had to look at him.

"You're not getting off the hook so easily, Miz Benefield," he said, drawling out his words lazily.

"But I'm not—"

"I'm not giving up on this. I want to know everything about you. What you like, what you hate. Are you a Democrat or Republican . . . a Braves fan? Do you like mustard on your hot dogs . . . Georgia Bulldogs or Georgia Tech?" His words, though light and teasing at first, had become intense, and now he stopped, pulling air through his teeth with a hissing sound, as if he'd been burned. "And most of all I want to know what bastard hurt you so badly and why."

His voice was hoarse, a mere whisper in the closeness of the truck cab. And his eyes seemed to shoot little sparks straight into her heart.

"Everyone," she said, so quietly he could barely make out her words. "Everyone I ever loved."

When she pulled away from him and slid out of the truck he sat for a moment, watching until she stepped up on the sidewalk and turned to look back through the truck's windshield at him. He clenched his teeth and took a long breath before getting out to join her.

Inside the store, Kurt was amazed by Anne's capacity to cover up her feelings. Her enthusiasm over the furniture was immediate and gay, and she laughed often at his comments about the things he didn't like. But she didn't fool him. He hadn't been wrong about the pain in her eyes. And if he wasn't mistaken, it was a deep, wrenching hurt, something that she lived with every day. If it took him the rest of his life, he intended to find out what it was, and then he intended to get rid of it, to banish it from her lovely, sad eyes for good.

He hadn't realized he was standing

still, staring at nothing, until he heard her voice.

"Kurt?" she said, smiling. "What about this for the family room?" She pointed to a homey-looking printed sofa with oak armrests and trim.

"Not wood," he said distractedly. "I guess I see visions of chipped teeth and bumped heads."

"Ah, you're the cautious type," she teased. "A worrywart."

He laughed then, giving in to her sweet pretense. If this was what she wanted, if she needed to cover up her pain to feel secure, then it was fine with him. But sooner or later he was going to find out exactly what made Anne Benefield tick.

"I confess—you've got me pegged," he said.

A gentleman walked over to them, a man with a wide, phony smile and a dark toupee that looked as artificial as his smile.

"Well," he said, in a calculated, salesmanlike voice. "Could we interest you folks in a couch today? That's a mighty nice one right there, ma'am. You have very good taste. Solid oak arms and frame. Look right here. Solid!" he said, lifting the skirt around the bottom of the sofa. "And see this . . . hypoallergenic filling and—"

"No, I don't think so," Anne said, winking at Kurt and walking on down the aisle. "He doesn't like wooden armrests."

"I see . . . I see," said the man. "Well, how about this? Now, I'll bet you're the type who likes eighteenth century. Am I right?" he asked Anne. "Classic Federalist furniture."

Kurt was smiling at Anne over the salesman's head and as he caught her eye, he lifted his brows in a funny, questioning way.

"Well, as a matter of fact, I do, but—" She looked toward Kurt, and the man turned around.

"Oh," he said, seeing Kurt's look and nodding wisely. "Your husband prefers something a bit more comfy . . . antique pine and plaid, I'll bet."

"No, we're not—"

"We got this in just yesterday," the salesman said, moving to another group of couches. "Top of the line. Made right next door in Burlington, North Carolina.

Distressed finish—solid pine. And see,"
he said, beaming, "covered armrests—and
I bet you like this plaid material, nice
and soft—great for a nap on Sunday afternoons or watching the Braves."

"Or those fishing shows you like, dear,"
Anne said, gazing up at Kurt with wide,
innocent eyes as she fluttered her lashes.

"And those cooking shows you like,"
Kurt said, joining in her charade. "What
do you think, hon?"

Anne laughed and shook her head. She
couldn't seem to stop laughing. Cooking
shows, indeed. She didn't think she'd
ever watched one in her life.

"Actually, I like it a lot. But don't you
think we should look around a bit? We
might see something else we like better."

"Now, sweetheart, you know how easily
confused you are when you have too
many choices to make," Kurt said in his
most husbandly voice.

Both of them began to laugh, and the
poor salesman stood frowning at them.
Anne supposed he thought that two es-
capees from an insane asylum had wandered into his store.

"We'll take it," Anne said, still laughing.

"Well," the salesman said, seeming stunned. "Wonderful. Now, we have pine end tables and matching lamps and that chair there—"

"We'll take that, too," Anne said, reaching inside her purse for a checkbook.

"Maybe you should wait before writing a check," Kurt said, giving her an odd look. His eyes were sparkling with mischief. "We need to look at bedroom furniture, too, don't we? And mattresses—something soft this time," he said, his voice lowering to a purposefully intimate tone.

Anne's eyes widened, and she could actually feel her cheeks burning. "Kurt," she said beneath her breath.

"Oh, I get it," the salesman said, beaming at them. "You two are newlyweds. I knew it all along."

"I . . . no, we're—" Anne glared at Kurt, wishing she didn't blush so easily, wishing that the look in his eyes didn't make her knees tremble.

"Come along, honey," Kurt said, taking her arm. "Let's look at the mattresses." He turned to the salesman. "If you don't mind, we'd like to do this alone."

Now, for the first time . . .

You can find Janelle Taylor, Shannon Drake, Rosanne Bittner, Sylvie Sommerfield, Penelope Neri, Phoebe Conn, Bobbi Smith, and the rest of today's most popular, bestselling authors

. . . All in one brand-new club!

Introducing KENSINGTON CHOICE, the new Zebra/Pinnacle service that delivers the best new historical romances direct to your home, at a significant discount off the publisher's prices.

As your introduction, we invite you to accept 4 FREE BOOKS worth up to $23.96

details inside . . .

We've got your authors!

If you seek out the latest historical romances by today's bestselling authors, our new reader's service, KENSINGTON CHOICE, is the club for you.

KENSINGTON CHOICE is the only club where you can find authors like Janelle Taylor, Shannon Drake, Rosanne Bittner, Sylvie Sommerfield, Penelope Neri and Phoebe Conn all in one place...

...and the only service that will deliver their romances direct to your home as soon as they are published—even before they reach the bookstores.

KENSINGTON CHOICE is also the only service that will give you a substantial guaranteed discount off the publisher's prices on every one of those romances.

That's right: Every month, the Editors at Zebra and Pinnacle select four of the newest novels by our bestselling authors and rush them straight to you, usually *before they reach the bookstores*. The publisher's prices for these romances range from $4.99 to $5.99—but they are always yours for the guaranteed low price of just *$3.95!*

That means you'll always save over $1.00...often as much as *$2.00*...off the publisher's prices on every new novel you get from KENSINGTON CHOICE!

All books are sent on a 10-day free examination basis, and there is no minimum number of books to buy. (A postage and handling charge of $1.50 is added to each shipment.)

As your introduction to the convenience and value of this new service, we invite you to accept

4 BOOKS FREE

The 4 books, worth up to $23.96, are our welcoming gift. You pay only $1 to help cover postage and handling.

To start your subscription to KENSINGTON CHOICE and receive your introductory package of 4 FREE romances, detach and mail the postpaid card at right *today*.

We have 4 FREE BOOKS for you
as your introduction to
KENSINGTON CHOICE
To get your FREE BOOKS, worth
up to $23.96, mail the card below.

FREE BOOK CERTIFICATE

As my introduction to your new KENSINGTON CHOICE reader's service, please send me 4 FREE historical romances (worth up to $23.96), billing me just $1 to help cover postage and handling. As a KENSINGTON CHOICE subscriber, I will then receive 4 brand-new romances to preview each month for 10 days FREE. I can return any books I decide not to keep and owe nothing. The publisher's prices for the KENSINGTON CHOICE romances range from $4.99 to $5.99, but as a subscriber I will be entitled to get them for just $3.95 per book or $15.80 for all four titles. There is no minimum number of books to buy, and I can cancel my subscription at any time. A $1.50 postage and handling charge is added to each shipment.

Name _____

Address _____ Apt. _____

City _____ State _____ Zip _____

Telephone ( ) _____

Signature _____

(If under 18, parent or guardian must sign)

Subscription subject to acceptance. Terms and prices subject to change.

KC1094

We have
4
FREE
Historical
Romances
for you!

(worth up
to $23.96!)

Details inside!

The salesman grinned at Anne, noting the stain on her cheeks and the way she glared at Kurt.

"Of course," he said, bowing slightly. "I understand perfectly. Just let me know if I can help. I'll go ahead and write up the ticket for the living-room furniture."

"Kurt Bonner," Anne said as they walked away, "I'm going to murder you."

"Well, how else was I going to get rid of him?" he replied, laughing. "Besides, you look so cute when you blush."

"Liar!" she said, giggling. "I hate blushing and I look terrible."

Anne supposed the salesman was more confused than ever later when they ordered fifteen new twin-size mattress sets and asked that everything be delivered to the halfway house.

She and Kurt were still laughing when they went outside to get in the truck.

"You are a terrible man," she said.

"But you're having fun," he said, turning to smile at her.

"Yes." She sighed. "I am having fun. Now, where shall we go for the nursery furniture?"

They decided on a store on Main

Street that specialized in children's furniture. They had just walked into the store when Anne saw Sylvia Jordan.

"Well, as I live and breathe," Sylvia said, eyeing first Kurt and then Anne. "How are you, Mr. Bonner?" she asked, stepping forward and extending her hand. She barely glanced at Anne.

"Fine, Mrs. Jordan. And you?"

"Doin' fine," she said in a coy Southern drawl. "I've been hearing some very nice things about your work at the halfway house. I do hope you'll be able to come to the charity ball at the country club in the fall. I know it's a little early, but it's such an event that it takes us this long to get things organized. I made sure you were sent a personal invitation—I even addressed it myself. Did you get it?"

"Yes, I did. And I'd like to come. It's always nice meeting the people who contribute to our work."

"Good," she said with a simpering smile. "And you, dear," she said, turning a cool gaze toward Anne. "Did your invitation arrive yet?"

"I don't remember seeing it," Anne said.

"Well, I'm sure it must be in the mail. I hope so, anyway. It would be a shame if it didn't arrive. The event is by invitation only, although I'm sure if there was an oversight we could manage to get you in somehow."

Anne thought she didn't sound at all as if that's what she wanted to do.

"I hope so, too," Kurt said quietly. "Especially since Anne is on the board of Angels Incorporated."

"Are you?" Sylvia said with a wide, innocent smile. "I didn't know that. Will is, too, and I don't recall his ever mentioning your being at one of the meetings."

"Perhaps that's because I've never been to one. I'm only on the board as Baxter's widow."

"Oh, I see. Well, I'll be sure and find out about your invitation, just in case you decide to come to the ball."

"Don't worry about it," Kurt said. "I intend to try and persuade Anne to come with me anyway." He smiled as Anne turned to stare at him and as Sylvia Jordan lifted her brow haughtily. "As my date," he added.

"Ah, I see," Sylvia said, pretending indifference. "Well, I'll let you two get on with whatever it is you're doing. I'll look forward to seeing you at the ball, Kurt. Oh, and you, too, of course, Anne."

"Oh, I can't stand that woman," Anne said when Sylvia left the store. "And I'm sure she can't stand me. Thanks for coming to the rescue about the invitation."

"No problem," he said, his eyes telling her he had meant what he said about her being his date. "Don't worry about Sylvia Jordan's opinion. She's interested in three things that I know of—her husband's career, their status at the country club, and herself." He laughed when he said it.

Anne stared up at him, a look of horror in her eyes.

"What?" he asked, laughing as he stepped closer to her. "What did I say that's so terrible?"

"She's just like me," she said, as if she had just realized it herself. "Everyone in this town must see me exactly the same way they do Sylvia. My God, what a horrifying thought."

"Huh uh," he said, shaking his head.

"No way are you anything like Sylvia Jordan."

"But I am, Kurt," she said.

Kurt was surprised at the agony in her voice, and in her eyes. Slowly his smile faded, and he reached out to touch her arms, running his hands slowly down to her wrists to capture her hands.

"Will you listen to me?" he said. "You might have tried to be a snob, for reasons that I admit I don't quite understand. But believe me, it hasn't worked."

"I don't want to be. I don't."

"Then don't be."

"Goodness," she said, attempting a smile. "Even at my age, I still don't seem to have it all together as far as who I am and what I want to be."

"You're getting there."

"Am I? I've discovered recently that I don't like myself very much, or the way I've been living."

"Well," he murmured, leaning back as if to study her. "I think this is something we should discuss . . . over dinner at the Riverside Grill. As soon as we pick out the nursery furniture. What do you say? Are you up to causing a scandal in town by being seen with your boss? A man decidedly beneath your social status?"

"Don't you say that," she whispered, frowning up at him. "Don't you ever say that again . . . not even in fun."

"Does that mean yes?" he asked, his eyes dark and serious.

"Yes," she said. "Definitely yes."

Nineteen

They sat at one of the back tables overlooking the river. It was early, and the restaurant wasn't crowded. After the waiter took their order Anne sat staring out the window and thinking about the last time she was here. And how she'd felt when she saw Kurt sitting alone, watching her.

"What are you thinking about?" Kurt asked.

"About when Cecile and I were here before," she said quietly.

"You seemed very troubled that night." He said the words easily, even though his gaze never left her face.

"I've not been entirely honest with you," she said.

"How's that?" His eyes were cool and filled with what Anne thought must be an infinite patience.

"When you came to my house that night."

His eyes changed then, grew darker . . . warmer. Anne had to force herself not to look away from the intimacy she saw there. She was afraid she wouldn't be able to say what she wanted to say with him looking at her that way.

"You have to understand," she began again, "how I've been . . . how I've lived for the past few years. I guess I didn't allow anyone in . . ." She glanced up at him again and saw him frown slightly.

"If you're trying to tell me that you made a mistake that night, Anne—"

"No," she said quickly. "No, that's not what I'm saying at all. I suppose I have some deep-seated need to explain everything . . . to myself, if nothing else. And to you," she added softly.

The waiter brought glasses of iced tea and Anne sat back in her chair, trying to compose her thoughts.

When he was gone she leaned forward again, hoping desperately that she could find the words to explain how she felt.

"I let myself become vulnerable with Tracy, Kurt. I didn't think I was at the time. But the night she left I actually thought I would die, it hurt so badly. I'd spent years telling myself I didn't need anyone . . . that I didn't really care about anyone but myself. But with Tracy . . ." Her longing for Tracy came back in one swift, bittersweet rush, and even though the pain was not as sharp as before, it surprised her. "I let myself care about her. That night, after I went home, for the first time in a long time I needed someone to talk to . . . to understand how I was feeling."

He waited, not saying anything, only watching her with that sweet patience in his eyes.

"And you came." She took a sudden deep breath and closed her eyes for a moment. God, the memory of that night . . . sitting here looking straight into his face, discussing what had happened. It was almost too much.

"Is it so hard to talk about . . ." he asked softly, "what happened between us that night?"

"Yes," she said, frowning at him. "You don't know . . . you can't imagine. The next morning I couldn't believe that I just fell into your arms without a moment's hesitation. I don't know what you think of me, Kurt, or what you've heard. But I don't make a habit of doing that."

"I know that. You don't have to explain that to me." He leaned forward suddenly, as if his patience was at an end. He reached across the table for her hands and she moved hers toward him.

"I didn't mean to be ugly to you the next day," she said. "I was looking forward to seeing you. But then you offered me the job and suddenly I felt—"

"Cheap," he said quietly.

"Not exactly," she said, searching for the word she wanted. "Rewarded, maybe. Your offer made me feel rewarded, and suddenly . . ." She pulled her hands from his, gesturing futilely as she tried to explain. "Suddenly I felt the way I did when I was young—as if I wasn't good enough, as if no one could love me for what I was. I was a lot like Crystal, you know. A lot more even than I let on before. I was a fat, miserable, unwanted little girl."

Kurt's face had an intensity now, an impatience, as he glanced around the room. For a moment Anne thought he might leave. But he reached forward for her hands again, grasping them so tightly, she almost cried out.

"Dammit, Anne—you can't tell me that what we shared that night made you feel miserable or unwanted. You're right—I did come there only to offer you comfort and sympathy. But we're adults, sweetheart—we both know that there are a lot of reasons for making love. That doesn't diminish it. It doesn't make it any less exciting." He shook her hand for emphasis. "I wanted you. I still want you. And you know it."

She felt the tingle of excitement run from her fingers all the way through her body. And as she looked into his eyes, she thought she had never managed to have this kind of connection with any man. Ever.

"I'm not saying I felt unwanted . . . not then, certainly not when we made love." Her voice was soft as she spoke. "And I'm not saying it's you, or anything you did. It's me, Kurt. Don't you see? I'm not capable of having a normal relationship with any man. I never have been. And I don't want to hurt you by having you think I can."

"Bull. I don't believe that for a minute."

She stared into his eyes, not knowing what she could do to convince him. The waiter brought their salads and there was an awkward silence in the isolated corner of the room where they sat.

"Let's try to enjoy our dinner," she said finally.

"I'm not going to just drop this, Anne," he said, picking up his fork. "You can't ignore what's happened and hope it will go away. We're going to settle this . . . sooner or later."

She felt the fear gripping her heart even as she nodded her agreement. She wished she could ignore it—ignore him. But she couldn't. For once in her life she was going to have to face what was bothering her. And only she knew that it was much more than what had happened at the halfway house. More even than having a sexual relationship with a man after years of self-imposed celibacy.

It wasn't long until the waiter brought Kurt's steak and her grilled catfish. And as they ate, she could see his attempt to brighten the mood. She was amazed at how he always managed to do that, how he seemed to put all their problems aside and talk about other things as if nothing was wrong. Before long she was smiling and laughing at his stories and wondering where in the world this man had been all her life.

"Do you see your sons often?" she asked.

"Pretty often," he said. "I certainly see more of Greg now that he's married and settled down, and that's nice. Tim is still on the go, although he does manage to spend the weekend with me once a month or so."

"You enjoy being a dad; I can hear it in your voice when you talk about them."

"Well," he said, smiling wistfully, "I guess it's every man's dream to have sons. Although sometimes I do wish that we'd had a daughter, too." He glanced up at her, his hazel gaze intense and sweet. "Maybe I'd have known more about figuring out the female psyche if I had."

She laughed then, enjoying his bantering and his company.

"I don't think you have any problems in that area, Mr. Bonner."

"No?"

"No. Definitely not." She leaned back in the chair, smiling at him. "Oh, don't give me that look. You know perfectly well how women react around you. Kathleen and Jessica, for instance, and Sylvia Jordan practically swooned over you today at the furniture store."

"Ah . . . you think so?" he said, his eyes twinkling. "Sylvia Jordan. Now there's an interesting woman. Remind me to tell you about her one day."

Anne's mouth flew open and she gasped. "Kurt Bonner. You didn't. You wouldn't!"

He laughed then, tilting his head back and letting a deep, easy laugh rumble up from his chest.

"Hardly," he said finally. "I guess I just wanted to see if you were listening . . . maybe even shock you a little." His look grew more sober, even though his eyes were still sparkling. "And make you jealous."

Anne took a sip of her tea, looking into his eyes and shaking her head at him.

"What about you?" he asked. "Vivian tells me you were married before Baxter Benefield, when you were younger."

"Yes, very young. It didn't work out."

"Why?" He saw her closed-off look. "That was a long time ago. Surely it doesn't bother you to talk about it now."

"I don't like talking about it."

"Tell me," he urged softly. "I want to know."

Anne sighed, hardly knowing where to begin. But she could see that Kurt wasn't going to give up.

"Ronnie was a big man on campus. But after graduation, after we were married, he couldn't afford to go to college. He always intended to, always bragged about what an athlete he was and that he probably could have gotten a scholarship if he'd really tried. But he was actually a nobody in a dead-end job, and he couldn't admit that for a long time, not even to himself. But you know how it is once you get stuck in that first job—you need the money to pay the bills, so you can't quit. It's a vicious cycle that continues for most people until they die. That's where Ronnie was going and he couldn't stand it. I guess he blamed me."

Kurt frowned, leaning toward the table. "What do you mean, he blamed you?"

"Kurt . . ." she began.

"Tell me."

She took a deep breath as the waiter came to clear the table.

"Would you like dessert?" he asked. "Coffee?"

"Just coffee," Kurt said, his eyes going back to Anne.

"Coffee," she repeated.

"It started at first with his pushing me, or shoving me against a wall. It only happened when he was drinking. But then, over the years, it seemed that he was drinking all the time. So . . . it got worse." She lifted her gaze toward him.

"God . . . Anne." Kurt's look was intensely understanding and sympathetic. "How long did this go on? Did he hurt you? Were you—"

"Ten years," she said. She felt her chin trembling, and she clasped her fingers together and pressed them against her lips. "He broke my fingers," she whispered. "And my wrist once. And my nose. See . . . how crooked it is," she said, touching her nose and trying to joke about it. But her eyes were sober. "One night . . . he beat me so badly, I thought I probably would die." She lifted her chin then. "That was the end of it. I don't know how I found the courage to get out, but I did, and I never looked back. I swore then that no man would ever get close enough to hurt me that way again."

Kurt reached forward, taking her tightly gripped hands and pulling them away from her lips. He couldn't stand seeing the sparkle of tears in her eyes.

"Will you look at me?" she said, attempting a laugh. "I don't know what's wrong with me. I haven't worried about Ronnie Gatlin in years, and I certainly haven't shed a tear for him. Or anyone else, for that matter," she added, feeling rather puzzled.

"Personally, I'd like to kill the bastard myself," Kurt said through tightly clenched teeth.

"Oh, no," she whispered, gripping his hands. "He isn't worth that. It was a long time ago. He doesn't even live here anymore. The last time I saw him he was a pathetic old man, divorced twice more and living in a run-down trailer on the outskirts of Granger. If I hadn't despised him so much, I might have felt sorry for him."

"Let's get out of here," Kurt said, getting to his feet and pulling her up from her chair.

He wanted to be alone with her and tell her that all men weren't like Ronnie Gatlin. He wanted to look into her eyes and find out everything there was to know about this sweet, wounded, mysterious woman. And most of all he wanted to hold her and comfort her. He wanted to kiss her until both of them were breathless. And even though he knew he shouldn't want it in light of all the things she'd told him—he wanted to make hot, sweet, passionate love with her. All night. Every night.

Twenty

They didn't say much on the way back to Anne's house. Kurt turned on the radio, letting the sound of some unknown orchestra drift lazily around them and into the night air. The melodies were nostalgic and soothing to Anne's restless mind.

Kurt parked and, instead of getting out of the truck to open Anne's door, reached across her. His arm brushed against her breasts and he pulled away, looking down at her as if he had been burned.

She could feel his gaze on her, close and compelling . . . more tempting than she ever dreamed any man's look could be. She didn't lift her eyes to him but slid away.

The lights had been left on in part of the house. From her upstairs bedroom it fell softly out onto the surrounding trees and across the driveway as she and Kurt walked slowly toward the porch.

She climbed up onto the porch and Kurt stayed one step below, one foot resting up near hers. Their eyes were almost level. He didn't take his eyes away from her face, and when he reached forward and put his hands on her waist she didn't move or protest.

"I can't ask you in," she whispered, hoping he would understand.

"Don't worry," he said. "I'm not the kind of man to push my way into a woman's bedroom . . . or her life."

"I know that," she said, stepping closer. She reached out to brush her fingers across his face, letting her hand move slowly down to his mouth. "I feel rather foolish . . . and guilty, asking you to wait. After that night . . . at our age—"

He laughed. "Our age, I'd say, is a distinct advantage in that department. If the years have taught me anything, it's patience." He laughed again at her look of distress. "Annie," he whispered, his hand at her waist, pulling her closer, "don't worry about this, or put too much meaning into it. I'm a healthy, warm-blooded male, and there's nothing I'd like better than to take you upstairs, but . . ." Suddenly he leaned forward, pulling her toward him at the same time.

Their lips met with a quiet, whispered sigh, and Anne couldn't decide if it was his or hers. She let herself drown in his kiss, savoring the taste, the feel of his mouth on hers, leaning into him with an urgency that surprised her. The same urgency that she felt time and again with him . . . and the same disbelief and surprise because of it.

"Oh, Kurt," she whispered when the kiss ended. "You tempt me more than any man I've ever known. But—"

His hand went to cover her lips, his fingers caressing, his eyes following like a kiss.

"Don't say it," he whispered. "Don't qualify that statement. I want to remember it just the way it is."

Anne leaned against him, letting her head rest on his shoulder, feeling his arms tighten, his hands running softly from her neck down to her waist.

"Don't give up on me," she whispered against his shirt. "I'd like you to still be here if I ever manage to get my stupid mind in order."

He pulled back and touched his mouth lightly to hers.

"I don't want to hear you say that again. There's nothing stupid about you. And I don't intend to give up on you. You'll have to get a lot meaner before that happens," he added with a smile.

"Oh, Kurt." She wrapped her arms around him, giving in finally to the urge to hold him tightly, to feel the length of his body against hers. He was all male, hard where she was soft, his skin warm where hers was cool.

How could she resist him? How could anyone?

In these first tenuous, fragile stages of their relationship, she was finding in him all the things she'd ever searched for in a man. He was the kind of man she had begun to think didn't even exist.

When she released him and stepped back on the porch his hands trailed away from her body, one reaching out to touch her hair and her face.

"Good night," she said.

He didn't move, but stood in exactly

the same spot while she moved out of his reach and backed toward the front door. He was still there when she unlocked the door and went inside.

She quickly reset her alarm system and hurried up the steps to her room. Standing at her bedroom window, gazing down, she saw Kurt open the door to his truck. He turned then, looking up toward her with a lift of his hand. She waved to him and watched as he started the truck and pulled away.

She turned back to her room, staring at it as if she had never seen it before. This was her sanctuary, her home, and she had rarely felt lonely here.

Until now. Until Kurt.

Now she was overcome with a longing, a tantalizing loneliness that ate away at her heart and left her feeling restless and dissatisfied.

She went to look in the mirror, seeing the confusion in her eyes, touching her cheek and her lips where he had kissed her.

"What has he done to me?" she whispered, staring at her reflection. "And what am I going to do about it?"

She was at work early the next morning and she had already faced the fact that it was because of Kurt. He was so much on her mind that she hadn't thought about the kids or the Howards. She just wanted to see him and be near him.

But as soon as she stepped through the front door, she knew there was a more urgent problem than seeing Kurt.

The house was eerily quiet, and although the children were seated at the long dining-room table as usual, they weren't eating, but were waiting silently.

Anne stepped to the door, wondering why they were staring toward the end of the room and why they weren't eating.

She stepped through the open doorway, stopping when she saw Crystal, sitting uncomfortably in a child's high chair in the corner, her face turned toward the wall.

"What on earth is going on?" Anne gasped, moving toward the girl.

Crystal's face was red and her eyes watery, but she wasn't crying. Instead she sat with her teeth clamped tightly together, her hands clasped into tight little fists in her lap. She was trembling.

"Get up," Anne said softly, turning the chair around and reaching for Crystal.

The door from the kitchen opened and Nancy Howard walked through carrying a tray with juice-filled glasses.

"Well, good morning, Anne," she said. But she stopped when she saw Anne's glare and saw that she had helped Crystal from the high chair.

"I'd like to know what this is all about," Anne said. She put her arm around Crystal and pulled her toward her protectively.

With a cool look, Nancy placed the tray on a side table and turned to Anne.

"I don't think it's anything you need to concern yourself with. Crystal has been acting like a baby, so we are treating her like one by letting her sit in a high chair."

Her look was so smug, so self-assured, that Anne wanted to reach out and slap her. She clenched her fists so tightly that her nails bit into the palms of her hands.

"Where is Kurt?" Anne asked. "He would never agree to such humiliating tactics."

"Mr. Bonner had to go to court to sign some papers. As for humiliation, we've found it is the most effective way to teach this kind of child," Nancy said. "Mr. Bonner has given me the authority to discipline the children any way I see fit. After all, he isn't here with them all the time, but I will be. I suggest, Mrs. Benefield, that you confine your activities to the kitchen where you're needed. Ed and I will handle the children."

"Not this way," Anne said, ignoring her remarks. "Not Crystal, or any of the children, is to be treated in this manner."

Nancy stared at Anne as if she had lost her mind.

"Do you know what she did?" Nancy asked, her voice becoming high-pitched and agitated. "Did she tell you what she did?"

"I don't care what she did," Anne said, her eyes sparking dangerously. "It doesn't deserve this."

"She stole food," Nancy continued, ignoring Anne's anger and frustration. "The refrigerator door was left open all night because she forgot to close it. All the food was warm and no doubt some of it will have to be thrown away . . . wasted! In the process she took food and hid it in her room. I found it this morning." She raised her brows and her chin in a haughty way, but it was her look of dislike directed at Crystal that angered Anne the most.

She looked perverse, Anne thought. Self-righteous and smug and perverse. She actually seemed to be enjoying this torment.

Anne saw Gabby come to the kitchen door. She thought she'd never seen such disgust in his eyes as when he looked at Nancy Howard.

"It don't matter how much food she took. If she's hungry, she's hungry. We don't hide food from the kids," he said, waving his wooden spoon for emphasis. "And as for the refrigerator," he said, turning his gaze toward Anne, "you know how it does if you slam it too hard; it just comes back open. Got a bad gasket. The girl didn't know that. Probably didn't even know it was left open."

"That's true," Anne said. "It's happened to me."

When Gabby turned to Crystal his eyes softened.

"Did you know the door was left open, girl?"

"No," she said, her voice so soft they could hardly hear it.

"All right, then," Gabby said with a quirk of his lips and a satisfied nod.

Nancy made a sniffling little noise, as if she wasn't convinced.

"Do you actually think I'm going to take the word of a child? Besides, just look at her. Does she look as if she needs to be eating in the middle of the night?"

"That's enough," Anne said. She could feel her face growing hot and flushed, and her jaw actually ached from being held too tightly. "I suppose we'll have to wait until Kurt gets back to settle this. In the meantime I suggest that you let the children eat in the manner they usually do, including Crystal."

She moved Crystal toward her usual chair, her arm still around her shoulders. "Go ahead, honey. I'll sit here and eat breakfast with you."

The look of relief on Crystal's face was so sweet that it was heartbreaking, and Anne wondered how anyone could be cruel to a child. How could Nancy Howard humiliate and embarrass Crystal this way, or any of them? Anne felt angrier than she had in years. She found that she didn't want to be reasonable or polite. She wanted nothing more than to punch the woman in the mouth.

"You may eat breakfast this once," Nancy said, as if Anne were a child herself. "But I'm afraid such informality is going to have to stop. You'll all find that we Howards run a ship-shape operation. No waste, no disorganization, and no unnecessary sentimentality with the children."

"Oh, I see," Anne said coolly, taking her seat at the table. "Kind of like a prison."

She heard Gabby's wheezing laughter behind her and smiled. She glanced around the table and saw the children were smiling, too, except Crystal. She was still quiet and withdrawn.

"All right, children," Anne said defiantly. "Let's dig in."

The dining room came to life suddenly, with the clatter of dishes and the children's voices, even though some of them were still muted and soft.

Anne could sense Nancy's tenseness as

she stood beside her, but she didn't look up. Instead, she passed around biscuits and scrambled eggs, leaning over to Crystal and putting food into her plate.

"What do you want to drink, sweetie?"

"I don't care," Crystal said quietly.

"Orange juice? Milk?"

She was quiet for a long time before she glanced up at Anne, and then she looked away. "Can I have chocolate milk?"

The plaintiveness in Crystal's voice, the embarrassed tone of indecision, made Anne want to hug her. Instead she turned around toward the kitchen door.

"Of course you can. Gabby, would you bring some chocolate milk? Does anyone else want some?"

Several of the children did, expressing their wishes so loudly and with such enthusiasm that Nancy finally gave an exasperated sigh and turned to march out of the room.

But Anne didn't feel a sense of triumph at Nancy's leaving. If anything, she felt afraid; afraid she had made a mistake, that she had overstepped her bounds here in this house. Afraid that

Kurt might even have authorized the woman to use any kind of discipline she deemed necessary.

Maybe she didn't know Kurt at all. Maybe she had let her sexual attraction color her view of him and distract her from being as cautious as she should have been.

Twenty-one

Anne thought Kurt would never return to the house. Every time she heard a noise beyond the kitchen door she would look to see if it was him. And every time the door opened she glanced up quickly from whatever she was doing.

"You tell Kurt to set that woman straight when he gets here," Gabby muttered.

She could see the agitation in the old man, in the jerky way he moved about the kitchen and the way he slammed pots and spoons down on the counter. His eyes were hard, looking straight ahead, no matter what chore he was doing. Anne knew he was as concerned about Crystal and the other children as she was.

"I will," she said. "You don't think he told her it would be okay, do you? You don't think he—"

"No, I don't think he told her it would be okay," he answered sharply. "I've knowed Kurt Bonner a lot of years and he ain't never treated nobody the way that woman treated them kids this mornin'. Why, it was pitiful. Seein' the look in their eyes. And that new girl—"

"Crystal," Anne said, smiling at him. She thought sometimes that Gabby felt if he didn't use someone's name, he wasn't getting involved. A bit like herself, she thought.

"Yeah . . . her. She ain't fat and she shore ain't ugly, and for the life of me I can't figure out why anybody would want to hurt the poor kid that way."

"Did Nancy actually say that to her?" Anne asked, a horrified expression on her face. "That she was fat . . . or ugly?"

"Said more'n that," he said, his eyes turning dark.

Anne could feel the anger and frustration building up in her, tightening her chest and making her head ache.

Vivian came into the kitchen just before noon and whispered, "He's back."

Anne almost jumped out of her skin, turning so quickly that she spilled water on the floor and then groaned at her own clumsiness.

"I'll do that," Gabby said, coming quickly to her side. "You go on. Talk to Kurt."

She touched him on the shoulder as he bent to wipe up the water, then she quickly dried her hands and hurried toward the dining room.

She heard Nancy Howard's shrill voice before she ever got to the hallway.

"She was rude, and her actions undermined my wishes and my authority. I can't have it, Mr. Bonner. I simply won't have it. Either she goes or my husband and I go."

"Mrs. Howard," Kurt said, his voice quiet and calming, "there is no question of Mrs. Benefield's leaving. She was sent here by the court."

"Then let them send her somewhere else."

"That's not possible. We need her and she's staying. What we have to do is figure out some way that the two of you can work together."

"I won't tolerate her interference."

"Sit down, Mrs. Howard."

"I don't want to sit down. I—"

"Mrs. Howard . . ." Kurt's voice sounded weary with impatience. "Please . . . sit down. There are other things we need to discuss. We might as well do it now."

Anne heard Kurt's footsteps as he got up from the desk and moved toward the door. Anne was standing in the hallway, directly in front of his door, and when he saw her he stopped.

The slow smile that replaced his frown was sweet, and so welcoming. But then he gave a little shake of his head and rolled his eyes before softly closing the door, leaving Anne standing outside.

She knew in her head that this was business, that Kurt couldn't throw the woman out or ask her to leave while he heard Anne's version first. But she thought in her heart that that was exactly what she would have liked. She knew she shouldn't feel rejected, and yet she did.

Her shoulders slumped and she went to sit on the bottom step of the staircase. It was then, while the house was quiet, that she heard a rhythmic thumping sound from upstairs.

She cocked her head to one side, listening more carefully and wondering what the noise was. Then she got up and moved up the stairs.

The sound was coming from Crystal's room.

She opened the door; now she could hear the quiet sobs of the girl who sat on the floor, rocking back and forth, her head hitting against the wall with each backward movement.

"Crystal," Anne said with alarm as she moved quickly into the room.

Crystal's eyes had been closed, but now she opened them, staring at Anne as if she were some monster. Tears streamed down her face unchecked.

"Sweetheart . . ." Anne held her arms out as she approached.

Suddenly Crystal jumped up from the floor, backing into a corner as if she didn't know Anne, as if she'd never seen her before.

"No!" she cried, softly at first. Then she bent forward and the scream came up from her stomach and chest, up, it seemed, from her very soul. "Nooooo!"

The sound, the anguish in Crystal's

voice, stopped Anne cold. She stood, arms still outstretched, staring at the girl and feeling a chill run down her spine as the sound echoed through the room.

"Sweetheart," Anne said, barely breathing. "What is it? Let me help you."

Crystal's sobs shook her entire body, and the words that came out were choked and hard.

"I don't need you to help me!" she sobbed. "I don't want any of you to help me. Just leave me alone! You lied to me. You said it would be all right." The girl stopped, bending over in her anguish, and finally sliding down to the floor.

Anne heard footsteps behind her, and when she turned she saw Kurt and Nancy Howard were coming into the room. She saw the horror in Kurt's eyes as he went to help Crystal, and she saw the accusation on Nancy's face.

Crystal tried to pull away from him, tried to fight his restraining arms. And all the while her tearstained eyes accused Anne.

"You were *never* fat like me," Crystal sobbed. "You only told me that to make me do what you wanted. I . . . I tried to eat good . . . the way you said. But I'm still fat. I weigh more than I did before I came here." The last sentence was a screaming accusation as her eyes glanced at the floor toward the end of the bed.

Anne saw what she was looking at: a set of bath scales, obviously the thing that had sent the girl into such an anguished tantrum.

"Where did that come from?" Anne asked. "Why should a ten-year-old girl even need bath scales, or be concerned about what she weighs?" Her face was hot and her head had begun to throb painfully.

"I gave them to her," Nancy said. "And I told her she is to weigh herself every morning until she gets some of that weight off."

Anne could only stare in astonishment as Nancy's words made Crystal's face crumple from embarrassment.

"I think you should go," Kurt said to Anne as he cradled the girl against him. "At least until we get her calmed down."

Anne saw the look of sympathy in his eyes and knew he wasn't accusing her, but it hurt nonetheless. And when she turned and walked past Nancy, who stood with her arms crossed, looking smug and secure, she felt like screaming herself.

Instead she walked quickly down the stairs and through the kitchen, not even bothering to stop when Gabby turned and muttered something to her. She ran out into the backyard, leaning against the old oak tree and trying to catch her breath.

Who did she think she was? An amateur psychologist? Did she actually think her meaningless talk and inept advice was going to help anyone, especially someone as seriously troubled as Crystal?

She had made things worse, and the pain of that realization hit her like a blow, making her bend over in agony.

Finally she straightened up. Her head was pounding and she felt as if she might actually be sick. She turned and went into the kitchen, silently going to get her purse before saying anything to Gabby, who stood watching her with a puzzled frown on his face.

"What happened?" he asked. "Did he straighten that woman out?"

"Gabby, I'm sorry," she whispered. "I . . . I just have to go home. I have such a headache that I think I'm going to be sick. Would you tell Kurt?"

She was already going through the door when she heard his reply.

"Why, shore," he said, his voice gruff and unusually kind. "You just take the day off . . . get some rest. We'll take care of everything here."

She began to run then, out the front door and to her car. She still felt the need to run when she parked the car at home and went into the house.

She was surprised to see Mrs. Hargis in the kitchen.

"Mrs. Hargis . . ." she said. "I . . . I thought you were taking the day off."

"Oh, my daughter is picking me up tonight and driving me over. I'll be off tomorrow if . . ." She stopped, staring hard at Anne. "Why, what are you doin' home this time of day? You don't look so good. Are you sick, Mrs. Benefield? You don't look well at all."

"Yes," Anne gasped. The pain in her head seemed to intensify with every word, every movement. "I have a migraine. I'm going to take a cool bath and go to bed. Do you know where I put my medicine?"

"Why, no, not right off hand, I don't. It's been such a long time since you've needed it . . ." Her eyes lit up then, and she lifted her finger as if she wanted Anne to wait. "Jessie will know. I'll go get her. You go on upstairs and take your bath. We'll bring the medicine right up to you."

"Thank you, Mrs. Hargis."

Later, just as she was getting out of the bath, she heard a soft tap on the bathroom door.

"I've put your medicine and a fresh pitcher of water on the nightstand beside your bed, ma'am." It was Jessica, and her voice sounded soft and sympathetic. "I've closed the blinds and turned down your bed. And I'm going to cut the ringer off your phone."

"Thank you, Jessica," Anne whispered. She could hardly talk for the pain.

"I'll come back in a little while to check on you, okay?"

Anne felt tears in her eyes. Jessica and Mrs. Hargis had always treated her with such kindness . . . such concern, even when she'd been less than friendly with them. She'd hardly noticed until lately, never really appreciated them.

The cool sheets felt heavenly and as she sank down into the bed's softness she sighed, closing her eyes and hoping that the medicine would take effect quickly.

She hardly remembered drifting off to sleep. She didn't know when Jessica stepped into the room and looked down at her with concern. And she didn't hear the phone ringing downstairs, or Mrs. Hargis talking to Kurt.

"She's gone to bed with a migraine," Mrs. Hargis said. "Although Lord knows what caused it. It's been at least a year since she's had one."

Kurt took a deep breath and closed his eyes.

"I think I know," he said. "Do you think she'll be all right?"

"Oh, yes," she said. "Jessica went up to check on her a little while ago and she was sleeping. More than likely when she wakes the headache will be gone. That's the way it usually works, anyway. Do you want me to tell her you called?"

"No," he said. He frowned and sat for a moment, thinking. "No, don't say anything. I'll come by the farm and see her before I go home."

Mrs. Hargis smiled broadly.

"I'm glad," she said. "And say, why don't you stay for dinner? I baked a nice stuffed pork roast yesterday. I'll warm it up and make a fresh salad and some creamed potatoes to go with it."

"Kathleen," he said, smiling, "you're a woman after my own heart. That sounds good to me. See you around six?"

"All righty," she said, beaming as she hung up the phone. She turned to Jessica, who had walked into the kitchen. "That was that nice Mr. Bonner. He's comin' over for dinner. You know, I think he likes our Annie. I think he likes her a lot."

"I hope so," Jessica said. "These migraine headaches are just a symptom, they say. There was a show on *Oprah* just the other day about it. They said stress and worry causes 'em. And you can't tell me that bein' unhappy all these years ain't had somethin' to do with it. No, sir . . . Mrs. Benefield needs a man more'n anybody I ever seen."

At Mrs. Hargis's shake of her head and soft, skeptical grunt, Jessica continued.

"Now, I don't mean she needs a man just to be havin' a man, though Lord knows, they ain't nothing wrong with that. She needs somebody to love her and make her feel special. You know what I mean?"

"Yes, I do," Mrs. Hargis said with a wise nod. "I sure do."

"I swear . . . I think she's about the saddest, loneliest woman I ever knew. She's a good person, deep down inside. She was good to Mr. Benefield, although she didn't make no bones about it bein' a marriage of convenience. But she was as good to him as could be. And she deserves a little happiness."

"Well," Mrs. Hargis said, smiling, "maybe she's about to find a little bit of that."

"I hope so. I really hope so."

Twenty-two

Anne wasn't sure what woke her. For a moment she didn't know what day it was, or what time. She glanced at the crystal clock on her bedside table and frowned, remembering what had happened and how upset she'd been. She took a long, deep breath, not attempting to get up before she tested her neck and head for pain.

The headache was gone, thank goodness. She couldn't believe she had slept until six o'clock.

She heard a soft tap at her door and sat up in bed.

"Yes?"

"You awake?" Jessica said, peeking in the door. "How's your headache?"

"Come on in," Anne said, smiling. "Yes, I'm awake, and I'm feeling much better. The headache is completely gone."

"I didn't mean to disturb you. Just wanted you to know that Mr. Bonner is downstairs and—"

"Kurt?" Anne said, feeling her heart accelerate. "Kurt is here?" She threw back the covers and swung her legs over the side of the bed.

"Now, don't get up too quick," Jessica said, coming to her side. "He ain't goin' nowhere," she added with a grin.

Anne quickly went to the mirror, smoothing her hair with jerky, distracted movements. She turned twice and then stopped when she saw the amused look on Jessica's face.

"Oh, Jessica," she said with a sheepish grin. "What am I doing? You and Mrs. Hargis must think I've completely lost my mind."

"We don't think anything of the kind," she said. "That Mr. Bonner is good-lookin' enough to make any woman get a little flustered. You're just a little out of practice, that's all," she continued, nodding wisely. "Just put on somethin' soft and comfortable—he knows you've been in bed with a headache all day. He don't expect glamour. He came because he's worried about you, and Kathleen thought he might like to stay for supper while he was at it."

"Oh," Anne said, turning around again as if she was looking for something. "All right," she said beneath her breath. "I can do this. I can."

"Do you need anything? Want anything pressed or—?"

"No," Anne said, turning back to Jessica. "No; it's late. I know Elmer must be waiting for his own supper. You go ahead. And Jessica—"

Jessica stopped and turned, looking at Anne expectantly. "Yes'm?"

"Thank you. Thanks so much for all you've done for me."

"Why, it's what I get paid for, Mrs. Benefield," the woman said.

There was a glint in her eyes when she said it; maybe even a bit of teasing, Anne thought. She groaned inwardly when she asked the next question.

"Oh, dear. I . . . I've never said anything like that to you before . . . have I?"

"Why, yes," Jessica said, with an amused grin. "I do believe you've mentioned it once or twice on occasion."

"I'm sorry, Jessica. Really." Anne touched her forehead and closed her eyes for a moment.

"Hey, now," Jessica said, stepping toward her. "I was just jokin' you a little. It ain't nothin' to get upset about."

Anne sighed and shook her head.

"I've been such a selfish bitch over the years, haven't I? I wonder how you and Elmer and Mrs. Hargis stood me. And I wonder how Bax ever put up with me."

"Why, ma'am," Jessica said, a troubled look in her eyes, "he loved you. Just the way we do." Then, with a little dip of her head, she averted her eyes and moved toward the door. "You get ready now and don't start frettin' about the past. I have a feelin' Mr. Bonner is anxious to see you."

As Anne watched her leave, she felt a little catch in her throat. She felt lately as if her life were in a whirlwind, with so many changes, so many revelations. And realizing that Jessica and Mrs. Hargis cared about her—had cared for years—gave her a confused mixture of feelings.

"It's all happening too fast," she murmured to herself as she slipped off her gown and began to dress.

All these new emotions and new discoveries were like a wall of water, rushing full force toward her. Going to work at the halfway house, meeting Kurt and Gabby and all the others, falling completely under little Tracy's spell and now Crystal's, it was all too much. She had opened her heart against her will, telling herself she would become only a little involved. And now, like the powerful waters against the proverbial hole in the dike, her emotions threatened to overwhelm her, to engulf her in their rushing wake.

She took Jessica's advice and dressed simply in silk pants and a soft blouse. She didn't bother with any makeup except a little mascara and a touch of pale lipstick. She was pleasantly surprised at the way she looked—softer and more feminine.

She hurried downstairs, taking a deep breath before stepping into the kitchen.

"Oh, there you are," Mrs. Hargis said. She'd been leaning against the kitchen counter, talking to Kurt.

Anne saw Kurt's lashes flicker and his

eyes open wide, revealing the smoky depths of his hazel gaze. His look grew warm and welcoming as he pushed himself away from the counter and came to her.

"How are you feeling?" he asked. His voice was deep and quiet, and for a moment there was silence in the spacious room.

"Better," she managed. Did he have any idea what his eyes did to her? How the sight of him, so strong and solid, made her knees go weak, made her long to wrap herself in his arms and hold on? "My . . . my headache's gone, at least."

"Good," he murmured, his eyes still intense and steady.

"Well," Mrs. Hargis said, clearing her throat. "I've got to get home. My daughter will be picking me up soon. Do you think I should be here tomorrow?" she asked. "In case you're still not feeling well? In case you need me?"

"No, Kathleen," Anne said, looking at the woman with genuine affection. "You go on and take your day off. Visit with your family and your great-grandchild. I'll be fine."

Mrs. Hargis's gaze was serious and concerned for a moment. "Now I've set the table for you here in the breakfast nook. The flowers out in the garden are real pretty lately. But if you'd prefer the big dining room, I can—"

"No, the breakfast nook is fine," Anne said, smiling at Mrs. Hargis's motherly ways. "You go ahead. And thank you. The food smells really delicious."

Mrs. Hargis nodded and smiled, turning with a girlish grin toward Kurt.

"I hope you enjoy it," she said, going to the door.

Anne didn't know why she felt so awkward. She'd thought she was beginning to know Kurt well, and after all, they did work together every day. But now, suddenly, after the scene at the halfway house this morning . . . his being here, the look of quiet concern in his eyes, made her feel exposed and vulnerable.

"Over here," Anne said, going to the cozy corner where the table was set with sparkling china and crystal water-filled goblets. The salad looked crisp and colorful, and she was happy to see that Mrs.

Hargis had made her favorite vinaigrette dressing.

She could see the steam rising from the buttery creamed potatoes, and the stuffed pork roast lay in thick slices, covered by a delicate mushroom sauce.

"My, this looks good," she murmured, smiling at Kurt as they took their seats.

As they ate, they chatted about inconsequential things: the weather, the flowers outside. Anything, Anne thought, except what had happened with Crystal. Or what was happening at this moment between them.

She would catch his eyes on her and look away, talking about something trivial and meaningless. He would smile that knowing little smile of his; she knew she hadn't fooled him at all.

"The new furniture arrived this afternoon," he said.

"Oh," she said. She'd completely forgotten about the furniture. "I'm sorry I wasn't there. I—"

"It's all right. Mrs. Howard and Vivian and I managed. But if it doesn't suit you where we've put things when you come back, we'll change them."

She frowned at him and shook her head.

"But I . . . I have no authority, really. I'm just the dishwasher," she added, smiling wistfully at him.

"You're much more than that, Anne," he said. He put down his fork and rested his arms on the table, staring at her across the small bowl of roses and daisies. "And it *was* your money that bought the furniture."

"Oh, yes," she said, pulling her gaze away from his. "Money."

He leaned back in his chair and sighed, staring at her and saying nothing until she was forced to look up and meet his eyes.

"Don't get defensive with me, lady," he said, his words deceptively quiet. "You know damned well that your money has nothing to do with how I feel, how I've felt from the beginning. So don't throw that up between us now."

"I wasn't," she said, frowning at him.

But she was. And both of them knew it.

"What is it, Anne?" he asked, not moving, not offering to get up and come around to her. "Is it Mrs. Howard? Crys-

tal? I'm not very good at guessing games—
I've never had the time. But that is why I
came . . . to see how you were and to find
out exactly what's going on." He leaned
forward, propping his forearms on the table, his head lowered as he stared intently
into her face.

"I want to help you, Anne," he said,
his voice low and intense. "But dammit,
I can't if you keep shutting me out. If
you keep running away every time something doesn't go to suit you."

"I . . . I had a headache," she said,
feeling an ache in her heart at his criticism. "A migraine."

"I know you did," he said, his gaze
turning soft with worry. "I'm not questioning that. But sweetheart, don't you
see? That's just another form of running
away; your body's way of shutting down
and forcing you to get away from whatever it is that's bothering you."

Kurt could see the pain in her eyes and
it hurt him, knowing he'd helped put it
there. But he couldn't back off now. He
couldn't let her crawl back into her
warm, protective cocoon and withdraw

from the world again. He was afraid he'd lose her if that happened.

"Talk to me, Anne," he said, his voice a command.

Tears sparkled in her eyes and she clamped her lips together. Suddenly she pushed herself away from the table and stood up, turning her back to him. Kurt made no effort to follow her, but sat at the table, watching her, giving her all the space she needed.

"I wish I was as certain about things as you are, Kurt," she said, her voice a whisper. "But I'm not. And I never have been." She didn't turn around to let him see the tears in her eyes. "I've been alone all my life. Really alone. So you'll have to excuse me if now, being thrust into a new situation, I'm a little rusty at dealing with people."

"Hell."

His softly spoken curse caused her to turn around, and when she did she saw him getting up from the table. In two strides he was beside her. His hands reached out to grasp her arms and he shook her as he stared down into her eyes.

"Stop feeling sorry for yourself. You're

not alone. You have Mrs. Hargis and Jessica and her husband. They all adore you, whether you've ever noticed it or not. Little Tracy reached out for you, and now Crystal. And I've never seen Gabby fall so completely under anyone's spell as he has yours. And what about your husband? From what I've heard about him, he spent the last years of his life wanting nothing more than to make you happy. It wasn't his fault that you shut him out."

"How dare you say that to me," she cried. She jerked away from him, anger sparking in her eyes. "You don't know anything about Baxter or how he felt. And you don't know anything about me."

"I know you let everyone think you married him for his money."

"I did!"

"No, you didn't. You married him because you'd be safe. And because at last you'd have respect and the home you always wanted . . . someone to take care of you the way your mother and father never did."

"Damn you," she whispered.

"I know you," he insisted softly, his hands digging into her arms and refusing to let her go. "I know you better than you know yourself. I know what you need and what you want. The only thing I can't figure out is why you're so afraid, Anne. Why you're so damned afraid to let anyone in . . . to let anyone love you."

"Because I'm not worth anyone's love," she said, practically shouting at him. "And I know that sooner or later anyone who loves me will only be disappointed, and I couldn't stand that. I couldn't stand being rejected again." She did pull away from him then, only because he let her go. She went to the door and stood staring out into the night, at the glow of security lights that lit the area in the back and beyond toward the barns.

"There," she whispered angrily. "Are you satisfied now?"

She felt his arms on her shoulders, felt him turning her. And she could hear the soothing murmur of his voice as he pulled her into his arms.

"Shh," he whispered, his hand stroking her hair. "It's all right, baby."

She shouldn't have let him hold her, comfort her. But his arms, his voice—this moment was everything she'd been longing for all day. For all her life, it seemed. And she couldn't resist the feelings any longer. She couldn't resist him.

She put her arms around his waist, sighing as her head rested on his chest. She felt his arms tighten around her. She felt his lips on her hair, and she lifted her face for his kiss.

All the anguish she'd been feeling, all the desperation was there in that kiss. She let herself go, simply gave in to all the pleasure of his touch. She had been empty for so long and now that Kurt had come into her life she wasn't sure she could ever go back to the long, agonizing nights of hunger and loneliness.

If she expected him to take her upstairs to bed, she was mistaken. He pulled away reluctantly, touching her face and looking down into her eyes with such tenderness that it took her breath away. Then he took her hand and glanced toward the back door.

"I thought I saw a gazebo out back," he said. "Want to take a walk? Show me around?"

"Yes," she whispered. But when he

went out the door she was frowning at
him, wondering what he had in mind.

Once outside in the fragrant air of the
summer night, he took her hand and
pulled her up beside him as they walked
past the glittering pool and through the
rose garden.

"What did you mean when you said
you didn't want to be rejected again?"

"I . . . did I say that?" she asked,
frowning. "I don't know. I was angry. I—"

"You do know," he said, stopping and
turning to take her in his arms again.

She could feel the length of his body
against hers. He couldn't hide his
arousal, or the fact that he wanted her,
needed her as desperately as she did him.
She couldn't understand why they were
standing here talking instead of doing
something about it.

"Kurt," she began, moving against
him.

She heard him laugh softly and felt
him pull away from her. He did know
her, and he knew exactly what her soft
entreaty meant.

"Do you know that I can't think straight
when I'm around you?" he asked, grin-

ning down at her. He took her hand and pulled her along the pathway again. "That I'm likely to do anything you say? Believe anything?"

How could he feel that way about her? How could this compassionate, wonderful, sexy man possibly feel about her the way she did about him? It was incredible and unbelievable.

"And right now I'd like nothing more than to kiss you and hold you . . ." He stopped, taking a breath, as if he needed to slow down. When he continued his voice was soft and husky with emotion. " . . . make love to you all night. But in the morning I still wouldn't know why you're the way you are. And I wouldn't know who hurt you so badly that now, after all these years, you still won't let anyone get close to you."

"You're close," she said, her voice soft and enticing in the darkness. "Closer than I've ever allowed anyone," she added quietly.

"Don't try to distract me," he said, reaching out to cup her face in his hand. "I want to know, Anne."

They were at the gazebo and now in

the dim glow of the nearby security lights Anne walked up the steps and stood looking down at him.

"Did you see what happened today?" she asked. "With Crystal? I made the mistake of reaching out to her, Kurt . . . of thinking I could help her. And instead I made things worse. She hates me for that."

He stood looking up at her, wishing he could see into her eyes but afraid to move. Afraid he would break the spell and she wouldn't tell him all the things he thought she was about to say.

"No," he said. "She doesn't hate you and you didn't make anything worse."

"Don't patronize me," she said, shaking her head at him. "You want me to be like you. To be caring and understanding and—"

"I want you to be you, Anne. Why do you think you need to be like anyone else?"

"Because I'm not good enough!" she snapped. "Because I always feel as if I'm in over my head. Just like with Crystal. I'm not qualified to help her. I should have known all along that I wasn't. But I wanted to so badly . . ." Her voice trailed away and she turned to go into the gazebo, sitting on the cushioned bench that ran all the way around the interior.

Kurt followed and sat beside her, taking her hands and forcing her to look at him. He could barely make out her features, except for the glint of light in her eyes.

"Baby," he whispered. "What qualifications do you think you need to be her friend? No one expects you to give her advice. Hell, we have a psychologist for that. What she needs is a friend, Anne. Someone who will listen to her, let her cry on her shoulder. Someone who will be good to her, and maybe even love her."

"Oh, Kurt," she whispered, leaning forward until her forehead was resting against his chest. She felt his hand at the back of her neck, strong and warm. "I'm not sure I'm qualified even for that."

"You are," he said, his voice firm and steady. "You're good and kind and compassionate, Anne. Stop being afraid of your own instincts. You're a warm, sweet . . ." He groaned then, pulling her toward him and capturing her soft lips beneath his. "So incredibly, irresistibly sweet . . ."

Anne felt as if she had been waiting for his kiss all her life, and she let herself drown in the sensations of it.

Kurt felt her surrender and knew he couldn't resist the emotions that surged between them any longer, that were always there just beneath the surface. Even at work, in their polite conversations, the power was there. He knew she wanted him just as hotly, just as desperately as he wanted her. And even though he hadn't gotten the entire story out of her, even as he recognized the fact that she always seemed to come to him out of desperation and a need for comfort, he couldn't hold out one second longer.

Twenty-three

Kurt pulled several long, flat cushions
off the benches and threw them into the
middle of the gazebo floor. This time
when they came into each other's arms
there were no preliminaries except their
hungry, breathless kisses and soft sighs.
There was no time and no need for anything more.

Anne thought she might actually die
from the ecstasy of the moment. Never
in her life had she felt the emotions, experienced the sensations she was feeling
with Kurt. The first time had been so
good, and just as surprising . . . but this
was something special and they both
knew it. They were ready, so attuned to
each other that it took only seconds to
reach the stars.

"Oh, Kurt," she gasped as he moved

and teased, as he brought her with him to new heights of sensation.

"Tell me," he whispered against her ear. "Tell me you want me . . . that you want this."

"I do," she answered, his husky, urgent whispers making her feel wild and out of control. "I want you. Oh, how I want you and I need. . . . Oh, Kurt . . . Kurt . . ." She was holding on to him, kissing him, urging him to hold back nothing as she felt herself just at the edge of heaven.

It was a quick, sizzling ride to the stars . . . an explosive, beautiful rocket ride that left Anne breathless and surprised. And then the slow, celestial ride back down.

It was a few seconds before Anne realized she was crying.

"Hey," Kurt whispered huskily, pulling her tight in his arms and reaching for his shirt to drape over them. "What's this?" he asked, feeling her shuddering sobs and touching his fingers to her wet cheeks.

"I . . . I've never felt like this before," she explained, feeling a little foolish.

"I've never experienced anything like this before."

"Never?" he asked. There was a hint of pleasure in his voice, and a touch of surprise as well.

"Not like tonight," she said, her voice soft and filled with awe. "Oh, I've had dreams; I knew what an orgasm felt like before I met you. But it's never happened to me with a man before. Can you imagine . . . I'll turn fifty in a few months. It's taken me this long to find out what the fuss is all about," she whispered, turning to look at him.

"Was it worth the wait?" he said, chuckling softly.

"*You* were worth the wait," she said. She turned her face against his chest. Even in the darkness, she felt a little awkward to be talking about such an intimate subject. "It was you," she whispered, feeling a bit shy.

"Well," he said with a satisfied sigh and a soft grunt of laughter.

He turned over and lay on his back, looking up at the hole in the center of the gazebo roof. They could see the stars now and the misty white trail of the Milky Way.

"I'd love to take the credit," he said, turning his head to look at her. "But it's you . . . you're changing, Anne. Did you ever think that you might be less inhibited now?"

"Not the way I felt today at the halfway house," she said. "I felt as if I'd stepped back forty years. All I wanted to do was crawl into bed and go to sleep and forget Angels Incorporated and the halfway house, forget Crystal and all the rest."

"Forty years?" he asked. "What happened forty years ago?"

For a moment there were only the quiet sounds of the night around them. The whisper of crickets and tree frogs, the lowing sound of cattle down by the creek, the soft murmur of a car now and then on the main road. Kurt almost held his breath as he waited, wondering if Anne would pull away again and retreat into the safety of her self-imposed shell the way she always did.

"It wasn't one specific thing, I guess. I just meant that today I felt like a child. A child who had done something wrong and knew she would be ridiculed and criticized even though she had done her best."

"You have done your best," he said, tightening his arm around her. "Who criticized you, baby?" he asked, his voice quiet and steady. "Was it your father?"

He didn't know why he asked that, except for her obvious distrust of men and that he wanted to give her a place to start.

"No," she whispered. "I never knew my father. He left when I was too young to remember. From what my mother said he was a sorry excuse for a man, and I'm probably better off for never knowing him."

"I don't know about that. I think a child needs a father," Kurt said. "Especially a daughter. Have you ever tried to find him?"

"No," she said, frowning into the darkness. "I never wanted to."

"Then it was your mother?" he asked. "The one who criticized?"

"Oh, yes," she said, letting the words hiss between her teeth with a sigh. "My mother."

"She's not still alive, though," he said, meaning it as a question.

"Yes," Anne said, her voice bitter and soft. "My mother is very much alive. She's in a retirement village near Stone Mountain. She's crippled with arthritis, but her mind is as alert . . . and as self-centered as ever. She's a cold, uncaring, unfeeling woman."

Kurt watched her eyes. This was it. This was what he wanted to know.

"Stone Mountain," he said casually. "That's more than a hundred miles from here. So I assume you don't see her often?"

"I don't see her at all," Anne said. "Well, a few times a year at the most."

"What did she do to hurt you so much?" Kurt asked. He propped up on one elbow, looking down into her face as she lay looking through the opening at the sky.

He could just make out in the dim light that she had closed her eyes. And that the look on her face was one of painful remembrance.

"Everything she could," she whispered. "She was never satisfied with me, and she let me know it in so many cruel, sarcastic ways. Every day of my life. I was never pretty enough or smart enough to suit her. I was overweight, like Crystal." She turned to look up into his eyes, seeing his understanding and sympathy, and loving him for it. She could trust him. This was the one man she knew she could trust. And even now, admitting that to herself, she was still reluctant.

"She tried everything to make me lose weight," Anne said. "She ridiculed me, told me how ugly fat girls were, just like Crystal's mother. I can't remember ever putting a bite of food into my mouth without her telling me I didn't need it. Consequently, I ate in secret. I hid food, just the way Crystal is doing. And the harder I tried to stop eating, the hungrier I became. I always felt hungry, as if I could never get enough to eat. Sometimes I still feel that way. It's something I have to fight every day of my life."

"I'm sorry," he whispered, touching her cheek and tracing his finger down to her lips. "I'd give anything if I could make it all go away."

"I know I should be over it by now," she said, frowning. "If I were stronger, I

would have been able to put all this behind me by now."

"Don't be so hard on yourself. You're
human. We all have something we have
to struggle with."

"Oh, yeah?" she asked, smiling finally.
"What's your cross?"

"Thinning hair," he said, grinning
down at her.

"Oh . . . you," she said, reaching over
to kiss him. "You're beautiful and you
would be even if you were bald."

"I'm glad you said that because I probably will be one day," he said, laughing.

She felt a little catch in her throat at
his insinuation that she would be in his
life if that day ever came.

"Actually, I was the athletic type when
I was growing up. Played football and
baseball all through high school and later
in college. Even ran a little track. And I
was quiet. A lot of people seemed to
think I was a bit slow . . . you know, not
quite as smart as someone who wasn't a
jock."

"Well, how foolish," she said. "You're
one of the brightest, most intelligent men
I've ever met."

"That's my point," he said. "Just because someone slaps a label on you, it doesn't necessarily mean that's what you are."

"Well, unfortunately, my mother's labels have stuck," she said with a sigh. "But I do understand what you're saying. When I look back at pictures of myself I can see that I wasn't really fat at all. Not more than a few pounds overweight, at least. Certainly nothing worth the agony I put myself through because of it. I've often wondered if my thinking I was fat made me that way. Does that sound crazy?"

"It doesn't sound crazy at all. What is it they call it—a self-fulfilling prophecy? Besides, you couldn't sound crazy if you tried." He pulled her close and brushed his mouth against her lips. "And you're pretty damned sexy, too," he teased.

"Kurt," she said, looking at him with a new intensity, "you mentioned a psychologist for Crystal. Do you think I could work with him . . . or her . . . that I could really help them with Crystal and her problems?"

He didn't say anything for a long while. But as he looked into her eyes, she could see the warmth and the look of pleased approval.

"I think that would be terrific. You see," he said, touching her cheek. "You understand Crystal and I'm convinced you can help her if you keep trying."

"Oh, I need you to keep telling me that," she said. Even now she was afraid she would fail. And more than that she was afraid she would disappoint him.

"I will," he promised. "I'll be here . . . until you tell me to get lost, anyway," he teased.

"I can't imagine that," she whispered, moving closer to him.

They lay for a long while in each other's arms, looking up at the night sky and feeling the warm breeze against their naked skin.

"Anne," Kurt said finally. "Have you ever talked to your mother about your childhood? Ever told her how you felt?"

"No," she said, moving her head against his shoulder. "We don't talk about things like that. If I ever brought up anything that was emotional, or hard to deal with, she'd just pretend I never said anything."

"Have you ever thought that this might be as hard on her as it is on you? That she might want to make her peace with you before she dies?"

"No," Anne said, frowning at him. "You just don't know her," she added. "Take my word for it, my mother has never considered her remarks or her aloofness as anything that would hurt me. She probably doesn't even remember it. She doesn't like me very much, that's all; she never has. If I learned anything from her treatment of me, it's that not every woman is a good mother."

"You don't have to convince me of that, not in the line of work I'm in. I see it every day."

Anne said nothing for a while, but Kurt watched her, seeing the thoughtful expression on her face.

"Is that why you never wanted children?" he asked softly.

She turned quickly to look at him, staring at his face and trying to see his eyes in the dim light.

"Is it any wonder? I swore I'd never do to a child what she did to me. Never."

"Do you really think you could ever be

that way?" he asked. His eyes told her he
didn't believe it.

"Of course I thought it. I was convinced of it. I'm her daughter," she whispered.

"You're not like that, Anne," he said,
his smile sweet and understanding.

"You didn't seem to think that when
you first met me."

He laughed. "Self-protection doesn't
count. I saw through that right away."

"No, you didn't," she whispered.

"Yes," he said, grinning. "I did."

She smiled then, shaking her head at
him.

"You always make me laugh," she said.
"And you always manage to make me see
that things aren't as dark as I think."

They were quiet for a long while, content to lie peacefully in each other's
arms, watching the stars twinkling above
them.

"Maybe we'll drive to Stone Mountain
one Sunday," Kurt said, breaking the silence. "I'll go with you to see her."

"No," Anne said quickly, pulling away
from him. "I don't want to go see her
and I'm not going to. I certainly don't

intend ever to confront her with how I feel. And please, don't think because I've told you all this that you can change it. You can't, Kurt."

"All right," he said, reaching for her again. "All right. It was just a suggestion."

But he could feel her withdrawing from him. Even though she had shared some of her deepest, most troubling feelings with him, she was stepping back again, pulling away into her own protective little world.

All he could do was wait. Wait and hope that he could help her finally get over it. And that working with Crystal would help her come to grips finally with her own similar childhood experience.

His ex-wife had often told him that he was an impatient man, that he was too emotional in his decisions and subject to acting too quickly. And he had to admit that he could be domineering and pushy, but it was only because there was so much to be done, so much to accomplish.

His divorce had changed a lot of that. It had forced him to step back and take a long, critical look at himself and his actions. He hadn't liked some of what he saw.

Even with Anne, he found himself feeling impatient, wanting to help her *now*. Wanting to see the pain gone from her beautiful eyes. Wanting to see a smile on her face all the time.

And he wanted to be the one to put it there.

He sat up and looked down at her.

"Hey," he said softly. "How are you at making coffee?"

"Me? Well, pretty good, if I do say so myself."

"Mrs. Hargis told me she left a blackberry cobbler in the oven. Do you know how long it's been since I had blackberry cobbler?"

She smiled up at him and reached for her clothes.

"With vanilla ice cream," she said.

"Ummm," he said, laughing. "I'll race you back to the house."

"Jock," she said, pushing against him, her smile teasing and warm.

"Come on, woman," he said, pushing his legs into his jeans. "Time's a'wastin' and this man's hungry."

When they were dressed and the cushions were back in place Anne came to him and put her arms around his waist. They stood beneath the roof opening with the stars sparkling high above them.

"Kurt," she whispered, suddenly serious, "I don't ever want to talk about this again . . . what I've told you tonight. It's too painful and—"

"You need to talk about it, Anne," he said, his voice infinitely patient but firm.

"I know you're right," she said. "I probably do. But it has to be on my own terms. When I decide."

"I won't push it," he promised. "But you know I'm always here if you want to talk. About that, or anything else that bothers you."

"Oh," she said, with a long, peaceful sigh. "You can't imagine how good it feels knowing that. You can't imagine."

"I think I can," he said, kissing her. "Now . . . let's go eat!"

They walked arm in arm back toward the house.

Twenty-four

It was late when Kurt finally left. Anne walked him through the house to the front porch, where he gently nudged her back against one of the huge columns and kissed her long and hard.

"I don't want you to go," she whispered against his mouth.

"Don't tempt me," he groaned. "I want to go by the house before going home. Just to make sure Mrs. Howard hasn't locked any of the children in the closet."

"Oh," she said, laughing. "Don't even say such a thing. I swear that woman really gets to me."

"She's not my favorite person either," he admitted. "But she's all we've got. But just between you and me, I'm looking for the Howards' replacement."

"Oh, thank goodness," she said. "I didn't want to interfere, but—"

"Go ahead—interfere," he said. He was still holding her against the column with his body and now he pressed against her. "I like it when you get bossy."

"And I like it when you get sexy," she murmured, putting her arms around his neck.

"Umm, I've gotta get out of here . . . quick." He laughed and gave her a light kiss at the corner of her mouth. Then he pulled away and trotted down the steps, looking back at her with a reluctant grin.

Anne followed him down the steps, not wanting him to go. He turned around and, with a soft laugh, swept her into his arms, kissing her as if he couldn't bear to leave her.

This time when he pulled away his look was serious.

"Lady," he murmured, his voice husky, "you've got my head in a spin."

"Me, too," she whispered.

He moved away from her, holding her hand until the last moment and looking into her eyes with a bemused smile.

"Don't come one step farther," he warned, his voice half teasing, half serious.

"I won't."

"I'll see you tomorrow."

She watched him drive around the circle toward the main highway, sighing when she saw the blink of the truck's taillights. For a moment she thought he might come back, and her heart accelerated. Then she heard the murmur of his truck's engine and saw the lights heading toward town. She sighed again and glanced up at the stars, the same stars that had shone above them in the gazebo. Then she ran back into the house.

It was different this time. She felt no guilt, no confusion about their lovemaking. It was all she could think about as she took a long, leisurely bubble bath. He was all she could see, all she could feel, and each time his face appeared before her she felt a little tingle of pleasure in the pit of her stomach.

She hadn't felt this way in years. In fact, she didn't think she had ever felt this way before.

"God," she murmured, sitting up in the tub. "I'm not falling in love, am I?" Then she slid back down, smiling and letting the warm water from her sponge run down her shoulders and arms.

"What if I am?" she asked, staring into space and considering all the possibilities. "Would that be so awful?"

Somehow tonight, with the memory of Kurt's hands and body, with the taste of him still on her lips, she couldn't imagine anything awful about it.

She couldn't remember ever being so happy.

The next morning at work, they were all very busy. Several new children had been brought in overnight and Vivian was busy helping Mrs. Howard prepare rooms.

Gabby and Anne did all the kitchen work. Over the past few weeks she had begun helping him with the cooking when he needed her to, and she found that she enjoyed it, although she had never done a lot before.

"You're gettin' downright good at this," Gabby said, tasting the soup Anne had made.

"Well, don't tell anyone," she said, smiling at him, "but I enjoy it."

"Guess your headache's gone away today," he said, lifting his brows in a curious look.

"Yes. The first migraine I've had in a long time."

"Hell, old prune face is enough to give anybody a headache. I don't like that woman one bit. And I like her weaseling little husband even less. If he was a real man he'd have put a stop to her crazy ways a long time ago. Heck, I was so mad I even thought about taking a drink last night."

Anne looked at him. He was concentrating on the soup, but she thought she heard a note of concern in his gruff old voice.

"Gabby? Are you serious? You . . . you didn't, did you?"

"Hell no," he snapped. "Do I look drunk to you? If I'da had one drink I wouldn't be here today. I'd be in a bar somewhere gettin' good and soused. I said I *thought* about it."

She walked to him and placed her hand on his frail arm.

"If you ever need someone to talk to."

"I know," he said gruffly. "I know." He

moved away from her, pretending to be busy at something else.

He didn't fool her. She understood him more than he might think; for all their obvious differences, they were alike—both scared to death of life.

But Anne said nothing. She knew he would only deny it, and it would embarrass him if she told him such a thing.

Anne had only seen Kurt a couple of times during the morning. When they looked at each other today there was a new warmth between them, a sweet intimacy that stirred Anne's heart and made her legs feel weak. She found herself longing to reach out and touch him. To run her fingers down his chest when he stood in the kitchen talking to her and Gabby.

She was sure he could see it in her eyes. Just as she was sure he felt it, too, what was between them—that sweet and hot, sensual feeling that hung in the air, that shared experience that no one else knew about. For one moment she felt a deep well of sadness that she'd had to wait so long to have this with a man. To share the most wonderful, intimate feelings of her life.

But Kurt's smile quickly shook that feeling away. How could she be sad when he looked at her that way? When he affirmed with his eyes all the good things she was feeling?

They ate lunch together in the backyard, even though the weather was sweltering. Vivian ate with them, and Anne was certain she saw the new excitement between them, but she said nothing.

"I think I should tell you," Kurt said after they'd finished eating, "Crystal's mother is out of jail and she's coming over this afternoon to see her daughter."

"No," Anne said, instantly alert. "How can that be? How can they let her do that after the way she treated Crystal?"

"She is her mother," Kurt said with a shake of his head. But his eyes told her he understood her fear. "I'm afraid there's nothing we can do about it. But I don't intend to leave the woman alone with Crystal. Not for one second. If you'd like to—"

"I would," Anne said, knowing what he was going to say before he finished. "I'll stay with Crystal every second that her mother is here."

"Good," he said. His hazel eyes twinkled in the sunlight, and there were tiny crinkled lines at the edges. "I was hoping you'd say that."

The afternoon seemed interminable. Every time Anne heard a noise she'd look toward the door or walk to the dining room and peek out toward the entry hall.

"Where is she?" she muttered to herself.

"Probably out gettin' herself a drink," Gabby said.

"Oh, Gabby, don't say that."

"Well, now, I'd be willin' to bet it's alcohol that makes the woman so mean. Booze changes a person's entire personality. Makes some meaner'n a pit bull."

Anne slumped down into a chair, exhausted from waiting and wondering. "Were you like that, Gabby?" she asked. She grinned at him suddenly, thinking how much she had grown to like him over the past few weeks. "I don't know how you could be much meaner."

"Huh," he grunted. "Nope, I wasn't a mean drunk, although my ex-wife might disagree about that. I can't remember much about bein' married to that woman. And that's a blessin', I reckon," he said with a cluck and a shake of his head.

Anne laughed out loud then.

"But my daddy was."

Gabby's voice had turned very soft, very low, and it captured Anne's complete attention. She sat still, waiting and watching Gabby as he worked.

"Meaner'n a son of a gun," he muttered. "When I was a little kid I swore that when I grew up I'd beat the livin' hell out of him, just for practice, and for all the things he done to us kids when we was little and helpless."

"And did you?" Anne asked, her voice quiet.

"Yeah, I did," he said. He looked up then, and there was a strange light in his eyes, a mixture of pride and regret.

"Come in one day, he was beatin' my ma. She was a little slip of a woman. She wouldn't never say nothin' back to him. I guess she knew if she did what she'd get. My daddy was drunk . . . and he was mad. Mad at the world, I guess," he said, glancing at Anne again. "I was sixteen and bigger than he was, though that wasn't sayin' much," he said with a humorless laugh.

"I tore into him, not even thinkin' that he was my pa, not thinkin' about nothin'." Gabby stopped and shook his head, and there was a terrible fear in his eyes.

"Lord, I was mad that day."

"What happened?"

"I beat the hell out of him, that's what," he said, looking at her with a kind of surprise that she didn't already know that. "And I told him if he ever touched my ma again or any of the littler kids, I'd kill him. And I meant it. He left a few days later . . . and he never came back."

"Oh, Gabby," Anne whispered.

How powerless they all seemed in stopping themselves from self-destruction, she thought. Here was Gabby, hating his father's drinking and yet becoming a drunk himself. And she wasn't much better, resenting her mother's coldness all these years and now, at the age of forty-nine, finding that she herself had become cold and withdrawn from the world. And so much of it was from some deep-seated fear that was directly related to their childhood.

"I'm not going to be like my mother," she whispered. "Not any more."

"What?" he asked.

"Just like you finally decided to stop drinking and not follow in your father's footsteps, I'm going to stop running from my mother's shadow. I don't want to be like her, Gabby, any more than you wanted to be like your dad."

"Then don't," he said, nodding his head with approval. "Don't know anything about your ma, but I know you, girl. And I'd say you can do anything you set your mind to."

"I can," she said, feeling empowered, really empowered for the first time in her life.

"Listen, I can finish up here in the kitchen if you want to go on up to that girl's room."

"Crystal," she said, smiling at him.

"Yeah, whatever," he said, grinning. "Go on, git outta here."

Twenty-five

Anne heard voices at the front of the house. Kurt's quiet, deep rumble and another—the strident, high-pitched voice of a woman. She glanced at Gabby and took a deep breath, then headed toward the dining room.

When she saw Crystal's mother she was surprised. The woman was young and rather frail-looking, with darkly tanned thin arms sticking out of a sleeveless blouse. Her hair was the same light color as Crystal's and it hung limply down over her ears and around her face.

But it was her eyes that captured all Anne's attention. They were hard and cold and filled with an almost uncontrolled rage.

"Where's my kid?" she asked. "I've come to see my daughter."

"She's upstairs in her room," Kurt said, his voice quiet and calm.

He saw Anne then and motioned her forward.

"This is Mrs. Benefield. She'll go with you and remain in the room while you talk to Crystal."

"Oh, no," the woman said, her sharp eyes turning toward Anne.

Anne shivered at the look of cold hatred directed toward her.

"Ain't nobody comin' between me and my kid. I don't need a watchdog. She's my daughter and it's my right and—"

"Let's get something straight, Mrs. Raburn," Kurt said. He stepped toward Crystal's mother, and Anne could see the slow clenching and unclenching of his jaw. His eyes bored into the woman, stopping her protests completely.

"As far as I'm concerned, you have no rights. You gave them up the first time you abused that little girl. Now, I know what the court said, and I can't stop you from seeing her, but I'll be damned if I'm going to leave you alone with her. Is that clear?"

"You can't—" she began.

"I can and I will. You're in my territory now, Mrs. Raburn, and like it or not, what I say here goes."

"I'll . . . I'll get a court order," she threatened, staring at him with hatred.

"Go ahead." Kurt waved a hand toward the front door, daring the defiant woman to do as she'd threatened.

Instead she clamped her lips together. She looked from Kurt to Anne; then, with a flounce, she stalked past them and up the stairs.

Anne followed, and as she passed Kurt, he reached out for her hand, giving it a squeeze that made her feel warm all over. But for all his assurance and the light in his eyes that told her he believed in her, she thought she was more nervous than she'd ever been in her life.

Crystal's mother stopped at the top of the stairs, waiting for Anne to show her to the room. Anne stepped around her and knocked on Crystal's door. When the door opened the girls who roomed with Crystal looked up with wide, curious eyes at the two women, then silently moved past them and down the stairs. They had known Crystal's mother was coming.

She saw Crystal then, sitting on the bed, her head bent, her hair hanging over her eyes.

"Crystal, honey?" Mrs. Raburn said. There was such a change in the woman's tone of voice that Anne could hardly believe it.

Anne sat down in a chair across the room, watching as the woman went to Crystal and sat on the bed beside her. She put an arm around the child's shoulders, and Crystal made no attempt to pull away. But her head came up and she looked directly at Anne. There was a pleading look in her eyes that took Anne by surprise. Crystal really was afraid of her mother. Anne smiled at Crystal, hoping her presence would somehow reassure her. But she wasn't at all certain it did.

"Baby?" Mrs. Raburn said. "Look at you. You're so pretty in that new dress. Did they give it to you?"

Crystal nodded and glanced at Anne.

"Well, it's real pretty. Makes you look more slender. You know, I bet if you tried, you could lose some more weight before I come to get you for good. Then we'll go out and buy you a whole new set of clothes. What do you say?"

Anne sat forward in the chair. "Mrs. Raburn," she said, "Crystal is only ten. I don't think at that age she needs to be concerned about her weight."

The woman whirled around, her eyes glittering. "You stay out of this," she hissed. "I don't need you or that high-handed man downstairs tellin' me anything about my own kid."

Anne could see the fear in Crystal's eyes, could see her pulling back from her mother. That fear was the only thing that kept Anne from making a reply. She didn't want to make things worse for the little girl than they already were.

"Now," Mrs. Raburn said, turning back to Crystal with an instant change in her voice. "You know, honey, what I did the other day, that was for your own good. You know that, don't you? You have to learn to listen to me, and I did it because I want you to be pretty. You'll like yourself better."

Crystal hung her head, saying nothing, and Anne felt the anger rising in her.

How could the woman manipulate her own child this way?

"When you don't mind your mama you have to be punished." The woman laughed then, as if the entire affair was a joke, but the sound of it was unreal and forced. "Why, you could have got back in the house any time you wanted if you tried. Now, ain't that the truth?"

Crystal shrugged her shoulders, still saying nothing.

"I have to go to court next week," the woman continued. "And if they find me guilty, they're going to stick me in jail. In a dark, lonely cell where—"

"Mrs. Raburn," Anne cautioned.

The woman glared at Anne, then turned her attention back to Crystal.

"I guess it won't be so bad, bein' in jail," Mrs. Raburn said. "But the worst part is, you won't have a home, or a mama to take care of you."

"Mrs. Raburn . . ." Anne said again. How was she going to get the woman to stop saying such hurtful, manipulative things to Crystal? And how could she confront her about it in front of the child without making things worse?

Crystal's head came up then, and Anne saw the tears in her blue eyes. She looked directly at Anne, her eyes pleading and filled with fear.

"It's all right, honey," Anne said, moving to the edge of her seat. "You don't have to do anything you don't want to do."

"Don't you listen to her, Crystal," Mrs. Raburn said, tossing her hair back from her face. She reached down to her purse and drew out a pack of cigarettes.

"I'm afraid there's no smoking in here," Anne said, her voice hard and filled with warning. She was growing more and more exasperated with the overbearing woman.

Mrs. Raburn made a small sound of disgust and cursed beneath her breath before sticking the cigarettes back in her bag.

"What you've got to do," she continued, turning back to Crystal, "is help me out of this mess, sweetie." Her voice had lost some of its phony sweetness and patience; now it was clipped and rang with anger, the way it had downstairs. "You can even go to court if you want to . . ." She leaned toward Crystal, her face only inches from her daughter's as she stared into her eyes. ". . . and you can tell the judge that it was all a mistake, that you went outside on your own after I was asleep and accidentally got locked out of the house."

Tears rolled down Crystal's face, but she shook her head. She was trembling from head to toe as she looked into her mother's eyes.

"Oh, for goodness sake," Mrs. Raburn said, taking Crystal's arm and shaking her. "Stop that damned cryin'. I swear to God, you cry almost as much as you eat."

"That's enough!" Anne was on her feet and in two steps she was beside the woman, standing over her like an avenging angel.

Without thinking, she reached down and grabbed the woman's shirtfront, pulling her up from the bed and dragging her toward the middle of the room. Mrs. Raburn stared at Anne with a shocked expression as she stood with her shirt gaping open and one of the buttons hanging by a thread. She didn't seem to know what to say.

"Get out of here," Anne hissed through her teeth, staring hard at the woman. "You get your things and get. And don't you ever—ever!—belittle Crystal that way again. And don't you ever ask her to lie for you, either."

It had happened so quickly that the woman seemed stunned. But now she fought back, pulling away from Anne and standing with her arms back and her chin jutting forward in a defensive stance.

"Why, you old bitch," the woman said, her eyes sparking dangerously. "You can't talk to me like this."

Anne could see Mrs. Raburn's hands clenching into fists, and although once the possibility of a confrontation would have frightened her, today it only made her angrier. She wasn't afraid. She was so mad, she thought she would beat the woman to a pulp if she took even one step toward her.

"Get out," Anne repeated quietly, stepping toward the woman. Anne was taller and heavier, and at the moment, while the adrenaline rushed through her body, she felt as if she could handle a cage full of tigers. "And don't come back. Crystal is loved here and she's going to be taken care of. And the last thing she's going to do is appear in court and lie to save your worthless neck."

The woman actually growled, a low, menacing sound as she stared into Anne's eyes.

Anne walked to the door and opened it, staring hard at the woman.

"I mean it," she said, motioning through the opening. "Out."

"You can't do this to me," Mrs. Raburn said, her eyes disbelieving. "I'll sue your ass. I'll—"

"You do that," Anne said. "But just re-member—you're not the only one who can get a court order."

"Why . . . you're . . . you're threaten-ing me," the woman said, her voice a whisper of disbelief.

"Yes," Anne said, smiling coldly. "That's exactly what I'm doing. The only difference is, I mean it."

"Well, damn you," the woman said. She walked through the door, turning to glare back at Anne. "You'll pay for this, lady. I'll see to it."

"Have at it, honey," Anne said, slam-ming the door with a loud bang in the woman's face.

She turned to Crystal, and suddenly she felt quite proud of herself. Crystal was still sitting on the bed but her face had changed. Her eyes were wide and disbelieving, her face open and animated for the first time. Suddenly she jumped up and ran to Anne, throwing herself into her arms and clamping her arms around Anne's waist.

She could feel the child trembling still, and slowly Anne began to relax, putting her arms around Crystal as she stroked her hair and murmured soothing words to her.

She heard the door open and saw Kurt come in, his brow furrowed as he looked at her, his eyes questioning.

"Are you all right?"

"You heard?"

"Yeah. I was right outside the door. You didn't think I was going to leave you up here by yourself, did you?"

Anne smiled, loving him more than she'd ever thought possible.

"We're just fine." She glanced down at Crystal, who still clung to Anne's waist. "It was a little scary, but we did just fine, didn't we?"

Crystal looked up, her head still against Anne's breast as she nodded, smiling shyly from Anne to Kurt.

"Whew," Kurt said. There was a warm look of admiration in his eyes. "I sure could use something to drink. How about you two? Want to go downstairs and see what Gabby has stashed in the refrigerator?"

Anne lifted her brows questioningly at Crystal. The girl smiled and nodded. Anne took her hand and the three of them went downstairs.

She could see the relief on Gabby's weathered old face when they entered the kitchen.

"Well," he said, looking from one of them to the other, "you three look like the cats that swallowed the canaries. Things went good?"

"Things went good," Anne said, meeting Kurt's glance.

Crystal actually giggled then, and it seemed to surprise even her. Anne imagined it was sheer nerves that made her do it, but the sound of it made Anne feel a warm rush of love and sympathy for the little girl. She was so young, yet already she had suffered so much.

"We're thirsty," Anne said, giving Gabby a meaningful look.

"Got just the thing," he said, turning to the refrigerator.

They watched as he took out four brown bottles with no labels. He opened the caps, which emitted a light hissing sound. With the necks of the frosty bottles between his fingers, he carried them to Anne and Kurt and Crystal.

Anne frowned, staring hard at the brown beer bottles.

"Gabby," she said, protesting quietly under her breath.

"Root beer," he said, grinning at her. "Made it myself. Best root beer this side of Chicago."

Anne began to chuckle. She felt silly and relieved . . . and happy. Soon Kurt and Gabby joined in the laughter, and Crystal stood smiling at them as if she didn't quite get the joke. But there was a sweetness in her eyes, a childlike sweetness that Anne hadn't seen until now.

They all took the icy bottles and Kurt held his forward, proposing a toast.

"To good homemade root beer," he said, smiling first at Anne and then at Crystal. "And even better friends."

"I'll drink to that," Gabby muttered, clinking his bottle against Kurt's.

There was an odd look on Crystal's face, one of wonder and discovery as she joined in, shyly reaching forward to clink her bottle against Anne's.

"To friends," Anne said softly, smiling down at the little girl.

"And feisty women," Gabby added, his look admiring and obviously meant for Anne.

She thought it was one of the best compliments she'd ever received.

Twenty-six

The elation Anne felt over her small triumph didn't last long. But then, she had suspected it wouldn't, realizing the kind of person Crystal's mother was.

The woman phoned several times that afternoon, demanding to speak to Crystal. Kurt told Anne that he had refused to let her speak to the girl, giving some excuse each time.

"But I can't continue doing that forever," he said, rubbing his chin worriedly. He sighed. "No matter what I think of the woman, or how Crystal feels about her, she has a legal right to see her and talk to her on the phone."

"Can't we do anything to change that?"

"Not until she's declared a ward of the court and eligible for foster care. And even then it's not a sure thing."

"But why? How can this woman do this

to an innocent child, Kurt? Crystal is so sweet, and I know she's intelligent. Did you know that she's been moved so much that she doesn't even know what grade she's in in school? That she's ashamed because she's so far behind the other kids her age?"

"I know," he said, shaking his head. "I'm having a tutor brought in for her. You'd be surprised how many of these children come here unable to read or write."

"I don't think I'm surprised about anything anymore," Anne said wistfully.

"Come here," Kurt said, moving closer to her.

They were in his office, and for a moment she wished they could close the door, close out the rest of the world and be alone together. She felt the spark the moment he touched her, the moment he looked into her eyes and smiled.

"You did a wonderful job today with Crystal and her mother," he said, touching her cheek. "But I know how much it cost you, so if you want to go on home, your boss is giving his wholehearted approval."

"I appreciate that," she said, teasingly. "But I'd appreciate it even more if the boss would go home with me. I have a gazebo I think he'd really be interested in seeing."

He groaned slightly, then laughed. "That is an offer I can't refuse . . . almost."

"Almost?" she asked, looking into his eyes and seeing his regret.

"I have to go to Smithville tonight. They want me to help set up the guidelines for the new halfway house there. I told you about it—remember?"

"Yes, I remember. But oh," she said, giving him a halfhearted smile. "I'm so disappointed."

"So am I," he whispered. He glanced toward the open doorway and only touched her cheek briefly as they heard the sound of the children in the family room.

"I'll call you when I get back."

"Good," she said, looking into his eyes and thinking how much she hated leaving him. "I'll be waiting. I do think I'll take you up on that offer to go home now."

Just then they heard Mrs. Howard's

voice at the doorway, and both of them turned toward her.

"Mr. Bonner?" she said. Her eyes took in their closeness and she lifted her brow disapprovingly as her gaze moved down Anne's body and back up again. "Vivian and I have the nursery ready now if you'd like to come up and see."

"Sure," he said. "Anne . . . go home. I'll see you in the morning."

"I'm on my way," she said, turning with a little wave and heading toward the door. She didn't bother looking at Mrs. Howard as she passed. She knew all she'd see on that woman's face was disapproval. And she was feeling too good for disapproval tonight. Much too good.

She hadn't been home long when the phone rang. Halfway hoping it was Kurt and that he hadn't had to go to Smithville after all, she sounded expectant when she answered.

"Hello?"

"Well, you're home," Cecile said. "I swear, every time I call you're either working or out to dinner with that very handsome man you call your boss."

"I've only been out to dinner with Kurt once," Anne said, laughing.

"Ah, I'm dying to hear all about it."

"And where have you been?" Anne asked. "I've tried calling you several times this week, too."

"That's one of the reasons I called. Barney and I have been out of town. He had some business in Atlanta and I went with him. Did a little shopping while he worked. I must say I enjoyed it very much."

"You too still have as much fun as when you were first married, don't you?"

"Well, it might be at a little slower pace now. We're not quite so frantic about having fun as we were when we were younger. But yes, we do," Cecile said, obviously delighted.

"I envy you," Anne said.

"Good Lord, am I hearing things?"

Anne laughed when she heard Cecile's nails tapping on her phone.

"Is this thing out of order? Anne Benefield is actually envious of an old— and I mean *old*—married couple."

"Hey, early fifties aren't so old. Not anymore. And yes, you heard correctly."

"That Kurt Bonner must really be getting to you." Cecile's voice sounded sly and mischievous.

"Hmmm," Anne said, laughing good-naturedly. "Could be."

"God, it's good to hear you laugh, hon. I want to hear all about it, and soon. If you ever decide to stay at home, give me a call."

"I will. Maybe this weekend. I'm glad you called."

Anne sighed as she hung up the phone. Just talking about Kurt and admitting to herself how happy she was brought a sharp little twinge of fear to her chest. But it was fainter, farther back in the recesses now, and she thought that was good. It was a beginning.

Imagine that—a new beginning for someone like her at this stage of her life.

Anne couldn't sleep. She supposed it was because she was waiting for Kurt's call, and she was restless. She felt lonely for him, as if he should be here, as if she had been used to sleeping in his arms forever.

"What has that man done to me?" she whispered, her thoughts going back to his sweet, powerful lovemaking.

She loved him; that was all there was to it. She had tried to remain aloof and uninvolved, but it hadn't worked. How could it have worked with a man like Kurt? She shook her head at the thought, feeling the old fears returning, the old reluctance to believe in anything or anyone. She didn't know him that well, she told herself. What if he didn't feel the same way? What if this was just an interlude for him . . . a passing physical attraction that would end when he grew tired of her?

But Kurt wasn't like that. She knew he wasn't. It was just her old inhibitions returning, her old self-doubts coming back to plague her because she dared to be happy for once in her life.

"It's going to be all right," she said. *"I'm* going to be all right. If it's meant to be, it will happen. And if not," she whispered, her eyes growing dark and stormy, "if not, then I'll still have some of the best memories of my life."

Just then the phone by her bed rang and she jumped, reaching to answer it in the same movement.

"Hello?"

"Hey, you sound sleepy. I hope I didn't

wake you." His voice was warm and close, and the sound of it sent tingles down her spine.

"No, I wasn't asleep," she said. "Just lying here thinking, and waiting for you to call."

"I wish I was there," he said, his voice husky with emotion.

"Oh, so do I," she whispered. "So do I."

There was a long pause and Anne realized that her fingers had tightened on the receiver as she held it tightly against her ear.

"Anne," he said slowly, "tell me if I'm going too fast. I know this is all new for you, and I don't want to do anything to scare you away."

"I think it's too late for that," she said, smiling to herself.

"God," he said, "I haven't been able to think of anything except you since—"

"I know," she said, holding the phone close. "Me, too."

"I can't believe you're admitting it," he said. There was a hint of laughter and surprise in his voice.

"I'm scared to death," she said. "But

yes, I'm admitting that I'm totally, completely involved with you, Mr. Bonner."

He laughed then, his voice a soft, husky sound over the phone. He was pleased; he couldn't hide that fact.

"Well," he said. "This is a red-letter day. The cynical, standoffish Mrs. Benefield is involved, at long last."

"Very involved," she whispered. She took a deep, shuddering breath. "All I know is that I have never felt this way about anyone in my life. I can't think about anything except you. I hate to leave you at night and can't wait to see you in the morning. I've lost my appetite; I can't sleep. I'm a mess."

"You're beautiful, and you're hardly a mess," he said. "You're kind and good and decent. And from now on I don't want to hear any negatives when you're talking about the woman I—"

Anne waited, holding her breath.

"I'm involved with," he said, his voice quiet.

"All right."

"Well," he said, laughing again. "That was easy."

"You're a powerful persuader, sir," she

teased. "How was Smithville?" she asked. "Let's change the subject before I do something I promised myself I'd never do."

"What's that?" he asked, his voice intimate and soft.

"Beg," she whispered. "I find myself wanting to beg you to come over even though I know we should wait . . . give ourselves a little time to take all this in."

"You don't have to beg me for anything," he replied, his voice tender. "Anything I have is yours . . . for the asking."

"Oh, my," she sighed.

"But maybe you're right," he said. "Maybe we should give ourselves plenty of time. And I'm only saying this because of you, Anne. Personally, if it was up to me—I'd be there in ten quick minutes, and I would never leave again. But I want you to be sure. Really sure about what you want. I don't want you hurt and I don't want you disappointed . . . ever. Not by anyone, but most importantly not by me."

She closed her eyes, feeling her lips

tremble at his words, at the genuine concern in his voice when he said them.

She wanted to say the words then because she actually felt them in her heart, in the deepest part of her soul. But her past had taught her to be wary and she held the words in, only managing to offer a sweet, soft goodbye.

"I'll see you in the morning," he said.

Only after she had hung up the phone and lay back in bed, staring at the ceiling, could she say the words that were in her heart, that had almost slipped past her lips a few moments ago.

"I love you," she whispered, testing the words and feeling a slight lurch in her chest.

She put her fingers to her trembling lips, feeling tears in her eyes. It felt so good to say the words aloud. And it felt even better to feel them in her heart.

She had no idea what would happen next, what would eventually happen between her and Kurt. But she knew one thing for sure—she was going to enjoy every minute of it.

Twenty-seven

Over the next two weeks Anne worked hard at the halfway house. Mrs. Howard was aloof and distant, but at least she had let up a little in her criticisms so that Anne was able to spend time with Crystal without the woman's constant presence. But there were still tensions between them about the way she treated the other children.

Unfortunately, Kurt was out of town the first week and part of the next. He called Anne every night, sometimes even at work, and Vivian would find Anne wherever she was and smile at her knowingly when she told her that Kurt was on the phone.

Those days of separation were all it took for Anne to see how much she wanted and needed Kurt. She realized that for the first time in her life she was ready, really ready, to have a full, normal, give-and-take relationship with a man.

And she could hardly wait for him to come home.

In the meantime she spent her days working with Crystal and her psychologist. She had dreaded it at first, knowing it would probably bring up unpleasant memories of her mother and her own painful childhood, but she soon found the sessions to be as helpful to her as they were to the little girl. The rest of the time she continued working in the kitchen with Gabby, and she decided it was the work she liked most. The physical work and the quietness gave her time to think, and Gabby's anecdotes made her laugh.

She'd even suggested before he left that Kurt give the assistant's job to Vivian and had been pleasantly surprised when he took her advice with no argument. Vivian had taken over the job as quickly and naturally as if she'd done it all her life.

Even Kurt had been surprised by Vivian's diversity and talent, and before he left he told Anne that it was the first time since coming to Angels Incorporated that he had been able to leave the children without worrying about them. Vivian also worked well with Mr. and Mrs. Howard, much better than Anne herself could have, and because of that Kurt had made Vivian their supervisor.

The only problem that none of them seemed able to handle was Crystal's mother.

She continued to come for unannounced visits, and even though they were all supervised Anne could see the toll it took on the little girl each time. When the woman didn't visit she called, and those conversations were impossible to control since they couldn't be monitored.

Anne wished that Kurt could be there for the woman's court hearing, but she understood that his job took him away at inopportune times.

She and Vivian went to the courtroom in his place and sat quietly as Mrs. Raburn's name was called.

Anne had called Roger Finnell before the hearing and asked him to be there, even though Angels had its own lawyer.

As expected, Judge Jordan delayed the

case, much to the dissatisfaction of Crystal's mother.

"I want it settled now," they heard her tell her lawyer. "I want something done about my kid and I want it done now!"

"I'm sorry, Mrs.—"

"Sorry don't cut it! You know what they're trying to do, don't you?" she said, turning accusing eyes toward Anne and Vivian. "They're trying to get Crystal declared a ward of the state, and this delay is just their way of buying time 'til they can do it. Then, by God, they're going to take her away from me . . . permanent!"

The woman's lawyer took her by the arm and pulled her with him down the aisle and away from the judge's hearing. But Anne noted that Will Jordan had stopped what he was doing and was staring at Mrs. Raburn.

"Counselor, kindly take your client outside," he said, his deep voice booming with authority.

"I think she might just have cut her own throat," Vivian said, leaning toward Anne. "But she's right. This delay is exactly what we need. I only hope the lawyers can work fast enough to get Crystal away from that woman before the next hearing date."

"I'll see to it," Anne said. She stood up and fell into step beside Roger Finnell as he and the other lawyer were leaving.

"Will you have enough time?" she asked. "Can we get Crystal away from her for good?"

"That's something I want to talk to you about, Anne, since you have a personal interest in the child."

"What?"

"Come outside," he said. "Let's sit down somewhere and discuss this."

"All of us?"

"Just you," Roger said, with an apologetic smile to Vivian.

"I'll see you back at the house," Vivian said.

Anne and Roger walked from the courthouse across the street to a small coffee shop. Only after they had ordered coffee and the waitress had left the table did her lawyer lean forward.

"Mrs. Raburn wants to make a deal."

"A deal? What kind of deal?"

"Money . . . what else? Apparently, she's found out who you are, and since it's pretty obvious that you like the kid and have a personal interest in her—"

"Then what was all that about back in the courtroom?" she asked. "Why did she pretend to be concerned because Crystal might be taken away from her?"

"A little added pressure, I'd guess. Something she and her lawyer thought might help us hurry their case along . . . before she changes her mind."

"I can't believe this," Anne said, fuming. "What does she want? She's willing to sell Crystal to the highest bidder—is that it?"

"That's about it," Roger said, leaning back in his chair and spreading his hands toward her.

"Can she do that? Is it legal?"

"Honey, you'd be surprised what's legal nowadays. And yes, she can do it if we agree to what she wants."

"Which is?"

"She wants the court to drop the charges against her and she wants enough money to leave town and establish a residence somewhere else. If we recommend it, the judge probably will go along with it; saves time and taxpayer money if it can be settled out of court."

"How much does she want?"

"Fifty thousand . . . more than Angels Incorporated is authorized to pay."

"Write her a check," she said. There was a glint in her eyes as she lifted her chin and stared at Roger.

"Just like that?"

"Just like that." She leaned forward, tapping her fingers on the table for emphasis. "But I want the deal ironclad, Roger. I don't want this woman ever coming back for more. And I don't want her popping up in Crystal's life unannounced in the future."

"I'll take care of it," he said smoothly.

"But I want you to hold up on any action until tomorrow. Don't tell her anything yet. There's something I have to do first."

"What's that?"

"I have to make sure it's what Crystal wants, and that she understands that her mother will be out of her life for good. And I have to tell Kurt."

"What if he disagrees?"

Anne took a deep breath and sat back

in her chair. To be honest, she had no idea how Kurt would react. He was so forthright and aboveboard in all his dealings that the idea of buying a child might offend him. He might not agree to it at all.

"Then we'll find another way," she said finally.

"We could go over his head, if that's what you want," he offered. "It would be done before he ever found out about it."

"No," she said quickly, frowning at Roger. "I would never do that . . . never."

"Well," he said, his smile slow and knowing. "There's something different about you, Anne. But I think I like it."

"Yes," she said with a rather bemused look on her face. "I guess there is."

"This guy's opinion is important to you, huh?"

"His opinion and his happiness mean everything to me," she whispered.

"Well," Roger said, his eyes wide and filled with disbelief. "My, my, my, Mrs. Benefield," he drawled.

With a quirk of her lips, Anne gave him a withering look. But then she smiled.

"You can wipe that smug look off your face, lawyer," she said. "I still pay your fees, so don't get overly confident about anything. And don't try taking advantage of my newly found good nature."

Roger laughed aloud. He shook his head, looking into Anne's eyes with open affection.

"You are one in a million, Anne Benefield. One in a damned million." He paused, looking at her and smiling until Anne blushed. "Whatever you want," he said. "You just let me know when and how you want me to proceed."

"I will. And by the way, you and Janet are invited to a party at the farm next weekend. I've decided to throw a benefit for the halfway house, so bring your checkbook. It's about time you spent some of that moldy old money the Benefield account has been paying you all these years." She smiled at him in a teasing, almost flirtatious manner.

"Well, I must say, I like your enthusiasm," he said, laughing at her uncharacteristic behavior. "When did you decide to do that?"

"Just now," she said, smiling. "So, if

you'll excuse me, I have a great deal to do before next week. I'll call you tomorrow."

He was still watching her and shaking his head with wonder as she walked outside.

Anne knew that Kurt would be home that evening, although she expected it might be late and that she would only talk to him on the phone. This was not something she wanted to tell him on the phone. And she didn't want to mention it to Crystal at all until she spoke to Kurt.

She invited Cecile over to the farm for a light supper, and the two of them sat for a couple of hours, catching up. Cecile wanted to hear all about Anne's relationship with Kurt.

"So, exactly how far has this progressed?" Cecile asked, looking warily at Anne.

"I'm in love, Cecile," Anne said, her voice soft with astonishment. "Really in love, for the first time in my life." She turned to look at her friend.

"Oh, honey," Cecile said, reaching forward to hug Anne. "That's wonderful.

Oh, I'm so happy for you . . . so happy. I can't wait to tell Barney."

"No," Anne said. "Please don't say anything. I . . . I haven't even told Kurt yet. And I'm not sure I will."

"What are you talking about? Of course you'll tell him."

"Not yet," she said. "Not until I'm sure. Goodness, I have no idea how he feels about me, and I don't want to—"

"Don't you think it's about time to stop playing these silly kid games?" Cecile asked. "What's the worst thing that could happen? He won't love you back? Does that mean you can't still love him . . . and enjoy his company? Life passes too quickly to give up something that makes you feel this good, Annie. Don't go borrowing trouble, as my mother always said."

"I know you're right," Anne said. "But this is so difficult for me."

"I understand that," Cecile said, her smile warm and sympathetic. "But don't worry. I have a feeling this is all going to work out, despite your doubts and worries."

"You know, the funny thing is, deep

down inside I think I believe that, too. But then that little voice comes back, telling me that anything this good is bound to go wrong."

"You're wrong," Cecile said. "I mean, Barney Loudermilk might not be Robert Redford, but we've had a pretty good time of it for over thirty years. So don't tell me that anything good is bound to go wrong, because I know better."

Anne took a deep breath. "Okay," she said. "Okay, you're right. I'll tell him. I'm going to tell him . . . soon."

"Good. Atta girl. Well, look, speaking of Barney, I promised I'd be home in time to watch the ballgame with him. So I'd better go."

Anne stood up and walked Cecile outside to her car, where she hugged her goodbye.

"I'm so glad you came, Cecile. You always help me put my thoughts in perspective."

"Call me," Cecile said, kissing Anne lightly on the cheek.

Anne locked up for the night and set the security alarms. She took a bath and found herself too restless even for that.

She was just dressing in a pair of silky lounging pajamas when she heard the sound of a car slowing down on the main road.

She went to the windows overlooking the lake and saw headlights turning into the house's driveway. She frowned, feeling a little of the fear that she always felt when she was alone at night in the big old house. She switched off the lights so she could see and not be seen.

Then she gave a soft murmur of delight when she recognized the red truck and saw it pull to a stop in front of the walkway leading to the front porch.

Quickly she turned the lights back on and ran as fast as she could down the stairs. Her fingers were trembling so badly, she could hardly decode the alarm system and open the door. And when she did Kurt was walking up the front steps.

He stopped and smiled, his gaze growing warm as it moved from her face down the silky, flowing pajamas. The breeze from the lake blew the material against her, outlining her breasts and thighs.

"Kurt," she whispered, moving toward him.

They were in each other's arms, her mouth finding his in a welcoming kiss that sent her head reeling.

"I'm so glad you're back . . . so glad you came here."

"I haven't even been home," he said, holding her tightly against him.

He looked tired from the long drive, but Anne thought she had never seen a more welcome sight in her life.

"Come in," she said, her arm still around his waist as she turned toward the house. "Are you hungry? I'll fix you something to eat while we talk. There's so much I have to tell you . . . about the hearing and Crystal, about a party I'm planning."

She stopped, seeing the bemused smile on his face.

"About us," she said quietly.

He pulled her into his arms again, kissing her thoroughly until she was forced to pull away to catch her breath.

"Forget the food," he said, his voice husky. "Forget everything except the *us* part."

Her eyes were sparkling as she took his hand. Slowly she pulled him into the house, and with their arms around each other they moved toward the stairs and her bedroom.

Twenty-eight

The house was quiet. There was only the sound of crickets outside, muted by the soft whisper of air from the air-conditioning ducts. Anne lay in Kurt's arms, feeling content and satisfied and thoroughly loved.

Her head rested on his chest and she could hear the strong, steady beat of his heart and feel the rise and fall of his breathing.

"Promise me it will always be this good between us," she said, half teasing, half serious.

"I promise," he said, his voice rumbling beneath her ear.

She moved her head, looking up into his face. Even though she couldn't make out his features in the darkness she could feel the warmth of his gaze.

"You said that awfully quickly," she said.

"That's because it's an easy promise to make," he whispered. He brushed a kiss against her hair as he gently pushed her head back down to his chest. "You worry too much."

"That's because this has never happened to me before." Her voice was quiet, muffled against his chest. "I'm afraid I'll wake up one morning and it all will have been taken away."

"Don't you know I won't let that happen?" he said, his arms tightening around her. *"We* won't let it."

"All right," she said. "I'm going to quit whining and complaining and just enjoy this."

"Well," he said, chuckling softly, "good."

"You know, Crystal's psychologist has helped me see that a lot of my problems are because of my own negativism, and my inability to forgive even the smallest slights done to me."

"That's because you're sensitive," he said. "There's nothing wrong with that."

"Crystal is sensitive, too. We are so much alike, Kurt," she said, turning her head to look at him. "I sensed it before, but I never realized until we began to see the psychologist just how much we're alike in the way we handle problems. By closing people out. I'm learning a lot."

"Just don't change too much," he said, teasing. "I kind of like you just the way you are . . . feisty, like Gabby says."

They laughed, and Anne sat up in bed, pushing her pillow behind her back and leaning against the headboard of the bed.

"I told you the hearing has been delayed," she said.

"Yes, you did."

"There's something else. Something I didn't want to tell you on the phone."

Kurt sat up in bed, too, and reached out to turn on the bedside lamp. He pulled the sheet up to his waist and Anne let her gaze wander over his bare chest, thinking that he made a very distracting listener.

She explained quickly about the deal that Roger Finnell had presented to her. And then she waited. Kurt was frowning, his fingers fiddling with the edge of the sheet.

"What did you tell him?" he asked.

"I told him to write Mrs. Raburn a

check." Her voice was soft, tentative, as she continued watching Kurt. "But I told him I wanted to tell you and Crystal before we did anything."

His head came up and he looked straight into her eyes. His look took her breath away.

"You're quite a woman—do you know that?"

"I . . . I wouldn't do anything without consulting you first," she said.

"No, it's okay," he said, pulling her into his arms. "You do what you think is right." He smiled at her and kissed her lightly on the mouth. "But I appreciate your wanting to tell me about it first. I love you for wanting to please me."

Anne felt her heart quiver, hearing the words *I love you,* even though they weren't spoken as a declaration.

"But this is your decision, sweetheart. That's a lot of money we're talking about. I happen to agree with you, but in the end you should do exactly what you want to do."

"I keep thinking of that phrase, follow your heart," she said, feeling a bit of surprise that it was exactly what she was doing, for the first time in so many years. "I guess I was always afraid of following my instincts."

"It's what you should do," he said.

She took a long, slow breath of air, feeling good about herself, feeling wonderful about the way Kurt had responded to the news.

"Oh, Kurt," she whispered. "Do you know how good this new life of mine feels? I'm like a bird out of a cage . . . a self-imposed cage, I might add."

"Come here, my little bird," he said, laughing as he pulled her into his arms and placed tiny kisses on her face and neck.

They laughed and rolled together in bed like two playful puppies. Then they lay quietly in each other's arms, breathless and happy.

"Now, all we have to do is tell Crystal. Oh, Lord, Kurt, what if she says no? What if she wants to go with her mother? It isn't unusual, they say. Most children still love their parents and want to stay with them no matter what they've done."

Kurt tapped his finger against her nose. "Stop worrying."

"I know," she said, sighing. "Borrowing trouble."

"We'll talk to her first thing in the morning. Speaking of which . . . I have to go."

Anne turned to him, accepting his kiss but catching his arm and holding him beside her.

"You don't have to go if you don't want to. There's no reason you can't stay here. Waking up in your arms every morning sounds very appealing to me at this moment."

"There is a reason," he said softly. "I care too much about you to do that. You're a respected woman in this community, and I don't intend to do anything to jeopardize that."

She looked at him oddly, not understanding at first what he meant. Then she laughed.

"Why, Kurt Bonner—you're old-fashioned. Do you think in this day and age anyone would really look on me as a fallen woman?"

"Does that bother you . . . my being old-fashioned about such things?"

"No," she whispered, the light shining

in her eyes. "It doesn't bother me at all. In fact, I love it."

"Besides," he said, standing up and going to retrieve his clothes. "Kathleen and Jessica would have my hide."

"Oh, I doubt that," she said, thinking of the way they talked about Kurt. "They think Mr. Kurt Bonner can do no wrong. Besides being one helluva sexy guy."

He looked wryly at her from the corner of his eye, his lips quirking to one side as he shook his head at her.

"You are," she said, her voice filled with delight at his modesty.

"Stop that."

She laughed out loud and lay back in the bed, spreading her arms out and stretching.

"I love it that you're modest about yourself. And that you're protective of me," she said, looking up at him. "And that you can laugh about your age and your thinning hair."

"Hey," he said, frowning at her and feigning anger.

"I love your sense of fairness and decency, the way you make friends with everyone you meet. And I love your compassion, not only with the children, but with Gabby and Vivian. With me." Her eyes were shining now as she stared up at him.

Kurt's gaze grew serious, and he walked to the bed and sat down, taking her in his arms and rocking her gently back and forth.

"I want you to marry me, Anne," he whispered against her hair.

She pulled away, looking up into his eyes with a mixture of fear and disbelief.

"Marry," she murmured. "Oh, Kurt . . . I hadn't . . . I didn't expect—"

"Don't tell me you haven't thought about it."

"Well, yes, but—"

"But you're still afraid," he said. His expression changed then, grew a bit cooler and more reserved. "Even after what we've shared these past few weeks, after tonight." His eyes were fierce as he stared at her. "Dammit, Anne—life is too short for indecision and waiting. We have to grab on and fight for every bit of happiness we can get."

"I know that. . . . I've been feeling it more and more lately. And it's not you,

Kurt," she said. "It's me. I've had two marriages already—one disastrous and the other . . . well, it wasn't fair to Baxter, and that's putting it mildly."

"Don't you think I've had those same fears? After ending a marriage that had lasted more than twenty-five years? After learning that I wasn't the perfect husband and father I always told myself I was?"

"You *are* perfect," she whispered. "More perfect than me. There's no comparison."

"We've both learned a great deal in the past few years, Anne. And despite my bitterness after the divorce I've discovered that I really like being married, having the stability of a home to come home to every night. And I want a woman who's a friend as well as a lover. I want you."

She took a deep breath and smiled into his eyes.

"We are friends, aren't we?" she asked, seeming to realize it for the first time.

"Think about it," he said. "How it could be. Think about this . . ."

She moved into his arms, sighing and feeling some of the confusion drifting away as she felt them tighten around her. She felt safe with Kurt. She felt warm and loved for the first time in her life. Not even Baxter's indulgences could compare to what she shared with Kurt, for this was a mutual giving, and there was a rightness to it that she had never known before.

"I will," she whispered, turning her lips up for his kiss.

It was the sweetest, most gentle kiss Anne had ever received. And she knew that Kurt was as moved by the moment, as touched, as she was, and he didn't seem to mind that she knew it or saw his vulnerability.

"I'll see you in the morning," he whispered as he stood up and backed away from the bed.

She sat up, her smile tremulous as she watched him go and as she whispered, "Good night."

The next morning there was no mention of Kurt's marriage proposal. Anne thought he made an effort to be light and teasing with her. But there was a look in his eyes that made her toes tingle, and she found that she was the one who wanted to talk about what was happening between them. But she wanted to give herself time. She thought she couldn't possibly survive later if what was between them didn't work out.

After breakfast Anne and Kurt took Crystal upstairs.

"Sit down, sweetie," Anne said. "We have something to tell you."

Crystal's eyes were immediately alert, filled with a wild kind of fear.

"She's not taking me away, is she? I don't have to leave here, do I?"

"No, honey," Kurt said, touching Crystal's hair. "No, of course not. But that is kind of what we wanted to talk to you about."

Kurt pulled a chair up to the bed and Crystal sat down. Anne sat on the bed beside her, her arms lightly around the girl's waist.

Kurt explained quietly and patiently about what had happened, except that he didn't mention the part about her mother demanding money for her end of the agreement.

"Your mother is willing to give you up and I think that's a very unselfish thing for her to do."

Crystal's eyes were wide and shining with intensity as she tried to take in every word that Kurt said.

"She's doing it because she loves you, honey. She's afraid that she'll never be able to take care of you the way you really need to be taken care of. Do you understand?" Kurt and Anne both knew that was a lie, but if it made Crystal feel better . . .

Crystal had begun to cry, her sobs quiet, shaking her body without a sound coming from her lips.

Kurt looked into Anne's eyes and saw tears there, too. He frowned and shook his head.

"This won't happen if you don't want it to, Crystal," Kurt said, taking out a handkerchief and wiping her tears.

"Will . . . will I ever see her again?" she asked.

"That's up to you. Whatever you want to do."

Anne held her breath. It would be so much better for Crystal if she didn't see her mother, if she could just start a new life and forget the woman ever existed. But how could they tell a ten-year-old child that and expect her to understand? She knew herself how impossible it was to forget. A girl's need for her mother was as deep and basic as any in the universe.

"I . . . I don't know," Crystal murmured, looking at Kurt for guidance.

"It's all right," he said. "You don't have to make up your mind right this minute. We'll give you all the time you need."

"This is an awfully big decision for a little girl," Anne added as she touched Crystal's hair.

Crystal's head was bent and when she spoke her words were muffled. "I know what I want."

"What?" Anne asked, bending her head to hear Crystal's softly spoken words.

"I said I know what I want," Crystal said, looking up into Anne's eyes. Her blue eyes were haunting, filled with tears and a quiet pleading that made Anne's heart turn over. "But I guess I shouldn't say that I wish my mom would go away."

"Oh, honey," Anne said. "I understand why you feel guilty about that. But it's not you who suggested it. You *should* say what you want. You don't have to be afraid of what Kurt and I will think. We're on your side, no matter what."

Crystal's gaze moved from Anne to Kurt and back to Anne again.

"Couldn't . . . couldn't I just be your little girl?" she asked, her eyes pleading, even ashamed.

Anne's mouth dropped open as she met Kurt's amazed look.

"Oh, Crystal," she whispered. "I . . . I'm honored that you think . . . that you. . . . But honey, I don't have any children. I've never been a mother and—"

"It's okay," Crystal said, closing her mouth tightly and looking away. "I didn't expect you to say yes."

Anne closed her eyes and sighed.

"Oh, Lord," she muttered beneath her breath. She opened her eyes and stared at Kurt, feeling anguished, feeling the guilt tearing at her own heart.

"We'll let you think about what you want to do, Crystal," Kurt said, standing. "Anytime you want to talk to either of us, just let me know."

"Crystal . . ." Anne murmured.

She put her arms around the girl. Crystal didn't pull away, but her body was stiff and unyielding. She tried to smile at Anne and managed only a small quirk of her lips. Her eyes were as pained and vacant as before.

Outside the door, Anne leaned against Kurt, trembling.

"What have I done?" she whispered against his shirt. "God, Kurt . . . what have I done to this little girl? I've made her love me and asked her to forget her own mother. And now . . ."

"Anne, Anne," he whispered, stroking her hair. "It's going to be all right. This is perfectly normal. I don't think we've had a child here who didn't look on one of us as a sort of surrogate parent. The younger a child is, the more likely it is to happen. Crystal is going to be all right, and much of the credit goes to you for your love and concern. We'll find her a good home, sweetheart. A really good, loving home."

Anne said nothing as they turned and went downstairs. But in her heart she knew something that Kurt didn't . . . that no one else knew. She didn't want

Crystal to have just a good and loving home with strangers. She wished she had the courage to take her herself.

piece of to those just beyond and below
bring with crayons... It wanted for too
the languages me ask how herself, so dif-

Twenty-nine

The next few days were filled with work and with preparations for the party. Anne turned much of the food planning and decorations over to Kathleen and Jessica, and they seemed pleased to be in charge.

"Why, shoot," Jessica said when Anne asked for their help. "No need for callin' in caterers when you got us. Me and Kathleen and Elmer can do most anything you want. The rest we'll hire it done."

"I know that," Anne said. "I guess I just always hated to burden you with any more work than you already had. But this party is special. It's for the kids, and I trust you all to know how they would like things fixed and what they would like to eat."

"We'll take care of it, Mrs. Benefield," Mrs. Hargis said, nodding. She pulled a piece of paper across the counter and began to write.

Anne smiled at the woman, at the diligent look on her face as she wrote.

"Don't you think it's about time you started calling me Anne?" she asked.

Mrs. Hargis looked up, her pencil poised in the air as she stared first at Anne, and then at Jessica. Jessica had a pleased look on her face, but she said nothing.

"Both of you," Anne said.

"Well, I'm not sure it's proper . . ." Mrs. Hargis began. ". . . you bein' our employer and all."

"Proper," Anne said, making a little face. "Who cares about what's proper? You two and Elmer have been better friends to me than some people I've known for years. You're the ones who have always been here, who've taken care of me when I was sick or depressed or just plain lonely. You're my family," she whispered, her voice growing hoarse.

Mrs. Hargis nodded, and even though she was smiling, there was a glimmer of moisture in her eyes.

"Well," Anne said, turning away quickly

and moving toward the door. "I have to get to work."

She was getting in the car before either of the women in the kitchen spoke.

"Well, what do you know about that?" Mrs. Hargis said, shaking her head and staring out the window.

Anne saw Kurt every night that week, except Monday, when he had to go to an Angels board meeting in town.

"Why don't you come, Anne?" he asked. "You're a member of the board. Call Roger and tell him he doesn't have to sit in for you tonight."

"No," she said, her eyes filling with doubt. "I can't. I wouldn't know how to act. Besides, I'd feel pretentious, going now, after all this time. Heavens, I didn't even know I was on the board until I started working for you."

He sighed and kissed her. "All right. I'll call you when I get home."

Anne knew Kurt was disappointed in her even though he had said nothing. How tired he must be of her constant indecisiveness—of her inability to become involved and personally committed to something once and for all. But she had to take things one step at a time, and she couldn't explain to him why that was so important to her. She wasn't sure she understood it herself. But she did know, despite Kurt's concerns, that she was going in the right direction. Slow, but right, she thought to herself with a quiet feeling of satisfaction.

She spent that evening addressing invitations to Saturday's party to the most prominent people in town. They would be hand-delivered tomorrow since time was so short. But, after all, she told herself, how much time does one need to get ready for a picnic?

Then she laughed at herself and sat back in her chair. She wouldn't have had such thoughts last year, even several months ago. A party invitation and the planning of it had to be precise, had to be the most perfect affair anyone had ever attended. Perfectly decorated, perfectly catered. And now she found herself thinking only of the children and what they would enjoy, and whether they would prefer hot dogs or hamburgers. In the end she'd decided to have both, as well as steaks, chicken, and ribs for the adults. She could hardly wait to see some of their faces when they arrived. Benefield Farms would look different this time. They would see the real Anne Benefield—the one all of them probably suspected all along. A country girl, unsophisticated and plain, struggling with her weight and inner doubts, hidden behind the facade of glittering designer gowns and perfectly styled hair and makeup.

"And I don't care anymore," she said, laughing aloud and feeling amazed at the changes since she'd met Kurt. "I really don't care what they think."

All that week at work Anne had noticed a difference in Crystal. She was talking more, becoming more involved with the other kids, sometimes even acting as big sister to some of the smaller children. She also seemed to be taking more pains with her hair and her clothes.

One morning Mrs. Howard asked Anne to sit in for her at breakfast. As Anne sat beside Crystal, she watched the girl tenderly as she helped one of the newer children with her food.

Crystal finished with the girl and turned toward Anne, seeing her affectionate look. She smiled shyly and glanced away, and Anne thought she even blushed.

"I'm so proud of you," Anne said quietly. "You're growing into a very nice, very mature young lady. Are you feeling better . . . about things?"

Crystal nodded, but she continued looking down at her plate.

"Are you looking forward to the picnic on Saturday?" Anne asked.

Crystal looked up then, her eyes sparkling brightly.

"Gabby says you live in a big, fine house."

"Yes, I'm very lucky," Anne said.

"And that you have horses and cows."

Anne smiled. "Ducks, too. And geese sometimes in the lake."

Some of the other children overheard the conversation and of course they were excited, too, about seeing Anne's farm. It was a happy, spirited breakfast, with all of them making plans for the picnic. When the children finished and began to clear away the dishes Crystal sat quietly, looking down at her hands in her lap, then back up at Anne.

"I . . . I have something to tell you," she said.

"What is it?" Anne said, turning her full attention to the little girl.

"I want to stay here," she said, her voice barely above a whisper. "I don't want to go back to my mom."

"Are you sure?" Anne said, understanding the quiet anguish in Crystal's voice.

She nodded. "I . . . I feel bad sometimes 'cause I don't miss her."

"Oh, baby," Anne said, getting up from her chair and moving to kneel beside Crystal's chair. She put her arms around the child's waist and hugged her. "I know. Honey, I know exactly how you feel. But sometimes, when something or someone hurts you so badly, you just have to get away from it. Then when you're grown and more able to handle everything, you might actually find yourself wanting to see her again."

Crystal was looking intently at Anne.

"How . . . how do you know?" she asked. "Did—"

Anne nodded and quickly told her about her own mother. "She's in a retirement home now and I feel guilty, too."

"You do?"

"Yes, I do."

"You're grown up," Crystal said. "Do you want to see your mom again now?"

Anne took a long breath and frowned. Then she stood up and moved back to her chair. She stared at Crystal, this little girl whose troubles had helped her understand so much about her own.

"Yes," Anne whispered, feeling surprised. "Yes, I guess I do want to see her." She smiled at Crystal, taking her hand and squeezing it. "And you know what? That's exactly what I'm going to do . . . real soon."

"Do . . . do you think it's the right thing?" Crystal asked. "For me not to see my mom anymore . . . 'til I'm grown."

"Sweetie," Anne said, trying to find exactly the right words, "I do think it's best for you right now. And I think you're a very brave and mature young lady for taking your time and making this decision."

"Mrs. Howard said I'm being selfish."

"Mrs. Howard . . ." Anne began, feeling her anger rise. She made herself remain calm and purposely lowered her voice. "Mrs. Howard is wrong, Crystal. You know in your own heart and your own mind what you really want. And don't listen to anything except that."

Crystal nodded, her eyes sparkling. Anne thought it was the first time she'd ever seen the girl actually smile.

"I want to be like other kids," she said. "I want a home and a mama and a daddy who love me."

"That will be easy," Anne said. She pulled Crystal out of the chair and brought her to sit in her lap, hugging her close and whispering against her clean-smelling hair. "What Mama and Daddy wouldn't love a sweet little girl like you?"

Anne could hardly wait to tell Kurt and to call Roger Finnell. She felt a need to hurry and send Mrs. Raburn the money, and for the court to draw up the papers, releasing Crystal into social services' care for adoption. After telling Kurt she used the phone in his office to call Roger.

"Be sure it stipulates that Crystal will stay here at the halfway house until adoptive parents can be found," Anne told Roger on the phone.

"Will do," he said. "I'll take care of it right away."

"Good. Are you and Janet coming out Saturday?"

"Wouldn't miss it. As usual, a Benefield party is the talk of the town."

"Oh, yeah?" she said, smiling. "Well, this one will be different. So be prepared." She hung up, still smiling.

"You look awfully pleased with yourself," Kurt said. But he was pleased, too. Anne could see it in the sparkle of his hazel eyes, and the grin on his handsome face.

"Roger is going to be surprised when he sees the farm. Everyone will be."

"It's going to be quite a day," he agreed.

On Saturday morning Kurt arrived early to help Anne with any last-minute preparations. He found her hurrying about the house, laughing and shouting with excitement as she helped Mrs. Hargis and Jessica transfer prepared food into large serving bowls. Already huge barbecue grills were set up outside beneath the trees, and men were busy carrying wooden barrels filled with ice and soft drinks. Balloons and streamers decorated every tree and bush and gallon containers of bright flowers lined the drive and walkway up to the front of the house. Tables with blue-and-white-checked tablecloths and red napkins sat beneath the trees.

Anne and Kurt were outside just before the time for everyone's arrival. She wanted to make sure everything was ready and that the live band's wiring was in working order. They were practicing beneath the trees on the platform set up for them, and the sound of fiddles and the twang of guitars filled the air.

"Oh, Kurt," Anne said, practically bouncing beside him. "Isn't this fun?"

"Yes, ma'am," he said, producing a Western drawl as his gaze turned toward her.

Seeing the mischievous look in his eyes, Anne laughed and reached out to put her arm around him.

"Whoa there now, little filly," he said,

giving her a look that made her laugh again. His eyes took in her jeans and boots. "Ain't right for a woman as purty as you to be makin' a man feel this way. Better not touch me like that—you know how we cowboys are—we believe in less talk and more action."

"Oh, Kurt, you goose," she said. Her eyes were sparkling as she leaned toward him and whispered, "You're downright purty yourself, cowboy."

Just then the first vehicle turned off the road toward the house, and Anne recognized Roger Finnell's car.

"Oh, they're here," Anne said, grabbing Kurt's arm. "Lord, I hope I don't look like a fool. And I hope Roger isn't wearing a three-piece suit."

He wasn't. Anne's eyes widened as she watched him and his wife step out of the car and hand the keys to the cowboy valet who stood waiting. Roger was dressed in the latest Western gear and even wore authentic-looking low-heeled boots.

"Love your boots," Anne said as she watched them walk toward her.

"Ropers," Roger said proudly, lifting his foot for them to see.

"Well, I declare," Anne said.

Then they all laughed. Anne thought it was the most relaxed she'd ever seen her lawyer, and she was pleased.

His arrival was only the beginning. Everyone seemed to be in the spirit, even Judge Jordan, who looked like a town marshal in his black striped pants and sparkling white shirt. Anne thought even Sylvia seemed comfortable with the attire and the casual atmosphere.

Anne was especially pleased with the welcome the children received when they arrived. There was applause as the van pulled up and the kids leapt out enthusiastically. Cecile made a point of going to some of the children and giving them a hug before pointing them in the direction of Anne and Kurt. Some of the other guests followed suit, and Anne could see how happy it made the children.

Anne's eyes searched for Crystal, and she was pleased when the girl saw her and Kurt and came quickly toward them. She was different today, hardly able to contain her enthusiasm as she ran to Anne and hugged her, then Kurt.

"This is the prettiest house I've ever

seen," she said, her eyes bright with wonder. "I can't believe anybody lives in a place like this. Can I see inside?"

"Of course you may. After the party I'll take you through the house. Now, go with the others," Anne said. "Get something to eat. The band's getting ready to play. Where's Gabby?" Anne asked, turning back toward the van.

"He's coming," Crystal said, turning to join the other children.

Anne and Kurt watched as Crystal dashed away and both of them laughed and looked at one another. It was a very special moment—almost, Anne imagined, like seeing one of your children happy at play.

"You look beautiful today," Kurt said, pulling her close and kissing her quickly.

"I'm happy," she said. "Really, really happy."

They saw Gabby then, coming toward them, carrying a large foil-covered box. Vivian and her husband were behind him, carrying others. Anne could see Gabby's eyes shifting from her toward the house, and then to the other guests. She thought he looked a little uncomfortable.

"What do you have?" she asked, nodding toward the boxes.

"Brownies," Gabby said, unsmiling. "The kids like my brownies. But I guess with all this fancy food you won't be needin' any of mine."

"Oh, nonsense, you old crab cake," she said, taking Gabby's arm and smiling into his eyes. "We're having barbecue and potato salad, baked beans . . . hamburgers and hot dogs. How fancy can that be? Brownies will be perfect, and you know I think you make the best brownies in the world. They're so good, they ought to have a patent."

Gabby gave her a wry look and grunted, but he had trouble concealing his pleasure.

"Where you want 'em?" he asked.

Anne could see Kurt smiling, shaking his head affectionately at Gabby's gruff behavior. But the old man ignored the look and continued to frown at Anne.

"You can go around to the kitchen and ask Mrs. Hargis to find plates for them."

"Hey, guys," Anne said to Vivian and her husband, "I'm so glad you're here.

After you deliver the brownies come back out and sit with us."

"Are you sure?" Vivian asked, her eyes going warily to the other guests.

"Of course I'm sure," Anne said, giving her a look of exasperation. "I want you to meet my best friend and her husband."

Vivian smiled and nodded, and Anne didn't miss the look that passed between her and her husband. She supposed they expected her to be different here at her farm, with her wealthy friends around her. And she couldn't say she blamed anyone for thinking that, after the way she had behaved when she first came to the halfway house.

The party was a rousing success. Many of the guests, some of whom Anne had considered stuffy and snobbish, came up to her during the day and told her how much they were enjoying it. A large collection box shaped like a cowboy hat sat on the front porch and was filled with checks and pledges by the end of the day.

But the highlight of the day for Anne was when Judge Jordan came to speak to her.

"Anne, you've outdone yourself today. This is the best party Clayburn County has ever seen. And it's even better considering it's for such a good cause."

"I'm glad you're enjoying it," Anne said, glancing toward his wife Sylvia, who stood silently at his elbow. "You two make a very handsome Western couple."

"Oh, we love the West," Sylvia said. "I got this outfit in Phoenix last year. And Will has folks in New Mexico."

"Really?" she said. "I didn't know that." She thought it was the first time she'd ever had a conversation with Sylvia Jordan that wasn't strained.

"I just wanted to let you know that the papers for Crystal Raburn have been filed," the judge said. "She'll be eligible for adoption in another week, ten days at the most."

"Oh, Will," Anne said, looking up at him, her eyes serious. "That's wonderful. Oh, thank you." Without thinking, she stepped toward him and hugged him, then laughed self-consciously. "I suppose the prisoner shouldn't hug her judge," she said lightly.

"I've been hearing real good things

about you, Anne. And about your work at the halfway house."

"I guess you did me a favor, Will, whether you knew it or not."

"Good . . . good. I'm always glad when things work out this way. And as for being a prisoner," he grinned as he glanced toward Kurt, who stood nearby, talking to Cecile and Barney, "you look like just about the happiest prisoner I've ever seen."

Anne could see Sylvia's eyes sparkle. She even leaned forward a bit, as if she expected to hear some juicy gossip.

"What's he like, Anne?" she asked. "Really?"

"He's wonderful," Anne said, her eyes growing soft as she looked at Kurt. He turned and saw her and smiled. "He's the best thing that ever happened to me."

"My," Sylvia sighed, glancing at Kurt from the corner of her eye.

Will Jordan laughed and took his wife's arm.

"Come on, woman," he said. "It's time for your husband to take you home."

They all laughed then, and Anne leaned

toward him, wanting to ask him one thing before he left.

"Will . . . before you go. You have a lot of experience with adoption, being a judge. Would it be difficult for an older woman—say a woman my age—to adopt a child?"

His eyes widened with curiosity. "No, not at all. In past years it might have been an obstacle, but not anymore," he said.

"Heavens, Anne," Sylvia said. "Surely you aren't thinking about actually adopting one of these children, are you? Why would anyone your age want to tie herself down that way? Now that our kids are married and out of the house, Will and I are free as birds. I enjoy my leisure," she said smugly, nodding in her self-satisfied way.

"Leisure," Anne murmured. "Sylvia, to tell you the truth, for the past fifteen years I've had just about all the leisure I can stand." She saw Kurt watching her and smiled at him, feeling the warmth all the way down to her toes. Suddenly nothing seemed more important than touching him.

"Excuse me," she said, not bothering to look back at Sylvia or Will Jordan. "I'm really glad you all could come today."

Thirty

Anne walked to Kurt and put her hand around his arm, feeling his muscles tighten until she was imprisoned against his side.

"If someone sees you looking at me the way you did a while ago . . ." she said, pleased beyond reason that he had.

"It's too late," he murmured, leaning close. "I've already told everyone who would listen that I'm crazy about you."

"Really?" she said, her voice quietly pleased.

He laughed and pulled her away from the crowd of people. Slowly he guided her down toward the lake as the sound of fiddles and laughter drifted away behind them. They stopped beneath a weeping willow and stood for a moment, watching the ducks swimming and diving beneath the water.

"I heard you ask Judge Jordan about adoption procedures," he said, watching her carefully.

"Are you surprised?"

"Yes, I am. I thought you told me you didn't like kids." There was a twinkle in his eyes as he looked at her.

"I've changed my mind," she said, smiling up at him. "I think I was more afraid of them than anything."

"Are you sure about this? Really sure?"

"It's something I've been thinking about more and more lately," she admitted. "I could hardly bear it when Tracy's foster parents came for her, remember?"

"I remember."

"And now, with Crystal, I'm even more concerned. I really care about her, Kurt," she said. "I like her, and I find that I want her to be happy at any cost. I don't want her ever to be afraid again. I want to give her that home she's always wanted, and all the attention to go with it. Besides, this isn't an entirely unselfish thing, you know. This house gets awfully big and lonely sometimes."

"Then you're really serious about this."

"Do you mind that I am?"

"Hell no," he said, his voice strong and steady. "I'm delighted, not only for you but for Crystal."

"But?"

"But," he said, turning her to face him, "I think you need to take this slow, baby. Real slow. This is a lifetime commitment you're thinking about making. Don't say anything to Crystal until you're sure."

"I know," she said. "Not my strong suit in the past—commitment." Her look was apologetic, and they both knew she was talking mostly about him.

"It's one thing, not being able to commit to a man. But it would be quite another if you told Crystal and then decided—"

"Is that what you think?" she asked, gazing up into his hazel eyes. "That I can't commit to you?"

"Can you?" he asked.

His eyes were wary, but there was a spark of hope deep down inside somewhere. Anne hated every moment of waiting that she'd made him endure, every doubt she'd made him feel about her intentions.

"I love you, Kurt," she whispered, hearing her own words and feeling the intensity of her love to the very depths of her soul. She did love him, more than she'd ever thought it was possible to love anyone. And now, finally having said it, she knew the rightness of it, too.

"Annie," he whispered.

His eyes darkened and he pulled her into his arms, kissing her with an intensity that took her breath away.

"I think I've always loved you," she said. "And I'm sorry it took me so long to get the words out."

"Baby, I love you, too," he said, his look intense and happy. "I've wanted to tell you so many times." He laughed aloud then. "God, I feel like shouting . . . like telling everyone I see."

"But I want to wait," she said, hoping he wouldn't be disappointed. "I'm still not sure about what I want . . . about adopting Crystal . . . about marriage." She looked at him from beneath her lashes, hoping he would understand.

"All right," he said slowly. There was only a hint of disappointment in his eyes. But then he smiled, that charming, sexy smile she had loved from the first moment she saw him. "I'll wait. My ex-wife would be shocked to hear that. I wasn't exactly known for my patience in those days."

"I love it that you're impatient," she said. "You make me feel loved . . . and wanted."

"You are that," he said, holding her close so that she could feel the evidence. Then he grinned and stepped away from her, taking a long, deep breath. "We'd better walk, before I make a complete fool of myself."

She reached up to touch his face. "You could never be a fool," she whispered. "And I want you to know that my reluctance has nothing to do with you. You're too good for me, Kurt Bonner, and I am so lucky to have you in my life. And no matter how we end up, you are the best, most exciting thing that's ever happened to me."

"I know how we're going to end up," he said, his eyes dark with intensity. "Together. You're going to have the life you've always dreamed of, and so will I."

As they turned to walk back to the party, Anne breathed a sigh of hopefulness. She hoped he was right. She hoped she would have the good sense and the courage to choose right this time.

It had been a long day, and although Anne was sorry to see the party ending, she felt a bit of relief as well. She wanted to spend some time with Crystal and the children . . . with Gabby and the others from the halfway house. And later, after they'd gone home, she looked forward to having Kurt all to herself.

She and Kurt walked into the kitchen and Anne looked from Mrs. Hargis to Gabby. Both of whom seemed agitated. Kathleen was standing at her full height, which made her only a bit taller than Gabby. Her arms were crossed as she stared at him.

"What's wrong?" Anne asked.

"Nothin'," Gabby said quickly. "Ain't nothin' wrong. 'Cept this woman here says walnuts don't belong in brownies."

Anne made a small sound of disbelief as she stared at him. "Is that all?"

"Is that all?" Gabby began to pace the kitchen. "I spent a long time crackin' them walnuts, diggin' out the meat—didn't want nothin' but the best for . . ." He hesitated a moment, his eyes turning shy as he glanced at Anne. ". . . for you and your party. And when I come in I heard this woman talkin' to that skinny one over there and makin' comments about my cookin'!"

"Good Lord," Kurt said, chuckling softly.

"I didn't say anything bad," Mrs. Hargis said, her eyes sparkling with resentment. "I was only expressing my opinion that pecans are better."

"I'm sure that's what she meant, Gabby," Anne said. "After all, everyone is entitled to their own taste and their own opinion."

"Well, which do you like better?" he asked in his cantankerous way.

"Me?" Anne said, her eyes growing wide. She glanced from Mrs. Hargis's waiting eyes to Gabby's combative ones.

"Huh . . . actually, I like both pecans and walnuts."

Kurt was biting his lower lip to keep from laughing out loud.

"Can't like both," Gabby said, clamping his mouth together stubbornly. "You have to choose."

"Gabby," Anne said, staring at him and rolling her eyes, "what are you trying to do, put me on the spot here?"

"It's all right, Anne," Mrs. Hargis said. "I know how partial you are to pecans. He's just jealous, that's all, because I work for you every day and I was talkin' about how much you like my cookin'. Anybody with eyes can see that's what he's mad about. You don't have to explain anything to the stubborn old coot."

"Who you callin' a stubborn old coot?" Gabby said, turning to face Mrs. Hargis.

"Oh, for heaven's sake," Anne groaned. "Kurt . . . don't just stand there . . ."

"Come on, Gabby," Kurt said. "Let's go outside and show the kids the barn and the horses."

"I hate horses," he muttered as Kurt pulled him toward the door.

Kurt looked over his shoulder and grinned at Anne. "Coming, dear?" he said.

"In a minute," she said. She couldn't keep from laughing at the ridiculousness of the situation, or at the look on Gabby's face as Kurt led him outside. He reminded her of Grumpy of the Seven Dwarfs.

She turned to Mrs. Hargis, who looked slightly sheepish, and Jessica, whose eyes were still bright with disbelief.

"I'm sorry," Anne said. "Gabby can be a bit territorial at times."

"Well, this isn't his territory," Mrs. Hargis said.

"I know it isn't. But believe me, he doesn't mean anything. When I first met him I thought he actually hated me. But since I've gotten to know him I—"

"You hate *him*," Mrs. Hargis finished with a look of self-satisfaction.

"No," Anne growled. She went to Mrs. Hargis and put her arm around the woman's ample shoulders. "Gabby has had a lot of problems in his life."

"Who hasn't?"

"Some of us are better at handling them, Kathleen," Jessica said, nodding her agreement. "That's all she's sayin'."

"Well, you got that right. I guess I'm better at anything than that flea-brained little man."

"Kathleen," Anne murmured. "Please stop this. For my sake."

Mrs. Hargis sniffed and looked away; then she crossed her arms over her chest and lifted her chin.

"All right," she said. "If it's what you want. But I don't like his attitude, and if he comes in my kitchen again, tellin' me what for, he's liable to get a pot upside his head."

Anne saw Jessica's grin and shook her head.

"Thank you, Kathleen," she said softly. As she turned to go out the door, she muttered to herself, "Pecans and walnuts, for heaven's sake."

She saw Kurt going past the gardens toward the gate that led to the barn. He turned and smiled at her as he waited.

"Where are the children?" she asked.

"Elmer took them to the barn to see the newest calf. Gabby went with them."

Anne pushed open the gate, and they began to walk together toward the barn.

"I don't know what gets into him sometimes," Anne said. "I've never seen Mrs. Hargis upset about anything. She's the calmest, most easygoing person I know."

"You have to admit, Gabby can be pretty agitating at times."

"Yes," she said, laughing. "I remember. But why today? And why such a silly, meaningless subject as what kind of nuts to use in brownies?"

"Because it's what he knows, I guess," Kurt said. "He does take a certain pride in his cooking skills. He isn't used to competition in that field." He looked at Anne as they walked. "He probably feels a little intimidated here at your home, where you have your own personal cook. He's jealous, Anne."

"But Mrs. Hargis is like family. He doesn't have to be jealous of her."

"I know that and you know that."

"In many ways he's like one of the children," Anne murmured thoughtfully. "Needy and insecure, and when something really bothers them they get mean and troublesome."

"Yeah," Kurt agreed, nodding. "You're right."

"Well," she said, sighing, "I know he doesn't mean it. Deep down inside he's as sweet and lovable as a puppy. I'll just have to work on making him feel more secure with me, I guess."

Kurt didn't say anything, but he put

his arm around her waist and pulled her close. She didn't understand the look in his eyes, but she thought she liked it very much.

Thirty-one

The children seemed to enjoy their time alone at the farm, without the distraction of guests or a party. They ran and played until they were completely exhausted; then they all decided to sit beneath the trees and eat again. But Crystal came into the house with Anne and Kurt.

"Would any of you like something to eat?" Mrs. Hargis asked when they came into the kitchen.

"Would you, Crystal?" Anne asked.

"No," the girl said with a shake of her head. She seemed too excited to eat as her gaze took in the kitchen. She looked with curiosity through the doorway into the large formal dining room. "Can I see your house now?" she asked softly.

"Of course you may," Anne said. "Come on. It's an old house, you know, and although it has two stories and looks big from the outside, it actually doesn't have that many rooms."

"I'll wait for you two here," Kurt said, sitting down in the breakfast nook. "I intend to have a tall glass of iced tea and a slice of Kathleen's pound cake."

Anne walked through the rooms slowly, letting Crystal look as long as she wanted at the pictures and various decorations. She watched the little girl with affection, pleased at her genuine interest in all of her possessions.

"Is this old?" Crystal asked, pointing to an oak umbrella stand near the front door.

"Yes, it is," Anne said. "You have a very good eye for antiques. That belonged to my husband's mother. I think it came from Kentucky."

"Was he nice?" Crystal asked. "Your husband?"

"Yes, he was," Anne said quietly, reaching out to touch Crystal's shining hair. "He was very good to me."

"As nice as Mr. Bonner?"

Anne smiled, guiding Crystal toward the stairs. "Baxter was a wonderful man and I cared about him very much. He and Mr. Bonner are different, that's all."

Her answer seemed to satisfy Crystal, who ran ahead up the stairs to stand at the top, looking down at Anne as she walked up.

"Which one is your room? Wait, don't tell me . . . let me guess." Crystal ran from door to door, opening them all and peeking inside. Then she came back to take Anne's hand, pulling her toward her own bedroom. "It's this one."

"Ah," Anne said, smiling. "How did you know?"

"It smells like your perfume," Crystal answered rather shyly.

"Come in," Anne said, opening the door and standing aside. "You can see the lake from up here."

Crystal stood at the window, staring out for a long time. It was dusk, and the sunset glimmered in the tops of the old trees and threw a golden shadow across the lake's surface. Finally Crystal sighed, still not turning around.

"You must feel like a princess . . . living here," she said quietly.

Anne thought about that statement for a long moment. She *had* felt like a princess at first, being surrounded by such elegance and beauty, living in the serenity of this quiet country setting. At first she'd been like a kid in a toy store with a fistful of money. She'd run from one thing to another, buying designer clothes and jewelry, a new car, new furniture. She'd had the gazebo built and the rose garden put in at the back. She'd probably driven Baxter crazy with her constant spending and her constant changing. But if he had ever disapproved or been sorry for the choice he'd made in marrying her and giving her free rein with his wealth, he'd never let on. And she loved him for that. For taking her in and giving her the first real home she'd ever had. For being kind and generous and for never telling her she needed to change her ways.

She had so many regrets about Baxter, but she realized that all she could do now was hope that, in return, she had played her role well.

"Sometimes I did feel like a princess," Anne said finally.

She looked at Crystal. Anne knew that she had the chance to do the same thing for this child that Baxter had done for her. And the thought of such an opportunity both frightened and excited her.

"Come on," she said, reaching out for Crystal's hand. "Let me show you the other bedrooms. There are only three more."

"Are you ever lonesome here?" Crystal asked. "Living alone in this big house?"

"You know," Anne said, "I never was until recently. But I guess that was because I never realized what I was missing."

"But now you do?"

"Oh, yes," Anne said, putting her arm around Crystal. "Now I do."

There was only one bedroom at the back of the house. It was the smallest of the upstairs rooms, with a sloping ceiling and a dormer window that looked out over the rose garden and faced the back pastures. Now, as Anne and Crystal sat in the window seat, they could see a mare and her foal as they romped playfully in the waning sunlight, their coats glimmering gold, like the lake. Their distant whinnying could be heard from upstairs, and the sound made Crystal smile and turn to Anne.

"I love it here," she said.

"I thought you would," Anne said. "You'll have to come and spend the night one night." Her heart was pounding as she made the suggestion, trying to appear casual. She thought she already knew what Crystal's reaction would be, but what if she was wrong? What if Crystal saw the house not as a home, but only as a big, empty place . . . frightening to a small child?

"Can I really?" she asked, her eyes shining.

"I'd love for you to," Anne said. "Maybe next week, before school starts. How about next Wednesday?"

"Okay," Crystal said. Her eyes were sparkling as she clasped her hands together and turned to gaze out the window again. "Can I stay in this room?"

"Of course," Anne said. "Any room you like."

"I'm going outside. Is it all right if I tell the other kids?"

"It's fine," Anne said. Her breath caught in her throat as Crystal hugged her and placed a quick kiss on her cheek. Then she ran out the door, and Anne could hear her muffled footsteps running along the hall and down the stairs. She heard her high-pitched voice as Crystal ran into the kitchen, no doubt telling Kurt all about the house and Anne's invitation.

Anne closed her eyes and placed her fingers against her cheek.

"Please," she prayed silently, "please let this be the right thing for her . . . and for me. And let me be a good friend . . . and a good mom," she said, barely whispering the last words.

When Anne came back down to the kitchen Crystal was gone. Kurt sat at the table, talking casually with Jessica and Mrs. Hargis. Vivian and Kevin were there, drinking tea, and even Gabby had come back inside. There was a lot of laughter and a lot of good-natured teasing, and Anne thought her home had never sounded happier.

"Diced green peppers," she heard Mrs. Hargis say, looking at Gabby haughtily.

"Nah," Gabby said. "Don't never put bell peppers in cole slaw. Flavor's too strong—that's all you can taste. You've got to blend the ingredients—a tablespoon of minced onion, that's what you want."

Anne rolled her eyes at Kurt.

"Not again," she mouthed, her eyes widening comically.

"Blend the ingredients, my hind leg," Mrs. Hargis scoffed, her eyes filled with disdain.

Vivian and her husband seemed to be enjoying the exchange between the two cooks. But Jessica shook her head and headed toward the door.

"I'm going out to make sure everything's cleaned up. Weatherman says it's going to rain tonight."

"We'll go with you," Anne said quickly, motioning to Kurt.

When the yard was spotless again and Jessica had gone home Anne turned to Kurt.

"I wish your sons could have come today. Then it would have been perfect."

"I wish they could have, too. Tim's still on his vagabond tour, as I call it. He wanted to see the country before he settled down to a steady job."

"You said he's riding a motorcycle cross-country?"

"Yeah. He calls once a week and he seems to really be enjoying the trip."

"Who wouldn't?" Anne said, sighing. "I always longed to take a trip across country, but Baxter was constantly tied down with business and with the farm." She glanced up at Kurt and smiled. "I envy Tim, and I hope I can meet him when he gets back and ask him all about it. And Greg, too."

"I promised Greg and his wife I'd come down to Atlanta next weekend. Why don't you come with me?"

"Really? You don't think they'd mind?"

"No, of course they won't mind. They have a nice little house outside the city, and Greg's wife, Misty, is a great cook and a good housekeeper. They love having company, and I know they'd like to meet you."

Anne bit her lip as she gazed up into Kurt's eyes.

"It's ironic," she said quietly. "I haven't told you, but I've been thinking about Mother a lot lately. About going to see her."

"Stone Mountain isn't too far from where Greg and Misty live. We can make it a weekend—I know a quiet lodge where we can stay near the mountains. We'll go shopping, and I'll take you out for dinner. Do you realize we haven't done much of that since we met?"

"I know. We've been too busy." She sighed and put her arms around his neck. "A weekend with you sounds heavenly."

"Then it's a date?" he asked, his eyes warm and teasing.

"Yes," she whispered. "It's a date."

"Hey, you two," they heard from behind them.

Anne turned to see Vivian and Kevin walking toward them.

"Looks like we need to take the kids back to the house so you two lovebirds can be alone," Vivian teased, her eyes moving from Anne's smiling face to Kurt's.

"Yeah, if we can ever get Gabby out of the kitchen," her husband said.

"Are they still at it?" Anne groaned. "I hope Gabby doesn't upset Kathleen too badly."

"Actually," Vivian said, leaning closer and giggling, "I think they're enjoying themselves. There's nothing wrong with a little competition."

"I don't know," Anne said, still skeptical.

"Well, we're going to round up the kids. By the time we get them back and they have their baths, it will be late. Mrs. Howard is probably back by now. I don't like leaving her and Mr. Howard alone for too long. Gives them too much time to think up problems."

Gabby finally came out and helped find all the children and put them in the van. Crystal ran up to Anne and threw her arms around her. She smelled of grass and fresh air, and her face was hot and stained with dirt.

"Thank you," she whispered as she hugged Anne. "This was the most fun I've ever had in my life."

Anne kissed her cheek and walked with her to the van. "There are going to be a lot of fun days for you, sweetheart. I promise."

" 'Night," Crystal said, blowing a kiss to her and Kurt. "See you in the morning."

"See you in the morning."

"Oh, Kurt," Anne murmured as the van drove away. "It was a good day, wasn't it?"

"A great day," he said with a contented sigh. "You know, life isn't going to be easy for most of those kids, but I think you gave them a day they're going to remember for the rest of their lives. A glimpse of how good life is really supposed to be."

"I hope so," she whispered. "I really hope that's true."

"When will Kathleen leave for home?" he asked. His voice was soft and intimate and there was no doubt as to his meaning as he pulled her toward him.

"Soon," she whispered. "Just enough time for me to take a nice cool bath and change clothes. Will you stay?" she asked, knowing he would.

"You couldn't run me away," he said.

"I wouldn't try."

Thirty-two

It was long past dark when Anne and Kurt left the house again and strolled through the garden toward the gazebo. She walked with her head against his shoulder, feeling the strength of his arm about her, feeling more secure and happy than she'd ever been in her life. After sunset the evening air had grown cool and there was a soft breeze that stirred the ancient trees to whisper about them.

"I don't think I've ever enjoyed this place more than I did today," Anne said quietly.

"It's a beautiful farm," he said. "You should be proud of it."

"I am. But you know, I've come to appreciate it in an entirely different way than when Bax was alive."

"Maybe that's because you're different."

"I guess you're right."

"I hate to leave you," he said, pulling her around into his arms. The dim light from the house spilled over them, and he could see her eyes, warm and alive.

"I can't wait until the weekend," she said. "I'll have you completely to myself for two whole days." Then she smiled and thought of their visit to his son and to her mother. "Well," she said wryly, "almost alone."

"Don't worry—I'll find some time for us to be alone," he whispered, kissing her.

They walked around the house to where his truck was parked and she kissed him again before letting him go. For a moment she felt like begging him to stay. She even thought about agreeing to marriage if that was what it would take to keep him there with her.

She was beginning to feel the effects of their constant separations: missing him when he wasn't around, longing for the feel of his body beside hers in bed at night, wondering where he was and what he was doing. That was the way it would be all the time once her stint at the half-way house was over. At least now she could see him at work. But later . . .

For a moment, when Kurt told her good night, there was a look in his eye, some deep, hidden doubt that he couldn't hide. And as she watched him drive away, she felt a wave of panic wash over her. A fear that it was ending, that she might never see him again, might never feel his touch or hear him tell her he loved her. And she knew . . . really knew for the first time that the reality of that loss was more than she could bear, especially if it was her reluctance that brought it on in the first place.

Had she really changed? Hadn't she always been the one to hold herself away, just as she was doing with Kurt . . . content to remain on the perimeter, watching but never joining in? Poor Baxter could attest to that.

But Baxter hadn't had the passion or the strength that Kurt had. She knew Kurt would never give in on all counts, even though he wanted to please her. But he wouldn't sacrifice his dignity for a woman; she knew that. And he wouldn't wait forever.

All the more reason she didn't want to lose him.

Was this an omen she was feeling? Was something about to happen? Something that would end this happiness she'd been feeling . . . put a stop forever to her one, last hope of having a family and a normal life?

"No," she whispered vehemently, shaking her head. "Not this time. I won't let anything or anyone keep this from me." Her hands were clenched tightly into fists as she walked to the house and upstairs to the bedroom where only moments before she and Kurt had lain together, had made breathtakingly sweet, passionate love.

"I'm not going to stand by and let it happen this time," she vowed, tracing her fingers over the pillow.

They were busy at the halfway house that week, and Anne's mind was often filled with thoughts of the coming weekend. Roger had paid the money to Mrs. Raburn and by this time next week Crystal would be free—an adoptable child. And this weekend Anne intended to make her final plans known about the girl . . . and about Kurt.

She took all the girls at the house shopping one day, and she promised the boys that next week would be their turn. Mrs. Howard, as usual, didn't approve.

"You're just asking for trouble," she said. "Taking these children shopping, buying them clothes, letting them think they have a normal life . . . it's a mistake. They're not normal, Mrs. Benefield, and they probably never will be. Do you know the statistics on what happens to children like these?"

"Yes, Mrs. Howard, I do. That's exactly why I'm trying to make their lives as pleasant as possible while they're here."

"It will only bring disappointment later when they go back to their own abusive homes and realize that what you gave them was all a dream."

"It isn't a dream!" Anne snapped. "This is real. If nothing else, these children will have this day and these possessions as a memory, something to hold on to if times get rough for them again."

"Not if . . . when. It's only a matter of time for most of them." The look in Nancy Howard's eyes was so smug, so self-assured, as if she was pleased that the children's lives would be hard.

"You know something, Mrs. Howard? I'm really glad I'm not as cynical and negative as you are. It must be a very miserable existence."

Anne turned and walked away, leaving Mrs. Howard staring after her, her eyes snapping with anger and resentment.

Later, after shopping, Anne was exhausted. She sat in the food court at the mall, giving the girls money and letting them buy whatever they wanted to eat. Crystal went with her, preferring, she said, to have whatever Anne wanted.

They sat together, eating and chattering about their purchases. When they'd finished Crystal took one of her shopping bags and pulled out a bright red pleated skirt and a white blouse sprinkled with tiny red polka dots.

"It's beautiful," Anne said. "Red is a good color for you."

"My mom would never let me wear red," she said quietly. "She said red makes you look fatter than you really are."

"Nonsense," Anne said. "There are many more considerations for buying clothes than that. Besides, you're not fat, Crystal. Remember what the counselor told you about that? About how you see yourself that way, even when it's not really true?"

Crystal sighed, but there was still doubt in her eyes.

"I just don't want to look stupid," she said.

"Sweetheart," Anne said, leaning toward her, "this red outfit brings out the color in your complexion and it complements your fair hair and blue eyes. You look like a million bucks in it."

"Really?" Crystal said.

"Yes, really."

The other girls sitting nearby were quiet as they listened to Crystal's and Anne's conversation.

"Doesn't she, girls?" Anne asked.

All the girls began to chatter at once, reassuring Crystal that she looked good in the red skirt and blouse.

"I wish I looked that good," one of them said guilelessly.

Finally Crystal grinned and stuffed the clothes back into the bag. "I'm going to wear it on the first day of school."

* * *

That weekend, as Anne and Kurt drove toward Atlanta, she related the story to Kurt.

"I think she's going to be fine," he said. "And now that Mrs. Raburn has her money, it's only a matter of time before Crystal has a real home and a real family. Does that bother you?"

"No," Anne said, smiling. It didn't bother her because she knew exactly where Crystal was going to spend the rest of her childhood—with her at Benefield Farms. And with Kurt, if Anne was lucky enough to have him still want her and a ready-made family.

They went first to the lodge where Kurt had made reservations. And he was right—Anne loved it. She loved the rustic wood-and-stone structure and the dark, rich-smelling hemlocks that surrounded the place. And she loved the peacefulness, the primitive beauty of being away from the traffic and the noise of the city.

Kurt unlocked the door to their cabin and turned to allow Anne to enter first. She stepped inside and stopped, her eyes growing wide, her lips turning up into a wistful smile.

"Oh . . . Kurt," she whispered. "Did you do this?"

"What?" he asked, peeking around her into the room as if he didn't understand what she meant.

The room was filled with flowers . . . large baskets of daisies and tiny pink rosebuds, vases of stately tulips. Even small wooden containers of azaleas and crape myrtle.

"We can have these planted at the farm," he said.

Anne felt overwhelmed as she turned and looked into Kurt's smiling eyes.

"You did this for me?"

"Do you like it?"

"Like it?" she whispered. "Oh, Kurt . . . I love it. And I love you."

Later they had coffee in the quaint restaurant and rested awhile before driving on toward Atlanta.

"Misty is making lunch for us. Then I thought we could visit your mother afterward, if that's all right with you."

"That's fine," she said. "I'm so glad you're going with me to see her. I have no idea how she's going to react. Sometimes she seems happy to see me and other times she's cold and rude."

Afterward they drove through the country, taking the back roads as Kurt pointed out the scenery and places of interest to her. It wasn't long until they reached a residential area, and Kurt pulled into the driveway of a pretty little ranch house, painted pale yellow and trimmed with dark green shutters.

"It's lovely," Anne murmured as she stepped out of the car and noted the well-kept lawn and mounds of blooming flowers along the walk.

Greg and Misty met them at the door, hugging Kurt and then Anne as if they already knew her.

Greg was tall and well-built, like his father. His hair was darker and his eyes were brown instead of hazel, but Anne thought they looked a great deal alike, especially their smile.

Misty was tiny and full of energy. Her pretty face was framed by a mass of curly blond hair and she never seemed to stop smiling.

Anne felt welcomed and comfortable

from the first moment she stepped into the small, immaculately kept house.

As they sat at the dining-room table, eating a crisp garden salad and one of the best casseroles Anne thought she'd ever eaten, the talk was light and easy.

The young married couple talked about their jobs and all the work they'd done on the house. They talked about their hopes for the future, about having children, and Anne noticed how warm Kurt's eyes were as he listened, and how proud he seemed.

"Dad tells us that your mother lives in Stone Mountain," Greg said as they sat talking after the meal.

"Yes, she does. In a very nice retirement complex." She glanced at Kurt, not knowing how much he had told Greg and Misty about her relationship with her mother. "I . . . I'm afraid I don't see her very often."

"We go shopping in Stone Mountain," Misty said. "If you'd like, I can run by and check on your mom anytime I'm over there."

"That's very nice of you," Anne said, feeling really touched by her offer.

They were a very nice young couple. And if there was any resentment from Greg about his dad's first serious relationship since divorcing his mother, it didn't show.

As they were leaving, Anne hugged Misty and thanked her for the meal.

"Kurt said you were a wonderful cook and housekeeper," she said, glancing at Kurt. "And he was right. I've enjoyed it."

"Well, we enjoyed it, too," Misty said. "And I hope you all will come back real soon."

Anne noticed that Greg and Kurt had walked out into the yard, and now they stood talking quietly. They were laughing, and when Kurt took Greg's hand, his son put his arms around him. The sight of those two grown men hugging made Anne's eyes grow moist and warm.

As they drove away, Anne sighed and leaned her head back against the seat's headrest.

"They are so nice," she said. "I can't remember when I've felt so welcome or enjoyed a meal more."

Kurt's eyes were sparkling as they turned to her, then back to the road. He reached across to touch her leg. "They liked you, too," he said. "They're good kids. I guess I'm lucky."

"You are," she said, remembering the open affection and the easy way he and Greg talked.

"And now for *my* family," she said ruefully, turning to gaze out the window.

Kurt said nothing, but he squeezed her knee as they drove on toward the retirement home.

It was late afternoon when they arrived, and Anne hoped her mother wasn't at supper. She hated having her routine disturbed by anyone. If Anne remembered anything about her mother, it was how every schedule had to be rigidly enforced and nothing was ever done spontaneously or for fun.

She breathed a sigh of relief when they walked into the main lobby and saw a posted sign stating meal times; supper was served at six. That would give them an hour—probably more than Anne needed if any of her other visits were any indication.

Kurt reached out and took her hand as they walked down the hallway, past a small room used for movie viewing and a large, open recreation room, empty now as most of the residents were in their rooms preparing for dinner. They walked past a lovely atrium filled with green plants and a glassed-in hallway that gave one the feeling of going outdoors. The apartments past that point were farther apart and more spacious.

She knocked on her mother's door and waited, feeling her heart beating rapidly.

When her mother opened the door and saw her she smiled and seemed surprised. She was leaning heavily on a walker, and Anne thought that she had grown more stooped than before. She looked frail, and her deep-set blue eyes seemed enormous in her thin, wrinkled face.

"Well," she said, seeming pleased. "Come in." Her efforts to move out of the way were a struggle. She stood back with a certain rigid formality, inviting them into her apartment as if both of them were strangers. She made no comment about Kurt. In fact, she didn't even seem curious or surprised to see a man with Anne.

They stood for a moment in the lovely living room. It reminded Anne of her childhood, with its bright, clean walls and sparse furnishings, and the almost overpowering scent of pine cleaner. Her mother was as conservative with her surroundings as she was with her time and her affections.

"Mother, this is Kurt Bonner."

"Hello," her mother said, nodding at Kurt. There was a curious glint in her eyes now, an odd smile of amusement on her weathered face, as if she knew some secret.

Anne recognized that look—that almost smug look of knowledge. Her mother always knew everything, did everything correctly. To hear her tell it, she had no faults and no weaknesses.

"How have you been?" Anne said, moving to a wing-backed chair and sitting on the edge of the seat. Kurt sat on the couch across from her.

"Fair," her mother said. "I've been fair. Is that a new dress?" she asked, her eyes moving down Anne's silk print dress.

"No, not really," Anne said. Just the hint of her mother's disapproval made

Anne feel breathless and angry. She didn't even have to say anything for Anne to know that she didn't like the dress and didn't find it particularly flattering to her.

"Mabel, my neighbor next door . . . she wears things like that," her mother said. "I never wore prints. They tend to make women look heavier than they really are."

Anne sighed and gritted her teeth. Her mother's words sounded just like the ones Crystal had related about wearing red, and they made Anne so angry that she wanted to lash out at her mother and tell her how much she resented her, how much she had been hurt by such comments all her life. Then she glanced at Kurt and saw him watching her with a quiet warning in his eyes.

"It's one of my favorite dresses," Anne said, choking back her anger.

"Oh?" her mother said with a disinterested sniff. "Well, it's been hot, hasn't it? The air conditioning here doesn't always work right. Sometimes it's so hot in here I think I'll just suffocate. I told them I wasn't paying nearly a thousand dollars a month to live in a place that couldn't even provide proper air conditioning."

Anne said nothing. She was the one who paid the rent, although her mother never seemed to mention that, or thank her for it either, for that matter.

"We saw the movie theater as we came in. You must really enjoy that," Anne said, "being able to see new movies as soon as they come out."

"I used to like movies. But some of this stuff now is just trash. Pure trash. I don't watch anything much." She always sounded angry when she disliked or disagreed with something. "Not much to do here," she said, sighing, as if her boredom was someone else's fault.

"Mother," Anne said, looking at her intently and hoping to capture her complete attention, "there's something I've been wanting to talk to you about. You know I have all the room in the world at the farm. I've been thinking . . ."

Her mother's look of incredulity made Anne stop to catch her breath. There was actually a pleased look, a look of expectancy in her tired old eyes.

"Oh, you wouldn't want me living

there," her mother said in a falsely modest, wounded voice. "I'd just be in your way." Her eyes moved to Kurt, as if she was still curious about him.

Kurt smiled at the old woman.

"If you would be happier there," Anne began, hardly knowing what to say. She never knew what to say to her mother or what she wanted, whether she wanted to be persuaded or whether she wanted an excuse to say no. "We could put you in one of the rooms downstairs so you wouldn't have to worry about getting up and down the stairs."

"I don't have to worry about that here."

"No, I know you don't. I only meant . . ." Anne sighed and started over. "Mrs. Hargis still cooks for me. I could even hire a nurse for you if—"

"For heaven's sake, I don't need a nurse," her mother said in an insulted tone. "I'm not so old that I can't take care of myself."

"Yes, Mother, I know," Anne said. "But I'm your daughter—your only relative. It's only right that I—"

"Ah, you don't need an old woman

around," her mother said. "Getting in your way, causing you problems."

"You won't be in the way, Mother," Anne said, feeling the muscles in her neck tighten. "If anything, we'll probably be in your way. That's the only thing that might concern you—it wouldn't be as quiet and peaceful at Benefields as it is here."

"Why?" she asked, her eyes darting toward Kurt. "You getting married again? Does he have children?"

"My children are grown," Kurt said. His eyes, when they looked toward Anne, were filled with as much curiosity as her mother's as he waited to see what she would say about them being married.

"We aren't married yet, but we will be soon," Anne said. She smiled at Kurt and saw him frown, saw a little spark of curiosity in his beautiful eyes. "And I'm thinking of adopting a little girl, Mother."

"Adopting a girl?" her mother said. Her trembling old hand moved restlessly back and forth, smoothing the material of her dress from her thigh to her knee as she stared at Anne. "What in the world for? If you wanted kids, you should have had 'em years ago."

"You're right," Anne said. "I *should* have done it years ago. But I was afraid I might not be a good mother," she added. She wondered if her mother would even understand her reasoning or see that she'd had something to do with it.

But her mother only sniffed and shrugged her bony shoulders. Her look was one Anne remembered well . . . even feared as a child. That look of cold disinterest. Eyes that were hard and expressionless and uncaring. Anne had never been able to see past that look, any more than she could now.

"Well, you can think about coming to Benefields, Mother," Anne said, forcing herself to remain patient. "You're welcome, if it's what you want."

"You going to move in there, too, after you're married?" her mother asked Kurt.

Kurt was looking at Anne very intently. "We haven't really discussed that yet," he said.

The old woman sniffed again, her lips pulled down in an unpleasant scowl.

Anne rose and kissed her mother's cheek, and as she expected, her mother made no effort to touch her daughter or return the kiss.

Anne felt her chest tightening and wondered why on earth she bothered trying to please this woman.

"You have my number, Mother. Call me and let me know what you decide."

Thirty-three

Anne practically ran out of the room and started down the hall, three steps ahead of Kurt. Finally, with a muttered curse of exasperation, he caught up with her and reached out for her arm, halting her and turning her around to face him.

"Anne," he said, his voice slightly scolding, his look one of impatience, "stop this. Don't run away from me because you're angry with your mother."

They began to walk, and she didn't try to run anymore.

"She's rude and hateful and uncaring," Anne said. She was almost breathless with anger. "She's selfish and—"

"She's an old woman, Anne," he said. They passed several older women in the hall, who turned to stare at them.

"She was like that when she wasn't old," Anne snapped. She continued walking, barely glancing at the curious women who watched and listened. Soon they were in the lobby, and Anne didn't care anymore who heard.

"I don't like her very much, Kurt. God help me . . . I know she's my mother, but sometimes I can barely tolerate her high-handed ways and her cold attitude. And even though I know I'm doing my duty by inviting her to live at Benefield, I'm not sure I'll be able to stand her being there."

Kurt sighed and shook his head as he looked at her. He might have been looking at one of the children back at the halfway house. Anne's cheeks were flushed and her eyes, though dark and stormy, were filled with angry tears.

"Don't you think it's about time to let this all go?" Kurt asked softly. "Let all those resentments against your mother be in the past where they belong? You need to go on with your life now."

"I've tried," she groaned. "Really, I know I sound silly and immature. And honestly, I've tried to tell myself it doesn't matter anymore. But damn, she makes me so angry."

"Then be angry," he said. "Tell her you're angry."

"I can't do that—she's an old woman. Besides, she probably wouldn't say a word—she'd just sit there and look at me, silent and condemning for not being the kind of daughter she wanted."

Kurt sighed again and put his hands on his hips. Then he reached out for Anne and guided her toward the door.

She knew he was right. She knew she was being foolish and stubborn, but she couldn't seem to help it. Somehow, when she saw her mother with that same cold, disapproving look in her eyes, she lost all power to reason. And, worst of all, she always ended up feeling like a whipped puppy—or a powerless little girl.

"Come on. Let's get out of here," Kurt said. "Do you feel like eating? There's a really nice restaurant where I wanted to take you not far from here."

"Do they serve chocolate?" Anne asked, giving Kurt a sheepish grin as she looked up at him from beneath her lashes.

He laughed and hugged her as they walked.

"Yes, little girl, I'm sure they still have the best chocolate souffle in Atlanta."

When they got in the car Anne turned to him, smiling, but feeling rather foolish.

"You must think I'm the craziest person you've ever met."

"No, I don't," he said firmly. He glanced at her and smiled as he pulled out of the parking lot. "I understand your anger and your resentment. I wanted to say something myself when she made that remark about your dress. And I'd have to be totally blind not to be able to see how much she's hurt you. I knew someone had from the beginning."

He *had* known. It was one of the first things he'd asked—who had hurt her.

"You're unpredictable, though. I wasn't expecting to get an answer to my marriage proposal in exactly that way." His look was wry and just a little hurt.

"Oh, I know," she said. "But she just gets to me so. I should have told you first. I should—"

"Will you stop that, for God's sake?" he said. "Stop blaming yourself for everything that happens."

Suddenly Kurt pulled the car over to the

side of the road. They were in a residential area and he had stopped at a vacant lot. He turned to her and took her by the shoulders; then, looking into her eyes, he pulled her toward him and kissed her.

She could feel his impatience in that kiss, his frustration with her, and for a moment she wondered if she had finally done it, if she had finally managed to push him away and make him so angry that he would never want to marry her.

"I love you," he said, pulling away and staring down into her eyes. But despite his words she knew he was angry. "Do you understand that? I wanted this weekend to be special for us. And, yes, I would have liked to hear your answer in a more romantic setting, but damn it, don't you get it? I don't really care how or why or any of that other meaningless crap. I just want you, Anne. I want to sleep with you every night and wake up with you every morning. I want to enjoy every tiny moment with you that I can in the years that we have left. I want to have a home with you that is filled with laughter and happiness. I want to take you on a trip across country just the way you've always wanted."

At those last words Anne began to cry. She reached for him, grabbing him hard and clinging to him as she sobbed against his shirt. She felt his hand against her head, holding her tightly as he rocked her and whispered sweet, soothing words against her hair.

"I love you," she whispered, still crying. "Oh, how I love you."

He let her cry, holding her and murmuring to her until she finally grew quiet and still.

"Now," he said, pulling back and looking at her with a sweetly patient, wistful expression. "Let's start all over. Anne Benefield—will you marry me?"

"Yes," she whispered. "Even though I don't deserve it."

"Don't," he said, putting his fingers to her lips. "I don't ever want to hear you say you don't deserve anything again. You deserve it all, sweetheart. And you certainly deserve to have a little happiness."

"And what about Crystal?" she asked. "I want to adopt her, Kurt. I know I made the decision on my own and that—"

"I'm glad about Crystal," he said. "I told you that."

"But that was before you knew I was going to marry you and that you'd have to be the father of a ten-year-old girl."

"I knew," he said, smiling mischievously at her.

She smiled at him as he moved back beneath the steering wheel and started the engine.

"Pretty sure of yourself, aren't you?" she said, her voice still choked with tears.

"Yep," he said, grinning. "I knew you couldn't resist me from the first moment we met."

They both laughed as they drove along. Anne wiped her eyes and freshened her makeup, and by the time they reached the restaurant she felt as if a heavy burden had been lifted from her heart. She felt happy and secure . . . relieved and a tiny bit scared. But she knew that this time her happiness far outweighed any reservations she might have. And she was in love. For the first time in her life, Anne felt the giddy, overwhelming power of what it was to be in love and to be loved in return.

It was late when they arrived back at the lodge. They talked the entire way about their plans for the future, about Crystal and how happy she would be.

"My mother asked if you would move to the farm," Anne said. "I hope you will. I really love the farm and—"

"Is that what you want? After all, it was Baxter's family home."

"His family is all gone now. And, actually, Baxter wasn't much for living in the country. He did that for me, I think, and Benefield Farms is more mine now than it ever was his. I'd love for us to live there together. But I also know how some men are about such things. So if you don't want to, I'll understand, although personally, I think it's only practical. But if you—"

"Lord, woman." He laughed. "Will you let me get a word in?" He smiled at her look of happy chagrin. "I'd love it, too," he said. "Besides, I hardly think you could adjust to my small apartment."

She could see his grin in the dashboard lights.

"Really?" she asked.

"Really," he murmured, glancing at her tenderly.

"You won't mind about my money? There is quite a bit of it, I'm told. There's bound to be some people in Clayburn who will say you're a kept man."

Kurt tilted his head back and laughed aloud.

"Hell, let them," he said. "I think I might even get used to being kept," he said, still grinning. "Besides," he added, his look growing more serious, "you and I know what's between us. There isn't enough money in the world to make me marry a woman I didn't love."

She closed her eyes and took his hand, pulling it up to her lips.

"You are a very special man," she whispered. "In one fell swoop I'm making you a husband, a farmer, a son-in-law to a very cantankerous old woman, and a father. And you haven't even complained."

"I think I can deal with it," he said, smiling.

"I know you can."

They were both still giddy with happiness when they drove up to their cabin.

"Oh, I'm glad we came here," she said as they got out of the car. "It's so quiet and peaceful. We can sleep late in the morning and call room service."

"And go back to bed," he added with a wiggle of his brows. She laughed and put her arm around him as he unlocked the door and they went in.

The first thing Anne saw was the blinking red light on the phone. For some reason it filled her with an awful dread. She pointed to it, letting Kurt be the one to dial the desk and get the message. And she held her breath as she watched him.

"It was Vivian," he said, turning to dial the number.

"It's probably nothing," Anne said, clasping her cold fingers tightly together.

"Hey, Viv," she heard Kurt say, his voice light and unconcerned. "Got your message. We just got in from dinner."

He frowned then and seemed to be listening intently. His gaze moved to Anne as he listened.

Anne could feel her heart beating hard against her ribs. Her fingers were growing numb where she clasped them together so hard.

"When?" Kurt asked. "Well, how in the hell . . . ?" He listened again. "Godammit," he muttered, raking his hand through his hair. "Have you called the police? Yeah . . . yeah. We'll be there in a couple of hours. We're leaving right now."

"What is it?" Anne asked, finally forcing her legs to move her forward. "Is it Crystal?" she asked. Somehow she knew it was.

Kurt's troubled eyes answered her.

"Her mother took her. She came to the house this morning under the pretext of telling Crystal goodbye. Mrs. Howard let her see Crystal alone. Next thing Vivian knew, they were gone. They haven't heard from them since."

"Oh my God," Anne whispered, slumping down onto the bed. She put her head in her hands, leaning over and sighing loudly.

Kurt knelt on the floor before her, taking her hands and pulling them away from her face. He held her wrists as he looked intently into her eyes. She thought she'd never seen such anger, such determination on anyone's face.

"We'll find her," he said. His jaws clenched tightly together and his eyes were stormy and hard. "If it's the last thing I do, I'm going to find her. And when we do . . ." He stood up and walked to the closet, pulling out clothes and their luggage. "This will just about do it with Mrs. Raburn," he muttered. "Get your things, baby. We've got to go."

Anne got up, feeling as if her legs were wooden, as if her heart might beat out of her chest. But she did as he said, barely aware of what she was doing.

"When we find her and the judge learns what she's done, there's no way she'll ever get to see Crystal again." He turned to Anne, reaching into his pockets distractedly and pulling out a few bills. "Here, why don't you go to the restaurant? Get us some coffee while I put our things in the car."

She took the money, looking into his eyes and feeling as if everything had come crashing down around her.

Kurt saw her eyes and he took her into his arms.

"It's going to be all right," he whispered. "I promise you that. We're still going to find that dream, baby, and when we do Crystal is going to be there with us. You have to trust me," he said, lifting her chin and kissing her softly. "And you have to be strong and calm about this."

She took a deep breath and nodded, then turned and hurried out across the parking lot toward the restaurant.

Thirty-four

The drive along the narrow winding road from the lodge seemed interminable. Kurt drove too fast, and sometimes Anne had to grasp the door handle to keep from sliding over in the seat. She would glance at Kurt, seeing his determined look as he drove through the darkness. Normally such erratic driving would have frightened her into making some protest, but now she felt as much urgency, as much impatience as he did. And she said nothing.

It was hard to drink the coffee in the swaying car, so she simply held it in her hands, letting its warmth penetrate through her cold skin. By the time they were out on the main highway and onto a smoother road, the coffee was cool, but she sipped it anyway, hoping it would revive her and take away the numbness from her mind.

"Where do you think they went?" she asked.

"I don't know. They could be anywhere," he said. Kurt had finished his coffee and now he tossed the empty cup to the back floorboard and reached for Anne's hand. "You all right?" he asked.

"I'm fine," she said, drinking the cool, slightly bitter coffee.

"Not a very auspicious beginning for our new life together, huh?" he said quietly, his gaze moving from the road to her face.

"If we can find her," Anne said, looking at him with her heart in her eyes. "If we can just find her, Kurt, then everything will be all right."

"I know. We'll find her," he said, squeezing her fingers. "We've had children run away; we've even had parents take them before, just like Crystal."

"Did you find them?" she asked, her eyes wide.

"Every one," he said quietly. "Trust me, baby. This is one thing I know."

"I do," she said, her smile tremulous.

"Maybe I've never told you that, Kurt. But I trust you completely . . . with my life, even."

Still watching the road, he pulled her hand up to his lips, kissing her fingers, then holding it against his chest as he drove.

"Why don't you try to sleep? It's going to be a long night and you'll probably need it."

"I can't sleep," she said. But she knew he was right and she lay her head back, feeling the warmth and comfort of his hand around hers, and with a heavy sigh she closed her eyes.

When they arrived all the downstairs lights in the house were on, blazing brightly through the early morning darkness. Anne stepped out of the car, feeling the stiffness in her legs that sitting so long had brought. Kurt was beside her quickly, his hand on her back as they moved toward the house.

The door opened before they reached it.

"Oh, thank goodness," Vivian said, stepping out into the night.

"Have you heard anything?" Kurt asked. "Where are the police?"

"They say they can't do anything," Vivian said as Kurt and Anne walked past her. "Legally, Crystal is still Karen Raburn's daughter, and they say they won't get involved until it becomes a legal matter."

"Dammit," Kurt said. He hurried into his office and went to his desk, pulling out drawers and shuffling through the papers on top.

"Come in, Vivian," Kurt said. "Let's sit down and get all the facts straight before we begin."

Mrs. Howard came toward them then, and Kurt motioned her into the office as well, although she stood near the wall, her arms crossed over her chest.

"She had every right to see her daughter," Mrs. Howard said right away.

"How can you say that?" Anne asked, turning with fire in her eyes. "You know how the woman is. You should never have left her alone with Crystal."

"Where's Mr. Howard?" Kurt asked. "Shouldn't he be here, too? We are paying him a salary, as I recall," he said wryly.

"He's asleep," Mrs. Howard said, her look defensive. "He has to get up to go to his regular job in a few hours. But I'll get him if you really think—"

"Never mind," Kurt said with an impatient wave of his hand.

He pulled a writing pad across the desk and held his pencil poised. His eyes were bright and full of urgency as he looked from one of them to the other.

"What time was it?"

He wrote as Vivian and Mrs. Howard related the story. They told him how Crystal's mother had come, and they weren't sure exactly how long she had stayed or when she took Crystal. All they knew was that an hour later, when they went upstairs to check, both the little girl and her mother were gone.

"Are you telling me we aren't even sure that her mother took her?" Kurt asked, frowning. "That she might have run away on her own?"

"Well, we weren't sure at first," Vivian explained. "But we are now. One of the neighbors across the street saw Crystal getting in the car with Mrs. Raburn. They remembered Crystal because she had on a bright red skirt." Vivian glanced at Anne.

Anne groaned and closed her eyes. Then she took a deep breath, managing a weak smile to Kurt. She didn't want him to have to worry about her as well as Crystal.

"There was someone else in the car," Vivian said. "A man."

Anne sat up straighter and stared at Vivian.

"Did anyone get a license number?" Kurt asked. "What kind of car was it?"

"No tag number; the neighbor didn't think anything about it. You know how it is; kids come and go here all the time. All we know is that it was an older Oldsmobile, early eighties maybe, pale blue with a vinyl top."

"Vivian," Kurt said, writing something on a piece of paper. He ripped it out of the tablet and handed it to Vivian. "Call Mrs. Webb. Social Services should have a file on Mrs. Raburn. Tell her we want it and that you'll come over and pick it up."

"She's not going to like doing this in the middle of the night," Vivian said.

"I don't give a damn what she likes. If

she gives you any trouble, tell her we'll get a warrant if necessary. I want that file tonight."

He glanced at Anne. "Anne, why don't you go upstairs and go through Crystal's things? See if there's anything that could give us a clue, either about her mother's relatives or about who this man might be."

Without a word, Anne got up and headed up the stairs.

"What about me?" she heard Mrs. Howard say.

"You just sit tight," Kurt said coolly. "There'll be plenty to do as soon as we get the files. In the meantime, why don't you make us a pot of coffee?"

"Gabby's already seen to that."

"What's he doing here?" Kurt asked distractedly, barely glancing up.

"He was here when we discovered that Crystal was gone. And he refuses to go home until we find her."

Kurt smiled and got up from his desk. "Good old Gabby," he said. "Then I think I'll go get a cup of coffee from him. Want one?"

"No," Mrs. Howard said. "I still think

you're making a mistake, Mr. Bonner . . .
doing this, treating Mrs. Raburn like a
criminal," she said. "I feel sure that she
will bring Crystal back in the morning."

"Do you?" he asked, his voice clipped.
"Well, you're entitled to your opinion,
Mrs. Howard. But we had a deal—one
Mrs. Raburn fully agreed to. If I thought
she regretted it one minute or that she
cared enough about the girl to change
her lifestyle, I might be sympathetic, too.
But I don't. If we wait, she could be hun-
dreds of miles away by morning. I don't
intend to sit quietly and let that happen."

Within an hour Kurt had the files on
Mrs. Raburn and Anne had found some
pictures in Crystal's ragged purse.

They spread the pictures on Kurt's
desk, going through them one by one to
see if anyone recognized any of them.
They pushed aside the ones of Crystal
and concentrated on the ones with other
people in the picture.

Kurt singled out one picture, tapping
his finger on it and staring at the three
people who gazed toward the camera.
Crystal was much younger in the picture
and her mother had a different hairstyle,

but it was the man in the middle who caught his attention.

He turned the picture over and saw three names on the back.

" 'Me, Stony and Mom,' " he read aloud. "Stony . . ." he mused. "Any of you ever heard her mention him?"

"No," they all said.

He pushed the picture aside, keeping it within view, and began to sort through the rather voluminous file on Karen Raburn.

He divided the papers, handing part to Anne, part to Vivian, and part to Mrs. Howard.

"Check for relatives' addresses, recent addresses of Mrs. Raburn. We'll talk to her neighbors. And look for any mention of this Stony guy."

Suddenly Kurt took his coffeecup and stood up, walking the floor restlessly as he read through one paper, frowned, and stuffed it into his pocket. Then he took another paper, read it, and slammed it back on his desk. Anne glanced up intermittently from her stack of papers. Something was worrying him, something more than just Crystal's disappearance.

She had a headache, and when she got

up to go to the kitchen for aspirin, she touched Kurt's arm and motioned him to come with her.

Gabby sat at the kitchen table, reading a newspaper and drinking a cup of coffee. He glanced up at them when they came in, his smile forced, his old eyes filled with concern.

"Any news?" he asked.

"Nothing yet," Kurt said.

"Can I get you something to eat?"

"No, Gabby. Thanks," Anne said, patting his shoulder as she passed.

Kurt came with her to the cabinet and she lowered her voice as she turned on the water.

"What's wrong?" she asked. "Something's bothering you."

He took a deep breath and reached into his shirt pocket, bringing out a folded piece of paper and putting it down on the cabinet.

It was a report from Social Services, dated several months before Crystal came to the halfway house. As Anne's eyes quickly scanned the report, her hand came up to her throat and she was conscious of holding her breath.

"She . . . she told one of the social workers that she had been molested," Anne whispered, reading on. "Her mother denied it ever happened, and nothing further was done," she said, shaking her head in disgust as she continued reading. She felt a sick feeling wash over her, threatening to consume her as she read the sordid details of what one of Karen Raburn's boyfriends had done to Crystal.

"Oh, God, Kurt," she murmured, her voice etched with pain. "That poor baby."

"Read the name," he said, pointing to the bottom of the page.

"Darryl Stoneman," she read. "Do you think that's him? Stony?"

"Yeah," he said gruffly. "I have a feeling it is."

"But we don't know for sure that's who she's with now," Anne said hopefully, wishing the sick feeling in the pit of her stomach would go away. "That was almost a year ago. Surely Crystal's mother wouldn't—"

The look in Kurt's eyes stopped her words. She knew as well as he what Crystal's mother was capable of doing. And she also knew that when the woman needed a drink or drugs, she'd do anything to get it. Including selling her own child.

"If he touches her, Kurt. . . . If he hurts her . . ."

"I know, baby. I know."

Anne's hands were trembling so badly that she spilled the water as she took two aspirin. Kurt took her hand, holding it tightly against his chest.

"Are you all right?"

"I'm fine," she said, a glint of determination in her eyes. "Let's go back to the office . . . see if the others have found any leads. And I'm going to call Will Jordan and see if he can't put a fire under the police department."

Thirty-five

Kurt was proud of Anne as he listened to her phone conversation with Judge Jordan. She was factual and calm, and yet she was unyielding in what she asked him to do. When she hung up he could see by the look on her face that she had accomplished what she wanted.

"He's going to help," she said, breathing a long sigh.

Vivian came over to them, waving a piece of paper.

"Kurt, look at this. It's a copy of an arrest warrant for a man named Darryl Stoneman. It doesn't seem related to this case, except, I suppose, that he was a boyfriend of Karen Raburn's. But it gives his last address and his license number."

"That's him," Kurt said with a look toward Anne. "Vivian, you're a doll."

Kurt took the paper, and with Anne

and Vivian looking over his shoulder, he dialed Information and gave them the name and address shown on the warrant. He listened for a moment, then muttered one word, "Unlisted."

"Thank you, Operator," he said. "But can you confirm that it's still the same address?"

He nodded then, and there was a flash of hope in his eyes as he hung up the phone.

"I think this address is a trailer park on Highway 21, near the Clayburn County line."

"Why didn't you just tell the operator it was an emergency and get the unlisted number?" Vivian asked.

"I can't call. It would give it all away. Besides, we're going to need the police. We can't just go crashing into the man's home on our own." Kurt gritted his teeth as he spoke. "Although, believe me, I'd like nothing better."

Just then, as if on cue, they heard a car stop on the street outside and heard the slam of car doors. Anne ran to the window and looked out.

"It's the police," she said, her voice

full of relief and animation. She opened the door and stood waiting as the two officers walked toward the house.

Kurt explained the situation quickly.

"Crystal and her mother might not even be with this man," he said. "If she has any sense, she'll be miles from Clayburn by now."

One of the officers shook his head. "You'd be surprised how little sense people like this have," he said. "They know the first places we'll go to look, and yet nine out of ten times that's exactly where we find 'em."

"We're going with you," Kurt said, reaching out for Anne. "We were planning on adopting Crystal."

Anne heard Mrs. Howard's muttered disbelief and Vivian's excited gasp of surprise. Anne turned and smiled at her briefly before focusing her attention on the officer.

"We'll need to call the county in on this," one of the young men was saying. "This is outside our jurisdiction. You two get your things and follow us in your car. We'll radio County officers and have them meet us en route."

Anne thought it was the longest, darkest ride she'd ever taken. Her eyes felt strained and dry from watching the taillights of the police car so intently as it raced through the night, around curves and trees, sometimes moving out of her sight for a second or two.

"If Crystal is with him, he won't do anything to her," Anne said, gripping her fingers tightly together. "Not tonight . . . not so soon. . . ."

Kurt's look was sympathetic. She could see his face in the glow of the dashboard lights, and how the muscles of his jaw tightened. But she said nothing, concentrating instead on the narrow, winding road and the car lights ahead. He glanced up in the mirror, seeing lights behind them now, coming fast.

Anne glanced around, too.

"I think it's the County," she said. "I'm going to really owe Will Jordan for this one," she said wryly. "But whatever he wants, it will be worth it."

The car in front slowed as it reached the trailer court and turned onto the dusty road. Sand and dirt sprayed back against Anne's car as they followed slowly, twisting and turning down various streets and finally coming to a stop at a trailer almost completely covered by overgrown bushes and tall weeds. For a moment Anne thought the place was abandoned.

Then she saw a car beside the trailer and reached out to grab Kurt's arm.

"Look," she said.

He'd seen it, too, partially hidden at the side of the trailer—an old blue Oldsmobile with a ragged vinyl top.

"You two stay here," one of the police officers said as he sidled alongside the trailer and up to the front door.

A light went on in the trailer, and as the County officer, now in charge, motioned the two city policemen around to the back, he walked up the rickety steps and tapped on the door with his flashlight.

"Police officers," he shouted. "Open up."

Anne held her breath. The night was eerily quiet. Nothing moved as the officer stood waiting, glancing back over his shoulders at his partner.

"Police," he shouted again, banging harder. "We know you're in there. Ten seconds and we're coming in."

Anne closed her eyes, praying that they wouldn't shoot, praying that whoever was inside would come out peacefully and that Crystal would be all right.

The crash of the front door seconds later caused her to open her eyes, and when she saw the officers go in and heard a scream she pushed open her car door and jumped out.

"Anne," Kurt shouted, getting out on the other side. He caught her just before she went up the steps. They could hear the sound of a scuffle inside and the shouted protests of a woman.

The two officers who'd gone around back came back and pushed past Anne and Kurt, rushing into the trailer with pistols drawn. It was only a matter of minutes before they came out, pulling a thin, scruffy-looking man with them, his hands handcuffed behind his back. Anne couldn't be sure but she thought he was the man in the picture with Crystal and her mother, and she shuddered.

Anne recognized Crystal's mother as they led her out of the trailer. When she saw the look of indifference on the

woman's face she couldn't help herself:
She just reacted.

She leapt at the woman, wanting nothing more than to wipe the ugly smirk off
her face. All she could think about was
Crystal and what this woman had done
to her, the horrible life she'd been forced
to live because of Karen Raburn's selfish-
ness. This woman made Anne's own
mother look like a saint.

"Where's Crystal?" Anne growled.
"Where is she?" she shouted.

"Anne," Kurt said, taking her arm and
pulling her back against him. There was
something odd about his voice. In the back
of her mind she knew it was different . . .
happier.

Then she looked up and saw Crystal
standing in the doorway with one of the
County deputies. She was still wearing
her pleated red skirt, but her blouse was
hanging from the waistband and her hair
was in her eyes. The police officer had
his arm around her shoulders and he was
grinning down at Anne and Kurt.

But Crystal's head was bent and there
was that same sad, dejected look about

her as when she had first come to the halfway house.

Anne's heart lurched at the sight of her.

"Crystal," she said softly, feeling the tears choking at her throat.

Crystal looked up then, and when she saw Anne and Kurt there was a look of disbelief in her eyes. Her arms moved first, coming up in a joyful movement and propelling her down the steps.

"You came," she cried, running to Anne and wrapping her arms around her waist. "You came to get me."

"Of course we came," Kurt said.

Crystal released Anne and went into Kurt's arms, and when Anne looked up at him she wasn't surprised to see tears sparkling in his eyes, too. After all, she knew better than anyone what a compassionate man he was. And she knew that he loved Crystal as much as she did.

"Is . . . is it over?" Crystal asked, looking up from one of them to the other.

"Yes," Kurt said, rubbing her shoulders lightly. "It's over. You're coming back to the house with us."

"And I won't have to go with her

again . . . or with him?" Crystal shivered as she glanced at the patrol car where the man sat.

"Is that Stony?" Anne asked.

Crystal nodded, her eyes not quite meeting Anne's.

Anne wanted to ask her then if he had hurt her, if he had so much as touched her. But she could see the tiredness in the droop of Crystal's shoulders, the humiliation in the way her eyes darted away from Anne's questioning gaze.

"You don't ever have to go with them again," Anne said softly. "Kurt and I are going to take care of you and protect you. And we're going to see that nothing like this ever happens again. All right?"

Crystal looked up then. Tears ran down her cheeks, but there was a glimmer of a smile on her face. She nodded and put her arm around Anne, her head bent against her side as they walked to the car.

It was almost daybreak by the time they got back to the house. As soon as they drove up, the front door opened and Vivian stood looking toward them, trying to see into the car. Crystal was asleep on the back seat, and as soon as Kurt opened the door and carried her toward the house, Vivian came rushing out.

She threw her arms around Anne and they stood in the street, hugging one another and crying.

"Is she all right?" she asked, taking Anne's arm and walking with her behind Kurt.

"I think so," Anne said. "I hope so. But we can't be sure. We haven't really asked her anything yet about what happened. It was such an awful experience . . . such an awful place. We just wanted to get her away from there and back home."

Gabby stood at the door and, as she walked in, Anne was surprised when he walked to her and put his arms around her. There were rough, bony hands patting her back and she felt tears of thanksgiving welling in her eyes again.

"Welcome home," he said, his voice gruff and tired.

"Oh, Gabby," she said, "you don't know how good that sounds, or how good it is to have you and Vivian here waiting."

She glanced around.

"Where's Mrs. Howard? Didn't she

even stay up to find out if Crystal was all right?''

"They're gone . . . quit," Vivian said with a twinkle in her eye. "I think she thought it best to get out before Kurt threw her out. And he would have, too," she said. "Just as soon as this mess was over. She said she'd send for her furniture tomorrow . . . I guess that means today," she added, glancing out at the morning's approaching light.

"Oh," Anne said with a sigh. "Goodness, that means we'll have to find new house parents."

"And that I'll have to break the news to my husband about us being back on duty for a while." Vivian groaned, still smiling.

"Kevin can handle it," Anne said. "He doesn't seem like such a bad sort," she said, smiling at Vivian.

"Not a bad sort at all," Vivian said, nodding her head. "In fact, after tonight I'm going to go home and tell him what a terrific guy he really is. Well, listen, you go up to Kurt and Crystal. I'm going to help Gabby get started with breakfast."

"Oh, Viv," Anne said, glancing from

her to Gabby, who stood watching quietly, his eyes easy now and calm. "You two must be beat. I'm sorry you won't even get a break."

"We'll be all right," Gabby said. "Me and Viv," he said, nodding toward her, "we're tough. Why, we kept this place goin' when they weren't but the three of us. And now that we have you here, we'll manage even better." Then he grinned. "You two gettin' married?"

Anne laughed. "Yes, Gabby. As a matter of fact, we are. What do you think about that?"

"I think he's a lucky man," he said shyly.

"I'm the lucky one."

Anne went upstairs. She was anxious to see Kurt, to see what he thought about Crystal.

He was coming out of her room, and he stepped back inside with Anne when she peeked in the door toward the bed.

"She didn't even wake up," he said, chuckling softly.

"Do you think she's all right?" she asked, gazing down at the sleeping girl. "Do you think he—"

"Shh," he said, pulling Anne into his arms. "There you go again . . . borrowing trouble. We'll just have to wait and see, and whatever it takes to help her we'll do it."

She shook her head, then rested it wearily against his chest.

"Borrowing trouble . . . one of my worst faults," she said, grinning.

"Maybe I should have said it differently," he said, rocking her back and forth in his arms. "Maybe I should have said there you go again . . . caring."

"I think you make me sound good," she said, looking up at him.

He started walking toward the door, pulling her with him and closing the door so that they were alone in the dimly lit upstairs hall. The sun was coming up and its light lay in pale golden streaks through the windows and across the wooden floors of the entry hall downstairs.

"And you make me feel good," he said, holding her tightly, his hand cradling her head against him. "I love you, Anne Benefield. You've become a true Angel, as we say around this place. I love the way you care."

"I do, you know," she whispered. "I always have. It just took awhile for me to be able to show it. You did that. You changed my life."

"I didn't do anything," he said, kissing her lightly on the lips. "Except love you and want you. And need you more than I've ever needed anyone in my life."

"That was all it took," she whispered, snuggling against him and feeling all the love, all the contentment she'd ever longed for right there in Kurt's arms. "This place, these kids . . . Gabby and Viv. They're the real angels. I just came along for the ride," she said, smiling up at him. "And fell in love in the process."

Coming next month
from TO LOVE AGAIN:

Homefires by Joyce C. Ware
The Joy of Christmas story collection

WATCH AS THESE WOMEN LEARN
TO LOVE AGAIN

HELLO LOVE (4094, $4.50/$5.50)
by Joan Shapiro

Family tragedy leaves Barbara Sinclair alone with her success. The fight to gain custody of her young granddaughter brings a confrontation with the determined rancher Sam Douglass. Also widowed, Sam has been caring for Emily alone, guided by his own ideas of childrearing. Barbara challenges his ideas. And that's not all she challenges . . . Long-buried desires surface, then gentle affection. Sam and Barbara cannot ignore the chance to love again.

THE BEST MEDICINE (4220, $4.50/$5.50)
by Janet Lane Walters

Her late husband's expenses push Maggie Carr back to nursing, the career she left almost thirty years ago. The night shift is difficult, but it's harder still to ignore the way handsome Dr. Jason Knight soothes his patients. When she lends a hand to help his daughter, Jason and Maggie grow closer than simply doctor and nurse. Obstacles to romance seem insurmountable, but Maggie knows that love is always the best medicine.

AND BE MY LOVE (4291, $4.50/$5.50)
by Joyce C. Ware

Selflessly catering first to husband, then children, grandchildren, and her aging, though imperious mother, leaves Beth Volmar little time for her own adventures or passions. Then, the handsome archaeologist Karim Donovan arrives and campaigns to widen the boundaries of her narrow life. Beth finds new freedom when Karim insists that she accompany him to Turkey on an archaeological dig . . . and a journey towards loving again.

OVER THE RAINBOW (4032, $4.50/$5.50)
by Marjorie Eatock

Fifty-something, divorced for years, courted by more than one attractive man, and thoroughly enjoying her job with a large insurance company, Marian's sudden restlessness confuses her. She welcomes the chance to travel on business to a small Mississippi town. Full of good humor and words of love, Don Worth makes her feel needed, and not just to assess property damage. Marian takes the risk.

A KISS AT SUNRISE (4260, $4.50/$5.50)
by Charlotte Sherman

Beginning widowhood and retirement, Ruth Nichols has her first taste of freedom. Against the advice of her mother and daughter, Ruth heads for an adventure in the motor home that has sat unused since her husband's death. Long days and lonely campgrounds start to dampen the excitement of traveling alone. That is, until a dapper widower named Jack parks next door and invites her for dinner. On the road, Ruth and Jack find the chance to love again.

Available wherever paperbacks are sold, or order direct from the Publisher. Send cover price plus 50¢ per copy for mailing and handling to Penguin USA, P.O. Box 999, c/o Dept. 17109, Bergenfield, NJ 07621.Residents of New York and Tennessee must include sales tax. DO NOT SEND CASH.